THE ELEGANCE OF THE HEDGEHOG

Muriel Barbery was born in 1969. *The Elegance of the Hedgehog* is her second novel and has been translated from the original French into more than thirty languages.

Alison Anderson has translated many books into English and is herself a published novelist.

Praise for The Elegance of the Hedgehog

'Many authors dream of getting their books onto best-seller lists, but few pull it off with the panache of French writer Muriel Barbery.' *Time*

'A profound but accessible book… which elegantly treads the line between literary and commercial fiction… *The Elegance of the Hedgehog* is, by the end, quite radical in its stand against French classism and hypocrisy… Clever, informative and moving' *Observer*

'Its appeal is obvious… a feel-good book with philosophical aspirations' *The Guardian*

'At once absurd and lyrical, cheery and bleak, contemplative and tender…It is the revelatory joy the characters afford each other – with recognition, with friendship, with love – that quietly rises to the top.' *New Statesman*

'Muriel Barbery… commands the sophistication, polish and mental agility that often distinguish French fiction…Barbery has a warm heart and a heart moreover that knows that great art and the best philosophy may (just possibly) possess redemptive qualities, or at least make life bearable in a materialistic and self-indulgent world.' *Sydney Morning Herald*

THE ELEGANCE OF THE HEDGEHOG

MURIEL BARBERY

*Translated from the French
by Alison Anderson*

This book is published with support from the French Ministry of
Culture/Centre national du Livre

A Gallic Book

First published in France as *L'élégance du hérisson* by Éditions Gallimard, Paris

First published in Great Britain in 2008 by
Gallic Books, 134 Lots Road, London SW10 0RJ

A CIP record for this book is available from the British Library

ISBN 978-1-906040-18-5

Typeset in Simoncini Garamond and Arial by
SX Composing DTP, Rayleigh, Essex

Printed and bound by CPI Bookmarque, Croydon, CR0 4TD

6 8 10 9 7

CONTENTS

ON GRAMMAR

PALOMA

For Stéphane, with whom I wrote this book

MARX

(*Preamble*)

1. Whosoever Sows Desire

'**M**arx has completely changed the way I view the world,' declared the Pallières boy this morning, although ordinarily he says nary a word to me.

Antoine Pallières, prosperous heir to an old industrial dynasty, is the son of one of my eight employers. There he stood, the most recent eructation of the ruling corporate elite – a class that reproduces itself solely by means of virtuous and proper hiccups – beaming at his discovery, sharing it with me without thinking or ever dreaming for a moment that I might actually understand what he was referring to. How could the labouring classes understand Marx? Reading Marx is an arduous task, his style is lofty, the prose is subtle and the thesis complex.

And that is when I very nearly – foolishly – gave myself away.

'You ought to read *The German Ideology*,' I told him. Little cretin in his conifer-green duffel coat.

To understand Marx and understand why he is mistaken, one must read *The German Ideology*. It is the anthropological cornerstone on which all his exhortations for a new world would be built, and on which a sovereign certainty is established: mankind, doomed to its own ruin through desire, would do better to stick to its own needs. In a world where the hubris of desire has been vanquished, a new social organisation can emerge, cleansed of struggle, oppression and deleterious hierarchies.

'Whosoever sows desire harvests oppression,' I nearly murmured, as if only my cat were listening to me.

But Antoine Pallières, whose repulsive and embryonic whiskers have nothing the least bit feline about them, is staring at me, uncertain of my strange words. As always, I am saved by the inability of living creatures to believe anything that might cause the walls of their little mental assumptions to crumble. Concierges do not read *The German Ideology*; hence, they would certainly be incapable of quoting the eleventh thesis on Feuerbach. Moreover, a concierge who reads Marx must be contemplating subversion, must have sold her soul to that devil, the trade union. That she might simply be reading Marx to elevate her mind is so incongruous a conceit that no member of the bourgeoisie could ever entertain it.

'Say hello to your mother,' I murmur as I close the door in his face, hoping that the complete dissonance between my two sentences will be veiled by the might of millennial prejudice.

2. The Miracles of Art

My name is Renée. I am fifty-four years old. For twenty-seven years I have been the concierge at number 7, Rue de Grenelle, a fine *hôtel particulier* with a courtyard and private gardens, divided into eight luxury apartments, all of which are inhabited, all of which are immense. I am a widow, I am short, ugly and plump, I have bunions on my feet and, if I am to credit certain early mornings of self-inflicted disgust, the breath of a mammoth. I did not go to university, I have always been poor, discreet and insignificant. I live alone with my cat, a big lazy tom who has no distinguishing features other than the fact that his paws smell bad when he is annoyed. Neither he nor I make any effort to take part in the social doings of our respective species. Because I am rarely friendly – though always polite – I am not liked, but am tolerated nonetheless: I correspond so very well to what social prejudice has collectively construed to be a typical French concierge that I am one of the multiple cogs that make the great universal illusion turn, the illusion according to which life has a meaning that can be easily deciphered. And since it has been written somewhere that concierges are old, ugly and sour, so has it been branded in fiery letters on the pediment of that same imbecilic firmament that the aforementioned concierges have rather large dithering cats who sleep all day on cushions covered with crocheted cases.

Similarly, it has been decreed that concierges watch television interminably while their rather large cats doze, and that the entrance to the building must smell of pot-au-feu, cabbage soup or a country-style cassoulet. I have the extraordinary good fortune to be the concierge of a very high-class sort of building. It was so humiliating for me to have to cook such loathsome dishes that when Monsieur de Broglie – the State Councillor on the first floor – intervened (an intervention he described to his wife as being 'courteous but firm', whose only intention was to rid our communal habitat of such plebeian effluvia), it came as an immense relief, one I concealed as best I could beneath an expression of reluctant compliance.

That was twenty-seven years ago. Since then, I have gone every day to the butcher's to buy a slice of ham or some calves' liver, which I slip into my net bag between my packet of noodles and my bunch of carrots. I then obligingly flaunt these pauper's victuals – now much improved by the noteworthy fact that they do not smell – because I am a pauper in a house full of rich people and this display nourishes both the consensual cliché and my cat Leo, who has become rather large by virtue of these meals that should have been mine, and who stuffs himself liberally and noisily with macaroni and butter, and pork from the delicatessen, while I am free – without any olfactory disturbances or anyone suspecting a thing – to indulge my own culinary proclivities.

Far more irksome was the issue of the television. In my late husband's day, I did go along with it, for the constancy of his viewing spared me the chore of watching. From the hallway of the building you could hear the sound of the thing, and that sufficed to perpetuate the charade of social hierarchy, but once Lucien had passed away I had to think hard to find a way to keep up appearances. Alive, he freed me from this iniquitous obligation; dead, he has deprived me of his lack of culture, the indispensable bulwark against other people's suspicions.

I found a solution thanks to a non-buzzer.

A chime linked to an infrared mechanism now alerts me to

16

the comings and goings in the hallway, which has eliminated the need for anyone to buzz to notify me of their presence if I happen to be out of earshot. For on such occasions I am actually in the back room, where I spend most of my hours of leisure and where, sheltered from the noise and smells that my condition imposes, I can live as I please, without being deprived of the information vital to any sentry: who is coming in, who is going out, with whom and at what time.

Thus, the residents going down the hall would hear the muffled sounds indicating a television was on, and as they tend to lack rather than abound in imagination, they would form a mental image of the concierge sprawled in front of her television set. As for me, cosily installed in my lair, I heard nothing but I knew that someone was going by. So I would go to the adjacent room and peek through the spy-hole located opposite the stairs and, well hidden behind the white net curtains, I could enquire discreetly as to the identity of the passer-by.

With the advent of videocassettes and, subsequently, the DVD divinity, things changed radically, much to the enrichment of my happy hours. As it is not terribly common to come across a concierge waxing ecstatic over *Death in Venice* or to hear strains of Mahler wafting from her lodge, I delved into my hard-earned conjugal savings and bought a second television set that I could operate in my hideaway. Thus, the television in the front room, guardian of my clandestine activities, could bleat away and I was no longer forced to listen to inane nonsense fit for the brain of a clam – I was in the back room, perfectly euphoric, my eyes filling with tears, in the miraculous presence of Art.

Profound Thought No. 1

Follow the stars
In the goldfish bowl
An end

Apparently, now and again adults take the time to sit down and contemplate what a disaster their life is. They complain without understanding and, like flies constantly banging against the same old windowpane, they buzz around, suffer, waste away, get depressed then wonder how they got caught up in this spiral that is taking them where they don't want to go. The most intelligent among them turn their malaise into a religion: oh, the despicable vacuousness of bourgeois existence! Cynics of this kind frequently dine at Papa's table: 'What has become of the dreams of our youth?' they ask, with a smug, disillusioned air. 'Those years are long gone, and life's a bitch.' I despise this false lucidity that comes with age. The truth is that they are just like everyone else: nothing more than kids who don't understand what has happened to them, acting big and tough when in fact all they want is to burst into tears.

And yet there's nothing to understand. The problem is that children believe what adults say and, once they're adults themselves, they exact their revenge by deceiving their own children. 'Life has meaning and we grown-ups know what it is' is the universal lie that everyone is supposed to believe. Once you become an adult and you realise that's not true, it's too late. The mystery remains intact, but all your available energy has long ago been wasted on stupid things. All that's left is to anaesthetise yourself by trying to hide the fact that you can't find any meaning in your life, and then, the better to convince yourself, you deceive your own children.

All our family acquaintances have followed the same path: their youth spent trying to make the most of their intelligence, squeezing their studies like a lemon to make sure they'd secure a spot among the elite, then the rest of their lives wondering with a flabbergasted look on their faces why all that hopefulness has led to such a vain existence. People aim for the stars, and they end up like goldfish in a bowl. I wonder if it wouldn't be simpler just to teach children right from the start that life is absurd. That might deprive you of a few good moments in your childhood but it would save you a considerable amount of time as an adult – not to mention the fact that you'd be spared at least one traumatic experience, i.e. the goldfish bowl.

I am twelve years old, I live at 7, Rue de Grenelle in an apartment for rich people. My parents are rich, my family is rich and my sister and I are, therefore, as good as rich. My father is a member of parliament and before that he was a minister: no doubt he'll end up in the top spot, emptying out the wine cellar of the residence at the Hôtel de Lassay. As for my mother . . . Well, my mother isn't exactly a genius but she is educated. She has a literature PhD. She writes her dinner invitations without mistakes and spends her time bombarding us with literary references ('Colombe, stop trying to act like Madame Guermantes,' or 'Sweetie, you are a regular Sanseverina').

Despite all that, despite all this good fortune and all this wealth, I have known for a very long time that the final destination is the goldfish bowl. How do I know? Well, the fact is I am very intelligent. Exceptionally intelligent, in fact. Even now, if you look at children my age, there's an abyss between us. And since I don't really want to stand out, and since intelligence is very highly rated in my family – an exceptionally gifted child would never have a moment's peace – I try to scale back my performance at school, but even so I always come first. You might think that to pretend to be simply of average intelligence when you are twelve years old like me and have the level of a second-year university student is easy. Well, not at all. It really takes an effort to appear stupider than you are. But, in a way, this does keep me from dying of boredom: all the time I don't need to spend learning and understanding I use to imitate the ordinary good pupils – the way they do things, the answers they give, their progress, their concerns and their minor errors. I read everything that Constance Baret writes – she is second in the class – all her maths and French and history and that way I find out what I have to do: for French a string of words that are coherent and spelled correctly; for maths the mechanical reproduction of operations devoid of meaning; and for history a list of events joined by logical connections. But even if you compare me to an adult, I am much brighter than the vast majority. That's the way it is. I'm not particularly proud of this because it's not my doing. But one thing is certain – there's no way I'm going to end up in the goldfish bowl. I've thought this through quite carefully. Even for someone like me who is superbright and gifted in her studies and different from everyone else, in fact superior to the vast majority – even for me life is already all plotted out and so dismal you could cry: no one seems to have thought of the fact that if life is absurd, being a brilliant success has no greater value than being a failure. It's just more comfortable. And even then: I think lucidity gives your success a bitter taste, whereas mediocrity still leaves hope for something.

So I've made up my mind. I am about to leave childhood behind and, in spite of my conviction that life is a farce, I don't think I can hold out to the end. We are, basically, programmed to believe in something that doesn't exist, because we are living creatures; we don't want to suffer. So we spend all our energy persuading ourselves that there are things that are worthwhile and that that is why life has meaning. I may be very intelligent, but I don't know how much longer I'm going to be able to struggle against this biological tendency. When I join the adults in the rat race, will I still be able to confront this feeling of absurdity? I don't think so. That is why I've made up my mind: at the end of the school year, on the day I turn thirteen, the sixteenth of June, I will commit suicide. Careful now, I have no intention of making a big deal out of it, as if it were an act of bravery or defiance. Besides, it's in my best interest that no one suspect a thing. Adults have this neurotic relationship with death, it gets blown out of all proportion, they make a huge deal out of it when in fact it's really the most banal thing there is. What I care about, actually, is not the thing in itself, but the way it's done. My Japanese side, obviously, is inclined towards seppuku. When I say my Japanese side, what I mean is my love for Japan. I'm in year nine so, naturally, I chose Japanese as my second foreign language. The teacher isn't great, he swallows his words in French and spends his time scratching his head as if he were puzzled, but the textbook isn't bad and since the start of the year I've made huge progress. I hope in a few months to be able to read my favourite manga in the original. Maman doesn't understand why a little-girl-as-gifted-as-you-are wants to read manga. I haven't even bothered to explain to her that 'manga' in Japanese doesn't mean anything more than 'comic book'. She thinks I'm high on subculture and I haven't set her straight on that. In short, in a few months I might be able to read Taniguchi in Japanese. But back to what we were talking about: I'll have to do it before the sixteenth of June because on the sixteenth of June I'm committing suicide. But I won't do seppuku. It would be full of significance and beauty but . . . well . . . I really have no desire to suffer. In fact, I would hate to suffer; I think that if you have decided to die, it is precisely because your decision is in the nature of things, so you must do it in a gentle way. Dying must be a delicate passage, a sweet slipping away to rest. There are people who commit suicide by jumping out of the window of the fourth floor or swallowing bleach or even hanging themselves! That's senseless! Obscene, even. What is the point of dying if not to *not* suffer? I've devoted great care to planning how I'll exit the scene: every month for the last year I've been pilfering a sleeping pill from Maman's box on the bedside table. She takes so many that she wouldn't even notice if I took one every day, but I've decided to be particularly careful. You can't leave anything to chance when you've made a decision that most people won't understand. You can't imagine how quickly people will get in the way of your most heartfelt plans, in the name of such trifles as 'the meaning of life' or 'love of mankind'. Oh and then there is 'the sacred nature of childhood'.

Therefore, I am heading slowly towards the date of the six-teenth of June and I'm not afraid. A few regrets, maybe. But the world, in its present state, is no place for princesses. Having said that, simply because you've made plans to die doesn't mean you have to vegetate like some rotting piece of cabbage. Quite the contrary. The main thing isn't about dying or how old you are when you die, it's what you are doing the moment you die. In Taniguchi the heroes die while climbing Mount Everest. Since I haven't the slightest chance of taking a stab at K2 or the Grandes Jorasses before the sixteenth of June, my own personal Everest will be an intellectual endeavour. I have set as my goal to have the greatest number possible of profound thoughts, and to write them down in this notebook: even if nothing has any meaning, the mind, at least, can give it a shot, don't you think? But since I have this big thing about Japan, I've added one requirement: these profound thoughts have to be formulated like a little Japanese poem: either a haiku (three lines) or a tanka (five lines).

My favourite haiku is by Basho.

The fisherman's hut
Mixed with little shrimp
Some crickets!

Now that's no goldfish bowl, is it, that's what I call poetry!

22

But in the world I live in there is less poetry than in a Japanese fisherman's hut. And do you think it is normal for four people to live in four thousand square feet when tons of other people, perhaps some *poètes maudits* among them, don't even have a decent place to live and are crammed together fifteen at a time in two hundred square feet? When, this summer, I heard on the news that some Africans had died because a fire had started in the stairway of their run-down tenement, I had an idea. Those Africans have the goldfish bowl right there in front of them, all day long – they can't escape through storytelling. But my parents and Colombe are convinced they're swimming in the ocean just because they live in their four thousand square feet with their piles of furniture and paintings.

So, on the sixteenth of June I intend to refresh their pea-sized memories: I'm going to set fire to the apartment (with the barbecue lighter). Don't get me wrong, I'm not a criminal: I'll do it when there's no one around (the sixteenth of June is a Saturday and on Saturdays Colombe goes to see Tibère, Maman is at yoga, Papa is at his club and as for me, I stay home), I'll evacuate the cats through the window and I'll call the fire brigade early enough so that there won't be any victims. And then I'll go off quietly to Grandma's with my pills, to sleep.

With no more apartment and no more daughter, maybe they'll give some thought to all those dead Africans, don't you think?

CAMELLIAS

1. An Aristocrat

On Tuesdays and Thursdays, Manuela, my only friend, comes for tea with me in my lodge. Manuela is a simple woman and twenty years wasted stalking dust in other people's homes has in no way robbed her of her elegance. Besides, stalking dust is a very euphemistic way to put it. But where the rich are concerned, things are rarely called by their true name.

'I empty bins full of sanitary towels,' she says, with her gentle, slightly hissing accent. 'I wipe up dog vomit, clean the bird cage – you'd never believe the amount of poo such tiny animals can make – and I scrub the toilets. You talk about dust? Big deal!'

You must understand that when she comes down to see me at two in the afternoon, on Tuesdays after the Arthens, and on Thursdays after the de Broglies, Manuela has been polishing the toilets with a cotton bud, and though they may be gilded with gold leaf, they are just as filthy and reeking as any toilets on the planet, because if there is one thing the rich do share with the poor, however unwillingly, it is their nauseating intestines that always manage to find a place to free themselves of that which makes them stink.

So Manuela deserves our praise. Although she's been sacrificed at the altar of a world where the most thankless tasks have been allotted to some women while others merely hold their nose without raising a finger, she nevertheless strives relentlessly to maintain a degree of refinement that goes far beyond any gold-leaf gilding, *a fortiori* of the sanitary variety.

'When you eat a walnut, you must use a tablecloth,' says Manuela, removing from her old shopping bag a little hamper made of light wood where some almond *tuiles* are nestled among curls of carmine tissue paper. I make coffee that we shall not drink, but its wafting aroma delights us both, and in silence we sip a cup of green tea as we nibble on our tuiles.

Just as I am a permanent traitor to my archetype, so is Manuela: to the Portuguese cleaning woman she is a criminal oblivious of her condition. This girl from Faro, born under a fig tree after seven siblings and before six more, forced in childhood to work the fields and scarcely out of it to marry a mason and take the road of exile, mother of four children who are French by birthright but whom society looks upon as thoroughly Portuguese – this girl from Faro, as I was saying, who wears the requisite black support stockings and a kerchief on her head, is an aristocrat. An authentic one, of the kind whose entitlement you cannot contest: it is etched onto her very heart, it mocks titles and people with handles to their names. What is an aristocrat? A woman who is never sullied by vulgarity, although she may be surrounded by it.

On Sundays, the vulgarity of her in-laws, who with their loud laughter muffle the pain of being born weak and without prospects; the vulgarity of an environment as bleakly desolate as the neon lights of the factory where the men go each morning, like sinners returning to hell; then, the vulgarity of her employers who, for all their money, cannot hide their own baseness and who speak to her the way they would a mangy dog covered with oozing bald patches. But you should have witnessed Manuela offering me, as if I were a queen, the fruit of her prowess in *haute pâtisserie* to fully appreciate the grace that inhabits this woman. Yes, as if I were a queen. When Manuela arrives, my lodge is transformed into a palace, and a picnic between two pariahs becomes the feast of two monarchs. Like a storyteller transforming life into a shimmering river where trouble and boredom vanish far below the water, Manuela metamorphoses our existence into a warm and joyful epic.

'That little Pallières boy said hello to me on the stairs,' she says suddenly, interrupting the silence.

I snort with disdain.

'He's reading Marx,' I add, with a shrug of my shoulders.

'Marx?' she asks, pronouncing the *x* as if it were a *sh*, a somewhat slurping *sh*, as charming as a clear sky.

'The father of communism,' I reply.

Manuela makes a scornful noise.

'Politics,' she says. 'A toy for little rich kids that they won't let anyone else play with.'

She is thoughtful for a moment, frowning.

'Not his typical reading material,' she says.

The illustrated magazines that the young boys hide under the mattress cannot escape Manuela's shrewd gaze, and the Pallières boy seemed at one point to be consuming them assiduously, however selectively, as exemplified by one particularly dog-eared page with an explicit title: *The Saucy Marchionesses.*

We laugh and converse for a while longer about one thing or another, in the calm space of an old friendship. These are precious moments for me, and I am filled with anguish at the thought that a day will come when Manuela will fulfil her lifelong dream of returning to her country for good, and will leave me here alone and decrepit, with no companion to transform me, twice a week, into a clandestine monarch. I also wonder fearfully what will happen when the only friend I have ever had, the only one who knows everything without ever having to ask, leaves behind her this woman whom no one knows, enshrouding her in oblivion.

We can hear steps in the entrance and then, distinctly, the

cryptic sound of fingers on the lift's call button; it is an old wood-panelled lift with a black grille and double doors, the sort of place where, in the old days, if there had been room, you would have had an attendant. I recognise the footsteps, it is Pierre Arthens, the food critic who lives on the fourth floor, an oligarch of the worst sort who, from the very way he squints whenever he stands on the threshold of my dwelling, must think that I live in a dark cave – even though what he is able to see is bound to prove the contrary.

Well, I have read his brilliant restaurant reviews.

'I don't understand what he's talking about,' said Manuela; for her a good roast is a good roast and that's all there is to it.

There is nothing to understand. It's a pity to see such a worthy wordsmith blindly wasting his talent. To write entire pages of dazzling prose about a tomato – for Pierre Arthens reviews food as if he were telling a story, and that alone is enough to make him a genius – without ever *seeing* or *holding* the tomato is a troubling display of virtuosity. I have often wondered, as I watch him go by with his huge arrogant nose: can someone be so gifted and yet so impervious to the presence of things? It seems one can. Some people are incapable of perceiving in the object of their contemplation the very thing that gives it its intrinsic life and breath, and they spend their entire lives conversing about mankind as if they were robots, and about things as though they have no soul and must be reduced to what can be said about them – all at the whim of their own subjective inspiration.

As if on cue, the footsteps suddenly grow louder and Arthens rings at my lodge.

I stand up, careful to drag my feet: the slippers in which they are clad are so very typical that only the coalition between a baguette and a beret could possibly contend in the domain of cliché. In doing this, I know I am exasperating the Maître, for he is a living ode to the impatience of mighty predators, and this shall contribute to the diligence with which I very slowly open the door a crack to reveal my wary nose, which I trust is red and shiny.

'I'm expecting a courier package,' he says, eyes squinting and nostrils pinched. 'When it arrives, would you bring it to me immediately?'

This afternoon Monsieur Arthens is wearing a large polka-dot lavaliere that is too loose on his patrician neck and does not suit him at all: the abundance of his leonine mane and the floppiness of the silk cloth conspire to create a sort of vaporous tutu, causing the gentleman to forfeit his customary virility. Confound it, that lavaliere reminds me of something. I almost smile as it comes back to me. It's Legrandin, and his lavaliere. In *In Search of Lost Time*, the work of a certain Marcel, another notorious concierge, Legrandin is a snob who is torn between two worlds, his own and the one he would like to enter: he is a most pathetic snob whose lavaliere expresses his most secret vacillations between hope and bitterness, servility and disdain. Thus, when he has no wish to greet the narrator's parents on the square in Combray, but is nevertheless obliged to walk by them, he assigns to his scarf the task of floating in the wind, thereby signifying a melancholy mood that will exempt him from any conventional greeting.

Pierre Arthens may know his Proust, but, for all that, he has developed no particular indulgence towards concierges; he clears his throat impatiently.

To recall his question: 'Would you bring it to me immediately?' (The package sent by courier – rich people's parcels do not travel by the usual postal routes.)

'Yes,' I reply, beating all records of concision, encouraged by his own brevity and by the absence of any 'please', which the use of the interrogative conditional did not, in my opinion, entirely redeem.

'It's very fragile,' he adds, 'do be careful, I beg you.'

31

The use of the imperative and the 'I beg you' does not have the good fortune to find favour with me, particularly as he believes I am incapable of such syntactical subtleties, and merely uses them out of inclination, without having the least courtesy to suppose that I might feel insulted. You know you have reached the very bottom of the social food chain when you detect in a rich person's voice that he is merely addressing himself and that, although the words he is uttering may be, technically, destined for you, he does not even begin to imagine that you might be capable of understanding them.

'Fragile how?' I ask therefore, somewhat listlessly.

He sighs conspicuously and on his breath I detect a faint hint of ginger.

'It is an incunabulum,' he says and towards my eyes, which I try to render as glassy as possible, he directs the smug gaze of the propertied classes.

'Well, much good may it do you,' I retort with disgust. 'I'll bring it to you just as soon as the courier arrives.'

And I slam the door in his face.

The prospect that this evening Pierre Arthens will sit at his dinner table and entertain his family with a witty remark about his concierge's indignation over the mention of an incunabulum (no doubt she imagined that this was something improper) delights me no end.

God knows which one of us looks more of a fool.

Stay centred on yourself without losing your shorts

It's all well and good to have profound thoughts on a regular basis, but I think it's not enough. Well, I mean: I'm going to commit suicide and set the house on fire in a few months; obviously I can't assume I have much time at my disposal, therefore I have to do something substantial with the little I do have. And above all, I've set myself a little challenge: if you commit suicide, you have to be sure of what you're doing and not burn the house down for nothing. So if there is something on the planet that is worth living for, I'd better not miss it, because once you're dead, it's too late for regrets, and if you die by mistake, well, that is really, really stupid.

So, obviously, I have my profound thoughts. But in my profound thoughts, I am playing at who I am – hey, no way around it, I am an intellectual (who makes fun of other intellectuals). It's not always brilliant, but it's very entertaining. So I thought I ought to make up for this 'glory of the mind' side with a second journal that would talk about the body or about things. Not the profound thoughts of the mind, but the masterpieces of matter. Something incarnate, tangible. But beautiful and aesthetic at the same time. With the exception of love, friendship and the beauty of Art, I don't see much else that can nurture human life. I'm still too young to claim to know much about love and friendship. But Art . . . if I had more time to live, Art would be my whole life. Well, when I say Art, don't get me wrong: I'm not just talking about great works of art by great masters. Even Vermeer can't convince me to hold life dear. He's sublime, but he's dead. No,

I'm referring to the beauty that is there in the world, things that, being part of the movement of life, elevate us. The *Journal of the Movement of the World* will be devoted therefore to the movement of people, bodies, or even – if really there's nothing to say – things, and to finding whatever is beautiful enough to give life meaning. Grace, beauty, harmony, intensity. If I find something, then I may rethink my options: if I find a body with beautiful movement or, failing that, a beautiful idea for the mind, well then maybe I'll think that life is worth living after all.

In fact, I got this idea for a double journal (one for the mind, one for the body) yesterday. Papa was watching a rugby match on television. Up until now, at times like this I've looked mostly at Papa. I like to watch him roll up his shirtsleeves, take his shoes off and settle on the sofa with a beer and some saucisson, to watch the game as if declaring, 'Behold the man I also know how to be.' Apparently it doesn't occur to him that one stereotype (very serious Minister of the Republic) plus one more stereotype (Mr-Nice-Guy-all-the-same who likes his cold beer) makes a stereotype raised to the power of two. In short, on Saturday, Papa came home earlier than usual, threw his briefcase down any old place, took off his shoes, rolled up his sleeves, grabbed a beer in the kitchen and flopped in front of the television, and said, 'Sweetie, bring me some saucisson, please, I don't want to miss the haka.' As far as missing the haka went, I had plenty of time to slice the saucisson and bring it to him, the adverts were still on. Maman was sitting precariously on the arm of the sofa, to show how she was against the whole business (in her holier-than-thou-left-wing-intellectual pose), and she was badgering Papa with some complicated story about a dinner party where the idea was to invite two couples who'd fallen out, in order to reconcile them. Given Maman's psychological subtlety, this could be a very amusing undertaking. Anyway, I gave Papa his saucisson and, since I knew that Colombe was up in her room listening to music that was supposed to be enlightened avant-garde fifth arrondissement sort of stuff, I thought: after all, why not, let's watch a little haka. What I knew was that the haka is a sort of grotesque dance that the New Zealand team performs before the match. Sort of intimidation in the manner of the great apes. And I also knew that rugby is a heavy sort of game, with men falling all over each other on the grass all the time only to stand up and fall down and get all tangled up a few feet further along.

The adverts finally came to an end and, after credits showing a lot of beefcake sprawled on the grass, we had a view of the entire stadium with the commentators' voice-over and then a close-up of the commentators (all slavish cassoulet addicts) then back to the stadium. The players came onto the field and that's when I got hooked. I didn't really understand what was going on at first: there they were, all the usual images, but they had a new effect on me; they caused a kind of tingling, a sense of heady anticipation, sort of an 'I'm holding my breath' feeling. Next to me Papa had already knocked back his first barley beer, and was preparing to carry on in good Gallic fashion by asking Maman, who had just got up from her sofa arm, to bring him another. As for me, I was holding my breath. 'What's going on?' I wondered, watching the screen, and I couldn't figure out what I was seeing and what was giving me that tingling feeling.

Then when the New Zealand players began their haka, I got it. In their midst was this very tall Maori player, really young. I'd had my eye on him right from the start, probably because of his height to begin with but then because of the way he was moving. A really odd sort of movement, very fluid but above all very focused, I mean very focused within himself. Most people, when they move, well, they just move depending on whatever's around them. At this very moment, as I am writing, Constitution the cat is going by with her tummy dragging close to the floor. This cat has absolutely nothing constructive to do in life and still she is heading towards something, probably an armchair. And you can tell from the way she's moving: she is heading *towards*. Maman just went by in the direction of the front door, she's going out shopping and in fact she already is outside, her movement anticipating itself. I don't really know how to explain it, but when we move, we are in a way destructured by our movement *towards* something: we are both here and at the same time not here because we're already in the process of going elsewhere, if you see what I mean. To stop destructuring yourself, you have to stop moving altogether. Either you move and you're no longer whole, or you're whole and you can't move. But that player, when I saw him go out onto the field, I could tell there was something different about him. The impression that he was moving, yes, but by staying in one place. It's crazy, isn't it? When the haka began, I concentrated on him. It was obvious he wasn't like the others. Moreover, Cassoulet Number 1 said, 'And Somu, the formidable New Zealand fullback – what an impressive player, with a colossal build: six foot eight and eighteen stone, runs a hundred metres in eleven seconds, a fine specimen indeed, ladies!' Everyone was enthralled by him but no one seemed to know why. Yet it became obvious in the haka: he was moving and making the same gestures as the other players (slapping the palms of his hands on his thighs, rhythmically drumming his feet on the ground, touching his elbows, and all the while looking the adversary in the eye like a mad warrior), but while the others' gestures went *towards* their adversaries and the entire watching stadium, this player's gestures stayed inside him, stayed focused upon him, and that gave him an unbelievable presence and intensity. And so the haka, which is a warrior chant, gained all its strength from him. What makes the strength of a soldier isn't the energy he uses trying to intimidate his opponent by sending him a load of signals, it's the strength he's able to concentrate within himself, by staying centred. That Maori player was like a tree, a great indestructible oak with deep roots and a powerful radiance – everyone could feel it. And yet you also got the impression that the great oak could fly, that it would be as quick as the wind, despite, or perhaps because of, its deep roots.

So I watched the game attentively, constantly on the lookout for the same thing: compact moments where a player became his own movement without having to fragment himself by heading *towards*. And I saw them! I saw them in every phase of the game: in the scrums, with one clear point of equilibrium, a player who found his roots, who became a solid little anchor giving his strength to the group; then in the phases of deployment, with a player who would find the right speed without thinking any more about the goal, by concentrating on his own movement and running as if in a state of grace, with the ball stuck firmly to his body; and in the trance of the kicker, cut off from the rest of the world in order to find the perfect foot movement. But none of them came near the perfection of the great Maori player. When he scored the first try for New Zealand, Papa sat there dumbfounded, his mouth wide open, his beer quite forgotten. He should have been completely pissed off because he was rooting for the French team but instead, wiping his hand across his brow, he said, 'What a player!' The commentators were sort of hung over but they couldn't hide the fact that they'd seen something really beautiful: a player who was running without moving, leaving everyone else behind him. And the others, who seemed by comparison to move with frenzied and awkward gestures, were incapable of catching up with him.

So I said to myself: There, I have managed to witness motionless movement in the world: is that something worth carrying on for? And at that very moment a French player lost his shorts in a maul and suddenly I felt totally depressed because it made everyone else laugh so hard they cried, including Papa who had himself another beer to celebrate, despite two centuries of Protestantism in the family. I felt as if something had been profaned.

No, then, that won't be enough. Further movements will be necessary to convince me. But at least this one has given me an idea.

2. On Wars and Colonies

I have had no formal education, as I said in the preamble to these musings. Well, that is not exactly true. But my studious youth came to a halt at the certificate of studies, and before that time I was careful not to draw attention to myself – I was terribly frightened by the suspicions aroused in Monsieur Servant, my teacher, when he discovered that I had been avidly devouring his newspaper, which was filled with nothing but wars and colonies – and I was not yet ten years old.

Why? I do not know. Do you suppose I might really have continued? That's a question for the soothsayers of old. Let us just say that the idea of struggling to make my way in a world of privileged, affluent people exhausted me before I even tried: I was the child of nothing, I had neither beauty nor charm, neither past nor ambition; I had not the slightest savoir-faire or sparkle. There was only one thing I wanted: to be left alone, without too many demands upon my person, so that for a few moments each day I might be allowed to assuage my hunger.

For those who have no appetite, the first pangs of hunger are a source of both suffering and illumination. As a child I was apathetic, a virtual invalid, my posture so poor you would have taken me for a hunchback, and I only managed to get through my everyday life thanks to my ignorance of any alternatives. My lack of interest verged on the void: nothing spoke to me, nothing aroused me and, like a helpless wisp borne this way

38

and that upon some mysterious wind, I was not even aware of any desire to put an end to my existence.

There was very little conversation in my family. The children shrieked and the adults went about their business just as they would have had they been alone. We ate our fill, somewhat frugally, we were not mistreated and our paupers' rags were clean and sturdily mended so that even if we were ashamed, at least we did not suffer from the cold. But we did not speak.

The revelation occurred when, at the age of five, going to school for the first time, I was both astonished and frightened to hear a voice speaking to me and saying my name.

'Renée?' asked the voice, and I felt a friendly hand on mine.

This happened in the corridor where, for the first day of school, they had gathered the children, as it was raining outside.

'Renée?' I heard again the inflections of the voice above me, and felt the touch of the friendly hand – an incomprehensible language – still pressing lightly and tenderly on my arm.

I raised my head, an unusual, almost dizzying movement, and met a pair of eyes.

Renée. That meant me. For the first time, someone was talking to me, saying my name. Where my parents habitually merely gestured or grunted, here was a woman with clear eyes and a smiling mouth standing before me, and she was finding her way to my heart, saying my name, entering with me into a closeness I had not previously known existed. I looked around me and saw a world that was suddenly filled with colours. In one painful flash I became aware of the rain falling outside, the windows streaked with water, the smell of damp clothing, the confinement of the corridor, the narrow passageway vibrating with the press of pupils, the shine of the coat racks with their copper hooks where capes made of cheap cloth were hung close together, and the height of the ceiling which, to the eyes of a small child, was like that of the sky.

So, with my doleful eyes glued to hers, I clung to the woman who had just brought me into the world.

'Renée,' said the voice again, 'don't you want to take off your raincoat?'

And, holding me firmly so I would not fall, she removed my clothes with the agility of long experience.

We are mistaken to believe that our consciousness is awakened at the moment of our first birth – perhaps because we do not know how to imagine any other living state. It may seem to us that we have always seen and felt and, armed with this belief, we identify our entry into the world as the decisive instant where consciousness is born. The fact that for five years a little girl called Renée, a perfectly operational machine of perception blessed with sight, hearing, smell, taste and touch, could have lived in a state of utter unawareness both of herself and of the universe, is proof if any were needed that such a hasty theory is wrong. Because in order for consciousness to be aroused, it must have a name.

However, a combination of unfortunate circumstances would seem to confirm that no one had ever thought of giving me my name.

'You have such pretty eyes,' added the teacher, and I knew intuitively that she was not lying, that at that moment my eyes were shining with all their beauty and, to reflect the miracle of my birth, were sparkling with a thousand small fires.

I began to tremble and looked into her eyes for the complicity that shared joy can bring.

In her gentle, kindly gaze I saw nothing but compassion.

In the moment where I had at last come to life, I was merely pitied.

I was possessed.

As my hunger could not be assuaged by playing the game of social interaction – an inconceivable aim, given my social condition (and it was at a later point in time that I would grasp the meaning of the compassion I saw in the eyes of my saviour – for has one ever seen a girl raised in poverty penetrate the headiness of language deeply enough to share it with others?) – then it would be appeased by books. I touched one for the first time. I'd seen the older children in class look into books for invisible traces, as if they were driven by the same force and, sinking deeper into silence, they were able to draw from the dead paper something that seemed alive.

Unbeknownst to all, I learned to read. When the teacher was still droning away with the letters of the alphabet to my classmates, I had already been long acquainted with the solidarity that weaves written signs together, the infinite combinations and marvellous sounds that had dubbed me a dame in this place, on that first day, when she had said my name. No one knew. I read as if deranged, at first in hiding and then, once it seemed to me that the normal amount of time to learn one's letters had elapsed, out in the open for all to see, but I was careful to conceal the pleasure and interest that reading afforded me.

The feeble child had become a hungry soul.

At the age of twelve I left school and worked at home and in the fields alongside my parents and my brothers and sisters. At seventeen I married.

3. The Poodle as Totem

In the collective imagination, the couple formed by married concierges – a close-knit pair consisting of two entities so insignificant that only their union can make them apparent – will in all likelihood be the owners of a poodle. As we all know, poodles are a type of curly-haired dog preferred by retired petty bourgeois reactionaries, ladies very much on their own who transfer their affection to their pet, or residential concierges ensconced in their gloomy lodges. Poodles come in black or apricot. The apricot ones tend to be crabbier than the black ones, who on the other hand do not smell as nice. Though all poodles bark snappily at the slightest provocation, but in particular when nothing at all is happening. They follow their master by trotting on their stiff little legs without moving the rest of their sausage-shaped trunk. Above all they have venomous little black eyes set deep in their insignificant eye-sockets. Poodles are ugly and stupid, submissive and boastful. They are poodles, after all.

Thus the concierge couple, as served by the metaphor of their totemic poodle, seems to be utterly devoid of such passions as love and desire and, like their totem, destined to remain ugly, stupid, submissive and boastful. If, in certain novels, princes fall in love with working-class lasses, and princesses with galley slaves, between two concierges, even of the opposite sex, there is never any romance of the type that others experience and that might some day make a worthy story.

Not only were we never the owners of a poodle, but I believe I can fairly assert that our marriage was a success. With my husband, I was myself. I think back to our little Sunday mornings with nostalgia, mornings blessed with restfulness where, in the silent kitchen, he would drink his coffee while I read.

I married him at the age of seventeen following a swift but proper courtship. He worked at the factory, as did my older brothers, and stopped off on many evenings on his way home to drink a coffee and a drop of something stronger. Alas, I was ugly. And yet that would not have played the slightest role had I been ugly the way others are ugly. But I bore the cruelty of my affliction alone: this ugliness that deprived me of any freshness, although I was not yet a woman, and caused me at the age of fifteen to resemble the woman I would be at the age of fifty. My stooped back, thick waist, short legs, widespread feet, abundant hair, and lumpy features – well, features lacking any shapeliness or grace – might have been overlooked for the sake of the youthful charm granted to even the most unpre-possessing amongst us – but no, at the age of twenty I already qualified as an old biddy.

Thus, when the intentions of my future husband became clear and it was no longer possible for me to ignore them, I opened my heart to him, speaking frankly for the first time to someone other than my own self, and I confessed to him how astonished I was that he might conceive of wanting to marry me.

I was sincere. I had for many years accustomed myself to the prospect of a solitary life. To be poor, ugly and, moreover, intelligent condemns one, in our society, to a dark and dis-illusioned life, a condition one ought to accept at an early age. To beauty, all is forgiven, even vulgarity. Intelligence no longer seems an adequate compensation for things – some sort of balancing of the scales offered by nature to those less favoured among her children – no, it is a superfluous plaything to enhance the value of the jewel. As for ugliness, it is guilty from the start, and I was doomed by my tragic destiny to suffer all the more, for I was hardly stupid.

'Renée,' he replied, with as much gravity as he could muster, showing himself to be more loquacious during the long disquisition to come than he would ever be again, 'Renée, I don't want my wife to be one of those giddy young things who run wild and have no more brain than a sparrow beneath their pretty face. I want a woman who's loyal, a good wife, a good mother and a good housekeeper. I want a calm and steady companion who'll stay by my side and support me. In exchange, you can expect me to be a serious worker, a calm man at home and a tender husband at the right moment. I'm not a bad sort, and I'll do my best.'

And he did.

Small and dry like the stump of an elm tree, he had nevertheless a pleasant face and usually wore a smile. He did not drink, smoke, chew tobacco or gamble. At home, when work was over, he'd watch television, browse through fishing magazines or play cards with his friends from the factory. He was very sociable and often invited people over. On Sundays he went fishing. As for me, I looked after the house, because he didn't like the idea of me doing it for other people.

He was not lacking in intelligence, although his particular intelligence was not of the sort that an industrious society values. While his skills were confined to manual work, he displayed a talent that did not stem solely from mere mechanical aptitude and, however uneducated he might have been, he approached everything with a spirit of ingeniousness, something which, where small tasks are concerned, distinguishes the artists from the mere labourers and, in conversation, shows that knowledge is not everything. Having been resigned from an early age to the prospect of the life of a nun, I felt therefore that it was benign indeed of the heavens to have placed between my young bride's hands a companion with such agreeable manners and who, while not an intellectual, was no less clever for it.

I might have ended up with someone like Grelier.

Bernard Grelier is one of the rare souls at 7, Rue de Grenelle in whose presence I have no fear of betraying myself. Whether I say to him: '*War and Peace* is the staging of a determinist vision of history' or 'You'd do well to oil the hinges in the rubbish store,' he will not find that one is any more significant than the other. It even seems miraculous that the latter phrase manages to fire him into action. How can one do something one does not understand? No doubt this type of proposition does not require any rational processing and, like those stimuli that move in a loop through our bone marrow and set off a reflex without calling on the brain, perhaps the summons to apply oil is merely of a mechanical nature and sets in motion a reaction in one's limbs without inviting the mind to participate.

Bernard Grelier is the husband of Violette Grelier, who is the 'housekeeper' for the Arthens. She began working for them thirty years ago as a simple maid, and she rose through the ranks as they in turn became wealthier, and once she was a housekeeper she found herself reigning over a laughable kingdom whose subjects were the cleaning lady (Manuela), the part-time butler (an Englishman) and the factotum (her husband); she is as scornful of the lower classes as are her high and mighty upper-class employers. All day long she jabbers like a magpie, busily rushing here and there, acting important, reprimanding her menial subalterns as if this were Versailles in better days, and exhausting Manuela with pontificating speeches about the love of a job well done and the decline of good manners.

'She hasn't read Marx,' said Manuela to me one day.

The pertinence of this remark uttered by a Portuguese woman who is in no way well versed in the study of philosophy is striking. No, Violette Grelier has certainly not read any Marx, for the simple reason that he does not appear on any lists of cleaning products for rich people's silverware. She has paid the price for this oversight by inheriting a daily routine punctuated with endless catalogues vaunting the qualities of starch and linen dusters.

I, therefore, had married well.

To my husband, moreover, I had very quickly confessed my great sin.

Profound Thought No. 2

The cat here on earth
Modern totem
And intermittently decorative

I n any case, this is true at our place. If you want to understand my family, all you have to do is look at the cats. Our two cats are fat windbags who eat designer cat food and have no interesting interaction with human beings. They drag themselves from one sofa to the next and leave their fur everywhere, and no one seems to have grasped that they have no affection for any of us. The only purpose of cats is that they constitute mobile decorative objects, a concept which I find intellectually interesting, but, unfortunately, our cats have such drooping bellies that this does not apply to them.

My mother, who has read all of Balzac and quotes Flaubert at every dinner, is living proof every day of how education is a raging fraud. All you need to do is watch her with the cats. She's vaguely aware of their decorative potential, and yet she insists on talking to them as if they were people, which she would never do with a lamp or an Etruscan statue. It would seem that children believe for a fairly long time that anything that moves has a soul and is endowed with intention. My mother is no longer a child but she apparently has not managed to conceive that Constitution and Parliament possess no more understanding than the vacuum cleaner. I concede that the difference between the vacuum cleaner and the cats is that a cat can experience pain and pleasure. But does that mean it has a greater ability to *communicate* with humans? Not at all. That should simply incite us to take special precautions with them as we would with very fragile objects. When I hear my mother say,

47

'Constitution is both a very proud and very sensitive little cat,' when in fact said cat is sprawled on the sofa because she's eaten too much, it really makes me want to laugh. But if you think about the hypothesis that a cat's purpose is to act as a modern totem, a sort of emblematic incarnation, protector of the home, reflecting well upon its owners, then everything becomes clear. My mother makes the cats into what she wishes we were, and which we absolutely are not. You won't find anyone less proud and sensitive than the three aforementioned members of the Josse family: Papa, Maman and Colombe. They are utterly spineless and anaesthetised, emptied of all emotion.

In short, in my opinion the cat is a modern totem. Say what you want, do what you will with all those fine speeches on evolution, civilisation and a ton of other '-tion' words, mankind has not progressed very far from its origins: people still believe they're not here by chance, and that there are gods, kindly for the most part, who are watching over their fate.

4. Refusing the Fight

I have read so many books . . .

And yet, like most autodidacts, I am never quite sure of what I have gained from them. There are days when I feel I have been able to grasp all there is to know in one single gaze, as if invisible branches suddenly spring out of nowhere, weaving together all the disparate strands of my reading – and then suddenly the meaning escapes, the essence evaporates, and no matter how often I reread the same lines, they seem to flee ever further with each subsequent reading, and I see myself as some mad old fool who thinks her stomach is full because she's been attentively reading the menu. Apparently this combination of ability and blindness is a symptom exclusive to the autodidact. Deprived of the steady guiding hand that any good education provides, the autodidact possesses nonetheless the gift of freedom and conciseness of thought, where official discourse would put up barriers and prohibit adventure.

This morning, as it happens, I am standing, puzzled, in the kitchen, with a little book set down before me. I am in the midst of one of those moments where the folly of my solitary undertaking takes hold of me and, on the verge of giving up, I fear I have finally found my master.

His name is Husserl, a name not often given to pets or to brands of chocolate, for the simple reason that it evokes something grave, daunting and vaguely Prussian. But that is of little consolation. I believe that my fate has taught me, better than anyone, to resist the negative influences of world thought. Let me explain: if, thus far, you have imagined that the ugliness of ageing and conciergely widowhood have made a pitiful wretch of me, resigned to the lowliness of her fate – then you are truly lacking in imagination. I have withdrawn, to be sure, and refuse to fight. But within the safety of my own mind, there is no challenge I cannot accept. I may be indigent in name, position and appearance, but in my own mind I am an unrivalled goddess.

Thus Edmund Husserl – and I have concluded that this is a name fit for vacuum-cleaner bags – has been threatening the stability of my private Mount Olympus.

'All right, all right, all right,' I say, taking a deep breath, 'to every problem there is a solution, isn't there?' I glance at the cat, waiting for a sign of encouragement.

The ungrateful wretch does not respond. He has just devoured a monstrous slice of rillettes and, henceforth imbued with great kindliness, has colonised the armchair.

'All right, all right, all right,' I say again like an idiot and, puzzled, I stare at the ridiculous little book.

Cartesian Meditations – Introduction to Phenomenology. It quickly becomes clear, given both the title and the first few pages, that it is not possible to read Husserl, a phenomenological philosopher, if one has not already read Descartes and Kant. And yet one discovers with equal alacrity that even a solid mastery of Descartes and Kant will not, for all that, open the doors to transcendental phenomenology.

This is a pity. Because I have great admiration for Kant, for a number of reasons: his ideas are an admirable concentration of genius, rigour and madness, and however spartan the prose might be, I have had no difficulty in penetrating the meaning. Kantian texts are great works of literature, and I would like to prove this by demonstrating their ability to pass, with flying colours, the cherry plum test.

The cherry plum test is extraordinary for its disarming clarity. It derives its power from a universal observation: when man bites into the fruit, at last he understands. What does he understand? Everything. He understands how the human species, given only to survival, slowly matured and arrived one fine day at an intuition of pleasure, the vanity of all the artificial appetites that divert one from one's initial aspiration towards the virtues of simple and sublime things, the pointlessness of discourse, the slow and terrible degradation of multiple worlds from which no one can escape and, in spite of all that, the wonderful sweetness of the senses when they conspire to teach mankind pleasure and the terrifying beauty of Art.

The cherry plum test is held in my kitchen. I place the fruit and the book on the Formica table, and as I pick up the former to taste it, I also start on the latter. If each resists the powerful onslaught of the other, if the cherry plum fails to make me doubt the text and if the text is unable to spoil the fruit, then I know that I am in the presence of a worthwhile and, why not say it, exceptional undertaking, for there are very few works that have not dissolved – proven both ridiculous and complacent – into the extraordinary succulence of the little golden plums.

'I am truly up the creek,' I say to Leo, because my skills where Kant is concerned do not amount to anything when I contemplate the abyss of phenomenology.

I am left with no alternative. I will have to enlist the help of the library and attempt to unearth an introduction to the matter at hand. Ordinarily I am very wary of such glosses or short cuts which tend to place the reader in the iron grip of scholastic thought. But the situation is far too grave for me to allow myself the indulgence of equivocation. Phenomenology is beyond my reach and that I cannot bear.

Profound Thought No. 3

> *The strong ones*
> *Among humans*
> *Do nothing*
> *They talk*
> *And talk again*

I t's one of my profound thoughts, but it came from another profound thought. It was one of Papa's guests, at the dinner party yesterday, who said: 'Those who can, do; those who can't, teach; those who can't teach, teach the teachers; and those who can't teach the teachers go into politics.' Everyone seemed to find this very inspiring but for the wrong reasons. 'That's so true,' said Colombe, who is an expert at fake self-criticism. She's one of those who think that knowledge is power and forgiveness: if I know that I belong to a self-satisfied elite who are sacrificing the common good through an excess of arrogance, this liberates me from criticism, and I come out with twice the prestige. Papa also tends to think like this, although he's less of an idiot than my sister. He still believes that something known as duty exists and although in my opinion that's just pure fancy, it protects him from the cynic's weakness. Let me explain: nobody is a greater schoolgirl in spirit than a cynic. Cynics cannot relinquish the rubbish they were taught as children: they hold tight to the belief that the world has meaning and, when things go wrong for them, they consequently adopt the inverse attitude. 'Life's a whore, I don't believe in anything any more and I'll wallow in that idea until it makes me sick' is the very credo of the innocent who hasn't been able to get his way. That's my sister to a T. She may be a student at the École Normale, but she still believes in Santa Claus, not because she has a good heart but because she is totally childish. She started giggling like an idiot when Papa's colleague came out with his fancy phrase, as if to say, 'I'm an expert on the mise en abyme,' and that confirmed what I've been thinking for a long time: Colombe is a walking disaster.

As for me, I think that his sentence is a bona fide profound thought, precisely because it isn't true, or at least not entirely true. It doesn't mean what you think it does at the outset. If people could climb higher in the social hierarchy in proportion to their incompetence, I guarantee the world would not go round the way it does. But that's not even the problem. What his sentence means isn't that incompetent people have found their place in the sun, but that nothing is harder or more unfair than human reality: humans live in a world where it's words and not deeds that have power, where the ultimate skill is mastery of language. This is a terrible thing because basically we are primates who've been programmed to eat, sleep, reproduce, conquer and make our territory safe, and the ones who are most gifted at that, the most animal types among us, always get shafted by the others, the fine talkers, despite the latter being incapable of defending their own garden or bringing a rabbit home for dinner or procreating properly. Humans live in a world where the weak are dominant. This is a terrible insult to our animal nature, a sort of perversion or a deep contradiction.

5. In a Sorry State

After one month of frenetic reading I come to the conclusion, with immense relief, that phenomenology is a fraud. In the same way that cathedrals have always aroused in me the sensation of extreme light-headedness one often feels in the presence of man-made tributes to the glory of something that does not exist, phenomenology has tested to the extreme my ability to believe that so much intelligence could have gone to serve so futile an undertaking. As this is already the month of November, there are no cherry plums available. At times like this therefore – eleven months of the year in actual fact – I have to make do with dark chocolate (70%). But I know in advance the outcome of the test. Had I but the leisure to bite into the standard metre, I would slap myself noisily on the thighs while reading, and such delightful chapters as 'Uncovering the final sense of science by becoming immersed in science qua noematic phenomenon' or 'The problems constituting the transcendental ego' might even cause me to die of laughter, a blow straight to the heart as I sit slumped in my plush armchair, with plum juice or thin driblets of chocolate oozing from the corners of my mouth . . .

When you set out to deal with phenomenology, you have to be aware of the fact that it boils down to two questions: What is the nature of human consciousness? What do we know of the world?

Let's start with the first question.

For millennia now, by way of 'know thyself' to 'I think

therefore I am', mankind has been rambling on about the ridiculous human prerogative that is our consciousness of our own existence and above all the ability of this consciousness to make itself its own object. When something itches, a man scratches and is aware that he is scratching. If you ask him, What are you doing? he'll reply: I'm scratching myself. If you push your questioning a bit further (are you aware that you are conscious of the fact that you are scratching yourself?) he will again reply, Yes; thus, ad infinitum to as many are-you-aware-and-conscious questions as you wish. Does this, however, leave man with any less of an itch to know that he is scratching and is aware of it? Can reflective consciousness have a beneficial influence on the order of the itching? Nay, not in the slightest. Knowing that it itches and being conscious of the fact that one is conscious of knowing it has absolutely no effect on the fact of the itching. As an added handicap one must endure the lucidity that results from this wretched condition, and I would wager ten pounds of cherry plums that such lucidity merely serves to exacerbate an unpleasant condition which my cat, for example, can eliminate with a quick flick or two of his rear paw. But it seems so extraordinary to us – no other animal is capable of this and in this way we escape our own animal nature – that as human beings we are able to know that we are in the process of scratching ourselves; this pre-eminence of human consciousness seems to many to be the manifestation of something divine that is able to escape the cold determinism in us to which all physical things are subject.

All of phenomenology is founded on this certainty: our reflective consciousness, the sign of our ontological dignity, is the only entity we have that is worth studying, for it saves us from biological determinism.

No one seems aware of the fact that, since *we are* animals subject to the cold determinism of physical things, all of the foregoing is null and void.

6. Homespun Cowls

Which brings us to the second question: What do we know of the world?

Idealists such as Kant have an answer to this question.

What do they answer?

They answer: not a great deal.

Transcendental idealism holds that we can know only that which appears to our consciousness, that semi-divine entity that rescues us from our animal self. What we know of the world is what our consciousness can say about it because of what it has perceived – and nothing else.

Let us take an example, at random, a sweet cat by the name of Leo. Why? Because I find it easier with a cat. And let me ask you: how can you be certain that it really is a cat and likewise, how can you even know what a cat is? A sound reply would consist in emphasising the fact that your perception of the animal, complemented by a few conceptual and linguistic mechanisms, has enabled you to constitute your knowledge. But the response of the transcendental idealist would be to illustrate how impossible it is to know whether what we perceive and conceive of as a cat – if that which appears to our consciousness as a cat – is actually true to what the cat is in its deepest being. It may well be that my cat – at present I perceive him as an obese quadruped with quivering whiskers and I have filed him away in my mind in a drawer labelled 'cat' – is in actual fact, and in his very essence, a blob of green sticky stuff that does not meow. My senses, however, have been fashioned in such a way that this is not apparent to me, and the revolting blob of green sticky stuff, deceiving both my disgust and my earnest trust, is masquerading before my consciousness beneath the appearance of a silky and gluttonous house pet.

So much for Kantian idealism. What we know of the world is only the *idea* that our consciousness forms of it. But there is an even more depressing theory than that one, a theory that offers a prospect even more terrifying than that of innocently caressing a lump of green slime or dropping our toast every morning into a pustular abyss we had mistaken for a toaster.

There is the idealism of Edmund Husserl, which as far as I'm concerned now signifies designer-label homespun cowls for wayward monks sidetracked by some obscure schism in the Baptist Church.

According to Husserl's theory, all that exists is the perception of the cat. And the cat itself? Well, we can just do without it. Bye-bye kitty. Who needs a cat? What cat? Henceforth, philosophy will claim the right to wallow exclusively in the wickedness of pure mind. The world is an inaccessible reality and any effort to try to know it is futile. What do we know of the world? Nothing. As all knowledge is merely reflective consciousness exploring its own self, the world, therefore, can merrily go to the devil.

This is phenomenology: the 'science of that which appears to our consciousness'. How does a phenomenologist spend his day? He gets up, fully conscious as he takes his shower that he is merely soaping a body whose existence has no foundation, then he wolfs down a few slices of toast and jam that have been nihilised, puts on some clothes that are the equivalent of an empty set of parentheses, heads for his office and then snatches up a cat.

It matters little to our phenomenologist whether the cat exists or does not exist or even what the cat is in its very essence. The indemonstrable does not interest him. What cannot be denied, however, is that a cat appeared to his consciousness, and it is this act of appearing that is of concern to our good fellow.

And what is more, an act of appearing that is quite complex. The fact that one can explain, in detail, the way in which one's consciousness perceives a thing whose very existence is a matter of indifference is simply extraordinary. Did you know that our consciousness does not perceive things straight off but performs a complicated series of operations of synthesis which, by means of successive profiling, introduce to our senses objects as diverse as, for example, a cat, a broom or a fly swatter – and, God knows, isn't that useful? Have you ever wondered why it is that you can observe your cat and know at the same time what he looks like from the front, behind, above and below – even though at the present moment you are perceiving him only from the front? It must be that your consciousness, without your even realising it, has been synthesising multiple perceptions of your cat from every possible angle, and has ended up creating this integral image of the cat that your sight, at that moment, could never give you. And the same is true for the fly swatter, which you will only ever perceive from one direction even though you can visualise it in its entirety in your mind and, oh miracle, you know perfectly well without even turning it over how it is made on the other side.

You will agree that such knowledge is quite useful. We can't imagine Manuela using a fly swatter without immediately rallying the knowledge that she has of the various stages of profiling necessary to her perception. Moreover, you can't imagine Manuela using a fly swatter for the simple reason that there are never any flies in rich people's apartments. Neither flies, nor pox, nor bad smells, nor family secrets. In rich people's apartments everything is clean, smooth, healthy and consequently safe from the tyranny of fly swatters and public opprobrium.

But enough of phenomenology: it is nothing more than the solitary, endless monologue of consciousness, a hardcore autism that no real cat would ever importune.

7. In the Confederate South

'What are you reading?' asks Manuela, who has just arrived breathless from her Lady de Broglie's, feeling consumptive after preparing the evening's dinner party. She had just accepted delivery of seven jars of Petrossian caviar and was breathing like Darth Vader.

'An anthology of folk poems,' I say, closing the Husserl chapter forever.

Manuela is in a good mood today, that I can see. She eagerly unpacks a little hamper filled with almond sponge fingers that are still set in the frilly white paper in which they were baked, then sits down and smooths the tablecloth carefully with the flat of her hand, the prelude to a statement that will send her into transports of delight.

I set out the cups, join her at the table and wait.

'Madame de Broglie is not pleased with her truffles,' she begins.

'Oh, really?' I ask politely.

'They do not smell,' continues Manuela crossly, as if she held this shortcoming to be an enormous personal affront.

We indulge in this information for all it is worth, and I savour the vision of Bernadette de Broglie in her kitchen, looking haggard and dishevelled and doing her utmost to spray a potion of cep and chanterelle juice onto the offending roots in the ridiculous, insane hope that they might condescend to give off some faint odour evocative of the forest.

'And Neptune peed on Monsieur Saint-Nice's leg,' continues

Manuela. 'The poor beast must have been holding it in for hours, and when Monsieur Badoise finally got out the leash the dog couldn't wait, and in the entrance he went on Saint-Nice's trouser leg.'

Neptune, a cocker spaniel, belongs to the owners of the third-floor right-hand-side apartment. The second and third floors are the only ones divided into two apartments (of two thousand square feet each). On the first floor you have the de Broglies, on the fourth the Arthens, on the fifth the Josses and on the sixth the Pallières. On the second floor are the Meurisses and the Rosens. On the third, the Saint-Nices and the Badoises. Neptune belongs to the Badoises, or more precisely, to Mademoiselle Badoise, who is studying for her law degree at Assas, and who organises soirées with other cocker spaniel owners studying for law degrees at Assas.

I am very fond of Neptune. Yes, we appreciate each other a great deal, no doubt because of that state of grace that is attained when one's feelings are immediately accessible to another creature's. Neptune can sense that I love him; his multiple desires are perfectly clear to me. What charms me about the whole business is that he stubbornly insists on remaining a dog, whereas his mistress would like to make a gentleman of him. When he goes out into the courtyard, he runs to the very very end of his leash and stares covetously at the puddles of muddy water idling before him. His mistress has only to give one jerk to his yoke for him to lower his hindquarters down onto the ground, and with no further ado he will set to licking his attributes. The sight of Athena, the Meurisses' ridiculous whippet, causes Neptune to stick his tongue out like a lubricious satyr and pant in anticipation, his head filled with phantasms. What is particularly amusing about cocker spaniels is their swaying gait when they are in a playful mood; it's as if they had tiny little springs screwed to their paws that cause them to bounce upwards – but gently, without jolting. This also affects their paws and ears like the rolling of a ship, so cocker spaniels, like jaunty little vessels plying dry land, lend a nautical touch to the urban landscape: utterly enchanting.

Ultimately, however, Neptune is a greedy glutton who'll do anything for a scrap of turnip or a crust of stale bread. When his mistress leads him past the rubbish store, he pulls frenetically in the direction of said room, tongue lolling, tail wagging madly. Diane Badoise despairs of such behaviour. To her distinguished soul it seems that one's dog should be like the young ladies of antebellum high society in Savannah in the Confederate South, who could scarcely find a husband unless they feigned to have no appetite whatsoever.

But instead, Neptune carries on as if he were some famished Yankee.

Bacon for the cocker spaniel

In our building there are two dogs: the whippet belonging to the Meurisses who looks like a skeleton covered in beige hide, and a ginger cocker spaniel who belongs to Diane Badoise, an anorexic blonde woman who wears Burberry raincoats and who is the daughter of a very la-di-da lawyer. The whippet is called Athena and the cocker Neptune. Just in case you haven't yet understood what sort of place I live in: you won't find any Fidos or Rovers in our building. Anyway, yesterday, in the hallway, the two dogs met and I was fortunate to witness a very interesting sort of ballet. I won't dwell on the dogs, who sniffed each other's bottoms. I don't know if Neptune smells bad but Athena took a leap backwards while Neptune looked as if he were sniffing a bouquet of roses with a huge juicy steak in the middle.

No, what was interesting was the two human beings at the end of each leash. Because in town it is the dogs who have their masters on a leash, though no one seems to have caught on to the fact. If you have voluntarily saddled yourself with a dog that you'll have to walk twice a day, come rain, wind or snow, that is as good as putting a leash around your own neck. Anyway, Diane Badoise and Anne-Hélène Meurisse (same mould, twenty-five years apart) met in the hallway, each at the end of her leash. What a muddle when this happens! They're as clumsy as if they had webbed fingers and feet because they're incapable of doing the only truly practical thing in cases like this: acknowledge what is going on in order to prevent it. But because they act as if they believed they were walking two distinguished stuffed animals utterly devoid of any inappropriate impulses, they cannot bleat at their dogs to stop sniffing their arses or licking their little balls.

So here's what happened: Diane Badoise came out of the lift with Neptune, and Anne-Hélène Meurisse was waiting right outside with Athena. They virtually threw their dogs one on top of the other and, obviously, it drove Neptune utterly crazy. Here you come nicely trotting out of the lift only to find your nose right up against Athena's derrière, that's not something that happens every day. For ages now Colombe has been ranting on to us about *kairos*, a Greek concept that means roughly 'the right moment', something at which Napoleon apparently excelled. Naturally, my sister is an expert on military strategy. Anyway, *kairos* is the intuition of the moment, something like that. Well, I can tell you that Neptune had his *kairos* right in front of his nose and he didn't mess around, he made like a hussar, in the old style, and climbed right on top. 'Oh my God!' shrieked Anne-Hélène Meurisse as if she herself were victim of this outrage. 'Oh, no!' exclaimed Diane Badoise, as if all the shame were hers, though I'd bet you a chocolate truffle that it would never have occurred to her to climb onto Athena's rear end. And they both began pulling at their dogs' leashes but there was a problem, and that's what evolved into an interesting movement.

In fact, Diane should have pulled upwards and the other lady downwards, which would have released the two dogs but, instead of that, they each pulled sideways and as it's very narrow in front of the lift cage, they very quickly ran into an obstacle: one of them the lift grille, the other the wall on the left and as a result Neptune, who had lost his balance with the first tug, suddenly had a surge of energy and clung all the more solidly to Athena who was howling and rolling her eyes with fright. At that point the humans changed strategy by trying to drag their dogs away to a larger space so that they could repeat the manoeuvre more comfortably. But the matter was getting urgent: everyone knows there's a point at which dogs get stuck. So they really stepped on it, shouting simultaneously, 'Oh my God oh my God,' pulling on their leashes as if their very virtue was at stake. But in her haste, Diane Badoise slipped and twisted her ankle. And this was the moment of the interesting movement: her ankle twisted outwards and at the same time her entire body swerved in the same direction, except for her ponytail which went the opposite way.

It was magnificent, I assure you: it was like something by Bacon. There's been a framed Bacon in my parents' bathroom forever, a picture of someone on the potty, in fact, and in good Bacon style, you know, sort of tortured and not very appetising. I have always thought that it probably had an effect on the serenity of one's actions but anyway in my house we each have our own toilet so there was no point complaining. But Diane Badoise was completely thrown out of joint when she twisted her ankle, making weird angles with her knees, her arms and her head, and to top it off, her ponytail sticking out horizontally like that – and I immediately thought of the Bacon in the bathroom. For a very brief moment she looked like a disjointed rag doll, her body completely contorted and, for a few thousandths of a second (it happened very quickly, but, as I am very attentive to the movements of the body these days, I saw it as if in slow motion), Diane Badoise looked like a full-length portrait by Bacon. From that sudden impression to the consideration that the thing in the bathroom has been there all these years just so now I could fully appreciate her bizarre contortions, there is only a short step. And then Diane fell onto the dogs and that solved the problem because Athena, crushed on the ground, managed to wriggle free of Neptune. A complicated little ballet then followed, Anne-Hélène trying to help Diane and all the while keep her dog at a safe distance from the lubricious monster, and Neptune, completely indifferent to the shouts and pain of his mistress, continued to pull in the direction of his *steak à la rose*. But at that very moment Madame Michel came out of her lodge and I grabbed Neptune's leash and dragged him farther away.

He was so disappointed, poor mutt. And so he flopped down and started licking his little balls, making a lot of slurping noises, which only added to poor Diane's despair. Madame Michel called an ambulance because Diane's ankle was seriously beginning to look like a watermelon and then she took Neptune to her place while Anne-Hélène Meurisse stayed with Diane. As for me, I went home and said to myself, OK, a Bacon come to life before my very eyes, does that make it worth it?

I decided it didn't: because not only did Neptune not get his treat but, on top of that, he didn't even get his walk.

8. Prophet of the Modern Elite

This morning, while listening to France Inter on the radio, I was surprised to discover that I am not who I thought I was. Up until then I had ascribed the reasons for my cultural eclecticism to my condition as a proletarian autodidact. As I have already explained, I have spent every moment of my existence that could be spared from work in reading, watching films and listening to music. But my frenzied devouring of cultural objects seems to me to suffer from a major error of taste: brutally mixing respectable works with others that are far less so.

It is most certainly in the domain of reading that my eclecticism is least pronounced, though even there the variety of my interests is the most extreme. I have read history, philosophy, economics, sociology, psychology, pedagogy, psychoanalysis and, of course – above all – literature. While all these topics have always interested me, literature has been my whole life. My cat Leo was baptised thus because of Tolstoy. My previous cat was called Dongo because of Stendhal's Fabrice del. The first one was called Karenina because of Anna but I called her Karé for short, for fear of being found out. With the exception of my guilty lapse where Stendhal is concerned, my taste is most definitely partial to pre-1910 Russia, but it flatters my pride to note that the amount of world literature I have devoured is nevertheless considerable, given the fact that I am a country girl who, by ending up head concierge at 7, Rue de Grenelle, has witnessed her career expectations go far beyond what she anticipated – particularly when you think that such a destiny should surely have doomed her to the eternal worship of Barbara Cartland. I do confess to a guilty indulgence for detective stories – but the ones I read I consider to be true works of literature. I find it especially exasperating when, from time to time, I have to drag myself away from my Connelly or Mankell in order to go and answer the door for Bernard Grelier or Sabine Pallières, whose concerns are hardly shared by the likes of Harry Bosch, the jazz-loving LAPD cop, and all the more so when all they have to say is:

'How come the rubbish smells all the way out into the courtyard?'

That both Bernard Grelier and the heiress of an old Banque de France family could speak in so colloquial a manner and be preoccupied by the same trivial things sheds a new light on humanity.

Where the cinema is concerned, however, my eclecticism is in full flower. I like American blockbusters and art-house films. In fact, for a long time I preferred to watch entertaining British or American films, with the exception of a few serious works that I reserved for my aesthetic sensibilities, since my passionate or empathetic sensibilities were exclusively focused on entertainment. Greenaway fills me with admiration, interest and yawns, whereas I weep buckets of syrupy tears every time Melly and Mammy climb the staircase at the Butler mansion after Bonnie Blue dies; as for *Blade Runner,* it is a masterpiece of high-end escapism. For years my inevitable conclusion has been that the films of the seventh art are beautiful, powerful and soporific, and that blockbuster movies are pointless, very moving and immensely satisfying.

Take today, for example. I quiver with impatience at the thought of the treat I have in store – the fruit of exemplary patience, the long-deferred satisfaction of my desire to see, once again, a film I saw for the first time at Christmas, in 1989.

9. Red October

B y Christmas 1989 Lucien was very sick. We did not yet know when his death would come, but we were bound by the certainty of its imminence, bound to the dread inside, bound to each other by these invisible ties. When illness enters a home, not only does it take hold of a body; it also weaves a dark web between hearts, a web where hope is trapped. Like a spider's thread drawn ever tighter around our plans, making it impossible to breathe, with each passing day the illness was overwhelming our life. When I came in from running chores outside, it was like entering a dark cellar where I was constantly cold, with a chill that nothing could remedy, so much so towards the end that when I slept alongside Lucien, it seemed as if his body were sucking up all the heat my body might have managed to purloin elsewhere.

His illness was first diagnosed in the spring of 1988; it ate away at him for seventeen months and carried him off just before Christmas. The elder Madame Meurisse organised a collection from among the inhabitants of the building, and a fine wreath of flowers was delivered to my lodge, bound with a ribbon that bore no text. She alone came to the funeral. She was a cold, stiff, pious woman, but there was something sincere about her austere and rather abrupt manners, and when she died, a year after Lucien, I said to myself that she had been a good woman and that I would miss her, although we had scarcely exchanged two words in fifteen years.

'She made her daughter-in-law miserable right up to the

end. May she rest in peace, she was a saintly woman,' said Manuela – who professes a truly epic hatred for the younger Madame Meurisse – by way of a funeral oration.

Thus with the exception of Cornélia Meurisse, with her little veils and rosaries, Lucien's illness did not strike anyone as being worthy of interest. To rich people it must seem that the ordinary little people – perhaps because their lives are more impoverished, deprived of the oxygen of money and savoir-faire – experience human emotions with less intensity and greater indifference. Since we were concierges, it was a given that death, for us, must be a matter of course, whereas for our privileged neighbours it carried all the weight of injustice and drama. The death of a concierge leaves a slight indentation on everyday life, belongs to a biological certainty that has nothing tragic about it and, for the apartment owners who encountered him every day on the stairs or at the door to our lodge, Lucien was a nonentity who was merely returning to a nothingness from which he had never fully emerged, a creature who, because he had lived only half a life, with neither luxury nor artifice, must at the moment of his death have felt no more than half a shudder of revolt. The fact that we might be going through hell like any other human being, or that our hearts might be filling with rage as Lucien's suffering ravaged our lives, or that we might be slowly going to pieces inside, in the torment of fear and horror that death inspires in everyone, did not cross the mind of anyone on these premises.

One morning three weeks before that Christmas, I had just come in from shopping with a bag filled with turnips and lung for the cat, and there was Lucien dressed and ready to go out. He had even knotted his scarf and was standing there waiting for me. After weeks of witnessing my husband's agony as, drained of all strength and enveloped in a terrifying pallor, he would hobble from the bedroom to the kitchen; after weeks of seeing him wear nothing other than a pair of pyjamas that looked the very uniform of demise, and now to find him with his eyes shining and a mischievous expression on his face, the collar of his winter coat turned right up to his peculiarly pink cheeks: I very nearly collapsed.

'Lucien!' I exclaimed, and I was about to go to hold him up, sit him down, undress him and I don't know what else, everything that the illness had taught me in the way of unfamiliar gestures, which had become of late the only ones I knew how to make. I was about to put my bag down and embrace him, hold him close to me, carry him, all those things once more, when, breathless and feeling a strange flutter of expansion in my heart, I stopped in my tracks.

'We'll just make it,' said Lucien, 'the next showing is at one.'

In the heat of the cinema, on the verge of tears, happier than I had ever been, I was holding the faint warmth of his hand for the first time in months. I knew that an unexpected surge of energy had roused him from his bed, given him the strength to get dressed and the urge to go out, the desire for us to share a conjugal pleasure one more time – and I knew, too, that this was the sign that there was not much time left, a state of grace before the end. But that did not matter to me, I just wanted to make the most of it, of these moments stolen from the burden of illness, moments with his warm hand in mine and a shudder of pleasure going through both of us because, thank heavens, it was a film we could share and delight in equally.

I think he died right after that. His body held on for three more weeks, but his mind departed at the end of the film, because he knew it was better that way, because he had said farewell to me in the darkened cinema. There were no poignant regrets, because he had found peace this way; he had placed his trust in what we had said to each other without any need for words, while we watched, together, the bright screen where a story was being told.

71

And I accepted it.

The Hunt for Red October is the film of our last embrace. For anyone who wants to understand the art of storytelling, this film should suffice; one wonders why universities persist in teaching narrative principles on the basis of Propp, Greimas or other such punishing curricula, instead of investing in a projection room. Premise, plot, protagonists, adventures, quest, heroes and other stimulants: all you need is Sean Connery in the uniform of a Russian submarine officer and a few well-placed aircraft carriers.

As I was saying, this morning on France Inter Radio I learned that this contamination of my aspiration to high culture by my penchant for lower forms of culture does not necessarily represent the indelible mark of my lowly origins or of my solitary striving for enlightenment but is, rather, a contemporary characteristic of the dominant intellectual class. How did I come to know this? From the mouth of a sociologist, and I would have loved to have known if he himself would have loved to have known that a concierge in Scholl clogs had just made him into a holy icon. As part of a study on the evolution of the cultural practices of intellectuals who had once been immersed in highbrow culture from dawn to dusk but who were now mainstays of syncretism in whom the boundaries between high and low culture were irreversibly blurred, my sociologist described a classics professor who, once upon a time, would have listened to Bach, read Mauriac, and watched art-house films, but nowadays listened to Handel and MC Solaar, read Flaubert and John Le Carré, went to see Visconti and the latest *Die Hard,* and ate hamburgers at lunch and sashimi in the evening.

How distressing to stumble on a dominant social habitus, just when one was convinced of one's own uniqueness in the matter! Distressing, and perhaps even a bit annoying. The fact that, in spite of my confinement in a lodge that conforms in every way to what is expected, in spite of an isolation that should have protected me from the imperfections of the masses, in spite of those shameful years in my forties when I was utterly ignorant of the changes in the vast world to which I am confined; the fact that I, Renée, fifty-four years old, concierge and autodidact, am witness to the same changes that are animating the present-day elite – the little Pallières in their exclusive schools who read Marx then go off in gangs to watch *Terminator,* or the little Badoises who study law at Assas and sob into their Kleenex at *Notting Hill* – is a shock from which I can scarcely recover. And it is patently clear, for those who pay attention to chronology, that I am not the one who is aping these youngsters but, rather, in my eclectic practices, I am well ahead of them.

Renée, prophet of the contemporary elite.

'And well, why not,' I thought, removing the cat's slice of calves' liver from my shopping bag, and from beneath that, carefully wrapped in an unmarked sheet of plastic, two little fillets of red mullet which I intend to marinate then cook in lemon juice and coriander.

And this is when it all started.

Profound Thought No. 4

Care
For plants
For children

T here's a cleaning woman who comes to our house three hours a day, but it's Maman who looks after the plants. And it's an unbelievable rigmarole. She has two watering cans, one for water with fertiliser, one for special soft water, and a spray gun with several settings for 'targeted' squirts, either 'shower' or 'mist'. Every morning she inspects the twenty house plants in the apartment and administers the appropriate treatment to each one. She murmurs all sorts of stuff to them, oblivious of the outside world. You can say whatever you want to Maman while she's looking after her plants, she'll completely ignore it. For example: 'I'm going to buy some drugs today and maybe try for an overdose' will get you the following answer: 'The kentia's going yellow at the tips of the leaves, too much water, not good at all.'

With this we grasp the opening tenets of the paradigm: if you want to ruin your life by not listening to what other people are saying to you, look after house plants. But that's not all. When Maman is squirting water onto the plants, I can plainly see the hope that fills her. She thinks it's a kind of balm that is going to penetrate the plant and bring it what it needs to prosper. It's the same thing with the fertiliser, which she gives them by means of little sticks in the soil (in the mixture of potting soil, compost, sand and peat that she has made up especially for each individual plant at the nursery over at the Porte d'Auteuil). So, Maman feeds her plants the way she feeds her children: water and fertiliser for the kentia, green beans and vitamin C for us.

That's the heart of the paradigm: concentrate on the object, convey all the nutritional elements from the outside to the inside and, as they make their way inside, they will cause the object to grow and prosper. A little 'pschtt' on its leaves and there's the plant ready to go out into the world. You look at it with a mixture of anxiety and hope, you know how fragile life can be, you worry about accidents but, at the same time, you are satisfied with the knowledge that you've done what you were supposed to do, you've played your nurturing role: you feel reassured and, for a time, things feel safe. That's how Maman views life: a succession of conjuring acts, as useless as a 'pschtt' with the spray gun, which provide a fleeting illusion of security.

It would be so much better if we could share our insecurity, if we could all venture inside ourselves and realise that green beans and vitamin C, however much they nurture us, cannot save lives, nor sustain our souls.

10. A Cat Called Roget

Chabrot is ringing at my lodge.

Chabrot is Pierre Arthens's personal physician. He is one of those ageing beau types who are always tanned, and he squirms in the presence of the Master like the worm he really is. In twenty years, he has never greeted me or even given the least sign that he was aware of my presence. An interesting phenomenological experiment might consist in exploring the reasons why some phenomena fail to appear to the consciousness of some people but do appear to the consciousness of others. The fact that my image can at one and the same time make an impression in Neptune's skull and bounce off that of Chabrot altogether is indeed a fascinating concept.

But this morning Chabrot seems to have lost all his tan. His cheeks are drooping, his hand is trembling and as for his nose . . . wet. Yes, wet. Chabrot, physician to the mighty, has a runny nose. And on top of that he is uttering my name.

'Madame Michel.'

Perhaps it isn't Chabrot at all but some sort of extra-terrestrial mutant assisted by intelligence services that leave something to desire, because the real Chabrot doesn't clutter his mind with information regarding subordinates who are, by definition, anonymous.

'Madame Michel,' says Chabrot's flawed imitation, 'Madame Michel.'

Well, we'll find out. My name is Madame Michel.

'A terrible misfortune . . .' continues Runny Nose who, gadzooks, is sniffling instead of blowing his nose.

Well I never. He's sniffling noisily, expediting his nasal runoff to a place it never came from, and I am obliged, by the speed of his gesture, to witness the feverish contractions of his Adam's apple working to assist the passage of said nasal secretion. It is repulsive but above all disconcerting.

I look to the right, to the left. The hallway is deserted. If ET here has any hostile intentions, I am doomed.

He takes himself in hand, repeats himself.

'A terrible misfortune, yes, a terrible misfortune. Monsieur Arthens is dying.'

'Dying? Actually dying?'

'Actually dying, Madame Michel, actually dying. He has forty-eight hours left to live.'

'But I saw him yesterday morning, he was fit as a fiddle!' I am stunned.

'Alas, Madame, alas. When the heart gives way, it's like a bolt from the blue. In the morning you're hopping around like a mountain goat and by evening you're in your tomb.'

'Is he going to die at home, he's not going into hospital?'

'Oh, Madame Michel!' exclaims Chabrot, looking at me with the same expression as Neptune when he's on his leash. 'Who wants to die in hospital?'

For the first time in twenty years I feel a vague flutter of sympathy for Chabrot. He is, after all, a human being too, I say to myself, and in the end, we are all alike.

'Madame Michel,' he says again, and I am astounded by this profusion of Madame Michels after twenty years of nothing, 'a great many people will no doubt want to see the Master before . . . before. But he does not want to see anyone. With the exception of his nephew Paul. Would you be so good as to send the importunate boors on their way?'

I am torn. I realise that, as usual, my presence has only been acknowledged with the purpose of giving me a task to do. But then again, I concede, that is why I am here. I have also noticed that Chabrot speaks in a manner that I find absolutely enthralling – would you be so good as to send the importunate boors on their way? – and this troubles me. I do like this archaic, polite usage. I am a complete slave to vocabulary, I ought to have named my cat Roget. This fellow may be a nuisance but his language is delectable. And, finally, who wants to die in hospital? asked the ageing beau. No one. Not Pierre Arthens, nor Chabrot, nor Lucien, nor I. Chabrot, with his harmless question, has made us all human.

'I shall do what I can,' I say. 'But I cannot pursue them up the stairs either.'

'No,' he says, 'but you can discourage them. Tell them the Master has locked his door.'

And he gives me a strange look.

I must be careful, I must be very careful. I have been getting sloppy lately. There was the incident with the Pallières boy, my preposterous mention of *The German Ideology*, which, if the youngster had had half the intelligence of an oyster, could easily have betrayed some very awkward things. And now we have a geriatric sun addict the colour of toast who indulges in antiquated expressions and I am at his feet losing all my discipline.

I immediately wipe from my eyes the spark that had momentarily shone there, and adopt the glassy expression of the obedient concierge who is prepared to do her best even if she cannot pursue people up the stairs.

Chabrot's odd expression vanishes.

To further eradicate any trace of my lexical misdeeds, I allow myself a little heresy.

'Some kinda heart attack?' I ask.

'Yes,' says Chabrot, 'a heart attack.'

A moment of silence.

'Thank you,' he says.

'Don't mention it,' I reply, and close the door.

Profound Thought No. 5

Life
Everyone's
Military service

I am very proud of this profound thought. It came to me through Colombe. So at least once she will have been of some use in my life. I never thought I'd be able to say that before I die.

From the very start Colombe and I have been at war because as far as Colombe is concerned, life is a permanent battle where you can only win by destroying your opponent. She cannot feel safe if she hasn't crushed her adversaries and reduced their territory to the meanest share. A world where there's room for other people is a dangerous world, according to her pathetic warmongering criteria. At the same time she still needs them just a bit, for a small but essential chore: someone, after all, has to recognise her power. So not only does she spend her time trying to crush me by every available means, but on top of it she would like me to tell her, while her sword is under my chin, that she is the greatest and that I love her. So there are days when she drives me absolutely crazy. And the icing on the cake is that, for some obscure reason, Colombe, who most of the time is totally insensitive to what's going on with other people, has worked out that what I dread more than anything else in life is noise. I think she discovered this by chance. It would never have crossed her mind spontaneously that somebody might actually need silence. That silence helps you to go *inwards*, that anyone who is interested in something more than just life outside actually needs silence: this, I think, is not something Colombe is capable of understanding, because her inner space is as chaotic and noisy as the street outside. But in any case she worked out that I need silence and, unfortunately, my room is next to hers. So all day long she makes noise. She shouts into the phone, she puts her music on really loud (and that really gets to me), she slams doors, gives a running commentary on everything she does, including the most fascinating things like brushing her hair and looking for pencils in the drawer. In short, since she can't invade anything else because I am totally inaccessible to her on a human level, she invades my personal auditory space, and ruins my life from morning to night. You really have to have a pretty impoverished concept of territory to stoop this low; I don't give a damn about where I happen to be, provided nothing stops me from going into my mind. But Colombe won't stop at just ignoring the facts; she converts them into philosophy: 'My pest of a little sister is an intolerant and depressive little runt who hates other people and would rather live in a cemetery where everyone is dead – whereas *I* am outgoing, joyful and full of life.' If there is one thing I detest, it's when people transform their powerlessness or alienation into a creed. With Colombe, I've really lucked out.

But for the last few months Colombe has not merely been content with being the most dreadful sister in the universe. She has also had the poor taste to behave in a way that worries everyone. I really don't need this: a hostile lesion of a sister and the spectacle of all her little woes. For the last few months Colombe has been obsessed with two things: order and cleanliness. The infinitely pleasant consequence? From the zombie that I used to be, I have become a dirty swine; she spends her time shouting at me because I left crumbs in the kitchen or because there was a hair in the shower this morning. Having said that, it's not just me she's after. Everybody is harassed from morning to night because there's mess or crumbs. Her room, which used to be the most incredible shambles, has become clinical: everything shipshape, not a speck of dust, every object has its allotted space and woe betide Madame Grémond if once she's done the cleaning she doesn't put things back exactly where they were. It looks like a hospital. In a way it wouldn't bother me that Colombe has become such a neatness freak. But what I cannot stand is that she goes on acting as if she's really laid back. There's a problem here somewhere but everyone pretends they haven't noticed and Colombe goes on claiming to be the only one of the two of us to take life 'as an Epicurean'. I assure you however that there is nothing the least bit Epicurean about taking three showers a day and shouting like a lunatic because the lamp on your bedside table has moved two inches.

What is Colombe's problem? I really don't know. Perhaps all this wanting to crush everyone has turned her into a soldier, quite literally. She wants everything just so, she scrubs and cleans like in the army. Soldiers are obsessive about order and cleanliness, that's a well-known fact. For Colombe, cleanliness is a necessity, a way of combating chaos, of holding at bay the filth of war and all those little shreds of human being it leaves behind. But in fact I wonder if Colombe is not the extreme case that reveals the norm. Don't we all deal with life the way we do our military service? Doing what we can, while we wait either to be demobbed or do battle? Some will clean up the barrack-room, others will skive off, or spend their time playing cards, or trafficking, or plotting something. Officers command, soldiers obey, but no one's fooled by this comedy behind closed doors: one day, you'll have to go out and die, officers and soldiers alike, the morons along with the crafty ones who smuggle toilet paper or deal in cigarettes on the black market.

While I'm at it, let me give you the basic shrink's hypothesis: Colombe is so full of chaos inside, so empty and cluttered at the same time, that she is trying to create some order in herself by tidying up and cleaning her inner space. Very funny. I worked out a long time ago that shrinks are comedians who believe that metaphors are something for great wise men. In fact, any eleven-year-old can come up with one. But you should hear the scornful way Maman's psychiatrist friends laugh at the least little pun, and you should hear the absolutely idiotic things Maman tells us, too, because she tells everyone everything about her own sessions at the shrink's, as if she'd been to Disneyland: the 'family life' show, the 'my life with my mother' hall of mirrors, the 'my life without my mother' rollercoaster, the 'my sexual life' chamber of horrors (here she lowers her voice so I won't hear) and, in the end, for the tunnel of death, 'my life as a pre-menopausal woman'.

But what freaks me out about Colombe is that I often get the impression that she doesn't feel anything. Whenever she has to display some emotion it is such an act, so fake, that I wonder if she is feeling anything at all. Yes, sometimes that scares me. Maybe she's completely sick, maybe she's trying at any cost to feel something authentic, maybe she's going to commit some totally insane act. I can see the headlines from here: 'Nero of Rue de Grenelle: young woman sets fire to family apartment. Questioned on the motive for her act, she replied: I wanted to feel an emotion.'

Right, I know, I'm exaggerating a little. And I'm hardly the one to be denouncing pyromania. But still, when I heard her shouting her head off this morning because there was a cat hair on her green coat, I thought to myself, poor fool, the battle's lost before it's begun. You'd feel better if only you knew that.

11. The Rebellion of the Mongolian Tribes

There is a quiet knock on the door of the lodge. It's Manuela, she's just been given the rest of the day off.

'The Master is dying,' she says; I cannot tell whether she means to add a touch of irony to this echo of Chabrot's refrain. 'You aren't busy? We would have our tea now?'

Manuela's casual disregard for synchronising verb tenses, the way she uses a conditional interrogative without the proper word order, the way she can make free with her syntax because she is only a poor Portuguese woman forced into the language of exile, all have the same air of obsolescence about them as Chabrot's strict formulas.

'I met Laura on the stairs,' she says as she sits down. 'She was holding onto the banister as if she needed to go to the toilet. When she saw me, she left.'

Laura is the younger Arthens daughter, a nice girl who doesn't get many visits. Clémence, her older sister, is the awkward incarnation of frustration, a devout churchgoer who spends her time boring her husband and children with endless, mind-numbing days of holy mass, parish fêtes and cross-stitch embroidery. But Jean, the youngest, is a drug addict, a sad wreck. He was a lovely child once, with wide eyes filled with wonder, who would trot along behind his father as if his life depended on it. But when he started using drugs the change was spectacular: he ceased to move. After a childhood wasted running after God in vain, he now seems to be tripping over his own legs, moving along in fits and starts, stopping on the stairs or outside the lift or in the courtyard for increasingly lengthy spells, to the point of occasionally falling asleep on my doormat or in the rubbish store. One day he was stationed in a studied stupor over the bed of roses and dwarf camellias, so I asked him if he needed anything, and it occurred to me that he was beginning to look more and more like Neptune, with his tearful eyes, his damp, twitching nose and his scruffy curly hair straying across his temples.

'Uh, uh no,' he had replied, his words as detached and halting as his gestures.

'Wouldn't you at least like to sit down?' I suggested.

'Sit down?' he echoed, astonished. 'Uh, uh no, what for?'

'To rest a bit.'

'Ah, I seeee. Well, uh, uh no.'

I left him to the company of the camellias and kept an eye on him from the window. After a very long time he roused himself from his floral contemplation and headed at a snail's pace for my lodge. I opened before he foundered in his endeavour to ring the bell.

'I'll be on my way,' he said, without seeing me, his silky, unkempt locks flopping down over his eyes. Then, with what seemed an enormous effort: 'Those flowers . . . what are they called?'

'The camellias?' I asked, surprised.

'Camellias . . .' he echoed slowly, 'camellias . . . Well, thank you, Madame Michel,' he said eventually, his voice astonishingly firm.

And he turned on his heel. I did not see him again for weeks, until one morning in November when, as he was passing by outside my lodge, I scarcely recognised him, so great was his fall. Yes, a fall . . . We are all headed for one. But for a young man to reach that point before his time, the point where he cannot get to his feet again . . . such a fall is so visible and so brutal that your heart is seized with pity. Jean Arthens was no more than a tortured body staggering through life on a razor's edge. Horrified, I was wondering how he would even manage to make the simple gestures required to operate the lift when Bernard Grelier suddenly appeared, took hold of him and lifted him up as if he were a feather, and I was spared having to intervene. I had a brief glimpse of a frail mature man carrying a ravaged child in his arms, then they disappeared up the dark stairs.

'But Clémence will be coming,' said Manuela who, uncannily, always picks up the thread of my unspoken thoughts.

'Chabrot told me to ask her to leave,' I said, thoughtful. 'He won't see anyone but Paul.'

'The baroness was so upset she was blowing her nose into a dishcloth,' added Manuela, referring to Violette Grelier.

I am not surprised. Truth will out, when the end is near . . . Violette Grelier is to dishcloths what Pierre Arthens is to silk; we are all prisoners of our own destiny, must confront it with the knowledge that there is no way out and, in our epilogue, must be the person we have always been deep inside, regard-less of any illusions we may have nurtured in our lifetime. Just because you have been around fine linen does not mean you are entitled to it – no more than a sick person is to health.

I pour the tea and we sip in silence. We have never had our tea together in the morning, and this break with our usual protocol imbues the ritual with a strange flavour.

Yes, this sudden transmutation in the order of things seems to enhance our pleasure, as if consecrating the unchanging nature of a ritual established over our afternoons together, a ritual that has ripened into a solid and meaningful reality. Today, because our ritual has been transgressed, it suddenly acquires all its power; we are tasting the splendid gift of this unexpected morning as if it were some precious nectar; ordinary gestures have an extraordinary resonance, as we breathe in the fragrance of the tea, savour it, lower our cups, serve more and sip again: every gesture has the bright aura of rebirth. At moments like this the web of life is revealed by the power of ritual, and each time we renew our ceremony, the pleasure will be all the greater for our having violated one of its principles. Moments like this act as magical interludes, placing our hearts at the edge of our souls: fleetingly, yet intensely, a fragment of eternity has come to enrich time. Elsewhere the world may be blustering or sleeping, wars are fought, people live and die, some nations disintegrate, while others are born, soon to be swallowed up in turn – and in all this sound and fury, amidst eruptions and undertows, while the world goes its merry way, bursts into flames, tears itself apart and is reborn: human life continues to throb.

So, let us drink a cup of tea.

Kakuzo Okakura, the author of the *Book of Tea*, laments the rebellion of the Mongolian tribes in the thirteenth century not because it brought death and desolation but because it destroyed one of the creations of the Song dynasty, the most precious among them, the art of tea. Like Okakura, I know that tea is no minor beverage. When tea becomes ritual, it takes its place at the heart of our ability to see greatness in small things. Where is beauty to be found? In great things that, like everything else, are doomed to die, or in small things that aspire to nothing, yet know how to set a jewel of infinity in a single moment?

The tea ritual: such a precise repetition of the same gestures and the same tastes; accession to simple, authentic and refined sensations, a licence granted to all, at little cost, to become aristocrats of taste, because tea is the beverage of the wealthy and of the poor; the tea ritual, therefore, has the extraordinary virtue of introducing into the absurdity of our lives an aperture of serene harmony. Yes, the world may aspire to vacuousness, lost souls mourn beauty, insignificance surrounds us. Then let us drink a cup of tea. Silence descends, one hears the wind outside, the autumn leaves rustle and take flight, the cat sleeps in a warm pool of light. And with each swallow, time is sublimed.

Profound Thought No. 6

What do you drink
What do you read
At breakfast
And I know who
You are

E very morning at breakfast Papa drinks a coffee and reads the newspaper. Several newspapers, in fact: *Le Monde*, *Le Figaro*, *Libération* and, once a week, *L'Express*, *Les Échos*, *Time* and *Courrier International*. But I can tell that the most satisfying thing for him is his first cup of coffee with *Le Monde*. He is absorbed by his reading for at least half an hour. In order to enjoy this half-hour, he has to get up very early, because his days are full. But every morning, even if there's been an overnight session and he has only slept two hours, he gets up at six and reads his paper while he drinks a strong cup of coffee. In this way Papa constructs himself, every day. I say 'constructs himself' because I think that each time it's a new construction, as if everything has been reduced to ashes during the night, and he has to start from scratch. In our world, that's the way you live your grown-up life: you must constantly rebuild your identity as an adult, the way it's been put together it is wobbly and ephemeral, so fragile, cloaking despair and, when you're alone in front of the mirror, it tells you the lies you need to believe. For Papa, the newspaper and the coffee are magic wands that transform him into an important man. Like a pumpkin into a carriage. Of course he finds this very satisfying: I never see him as calm and relaxed as when he's sitting drinking his six o'clock coffee. But at such a price! You pay such a price when you lead a false life! When the mask is taken away, when there's a crisis – and there's always a crisis at some point among mortals – the truth is terrible! Look at Monsieur Arthens, the food

88

critic on the fourth floor, who is dying. At noon, Maman whirled in from her shopping like a tornado and the moment she was in the hallway she shouted for everybody to hear: 'Pierre Arthens is dying!' By everybody, of course I mean Constitution and me. Needless to say, her effort at drama was a flop. Maman, who was a bit dishevelled, looked disappointed. When Papa came home this evening she jumped on him to tell him the news. Papa seemed surprised: 'His heart? What, already?' he asked.

I have to admit that Monsieur Arthens is a truly nasty man. Papa is just a kid who's playing the deadly serious grown-up. But Monsieur Arthens . . . a first-class truly nasty man. When I say nasty, I don't mean unkind or cruel or tyrannical, though there is a bit of that too. No, when I say, 'he's a truly nasty man,' I mean he has so thoroughly renounced everything good that he might have inside him that he's already like a corpse even though he's still alive. Because truly nasty people hate everyone, to be sure, but most of all themselves. Can't you tell when a person hates himself? He becomes a living corpse, it numbs all his negative emotions but also all the good ones so that he won't feel nauseated by who he is.

Pierre Arthens really was truly nasty. They say he was the pope of food critics and a worldwide champion of French cuisine. Well, that doesn't surprise me. If you want my opinion, French cuisine is pitiful. So much genius and wherewithal and so many resources for such a heavy end result . . . And so many sauces and stuffings and pastries, enough to make you burst! It's in such bad taste . . . And when it isn't heavy, it's as fussy as can be: you're dying of hunger and before you are three stylised radishes and two scallops in a seaweed gelée served on pseudo-Zen plates by waiters who look as joyful as undertakers. On Saturday we went to a very fancy restaurant that was just like that: 'Napoléon's Bar'. This was a family outing, to celebrate Colombe's birthday. And she chose her dishes with all her usual grace: pretentious thingummies with chestnuts, lamb prepared with some herbs with an unpronounceable name, a Grand Marnier sabayon (how horrible can you get). Sabayon is the emblem of French cuisine: it pretends to be light but would asphyxiate any common Christian. I didn't have a starter (and I'll spare you Colombe's remarks about my 'irritating-little-sister anorexia') and then, for the price of sixty-three euros, I had some fillets of mullet in a curry sauce (with diced al dente courgettes and carrot tucked under the fish) and then, for thirty-four euros, the least evil thing I could find on the menu: a bitter chocolate fondant. Let me tell you: at that price, I would have preferred an annual season ticket at McDonald's. At least it's in bad taste without being pretentious. And I won't even get started on the decor in the dining room and on the table. When the French want to get away from the traditional 'Empire' style with burgundy curtains and gilt galore, they go in for hospital style. You sit on these Le Corbusier chairs ('By Corbu,' says Maman) and you eat off these white plates in very Soviet-bureaucracy geometrical shapes, and you dry your hands in the toilets on towels so thin that they don't absorb a thing.

Clean lines, simplicity; no, that's not it. 'But what would you rather have?' asked Colombe, exasperated, because I didn't manage to finish my first mullet. I didn't answer. Because I don't know. I'm still only a little girl, after all. But in my manga, people seem to eat differently. It looks simple, refined, moderate, delicious. You eat the way you look at a beautiful picture or sing in a beautiful choir. Neither too much nor too little: moderate, in the good sense of the word. Maybe I'm completely mistaken; but French cuisine seems old and pretentious to me, whereas Japanese cuisine seems . . . well, neither young nor old. Eternal, divine.

Anyway, Monsieur Arthens is dying. I wonder what he used to do in the morning to prepare for his role as a truly nasty man. Maybe a strong little coffee while he read the competition, or an American breakfast with sausages and home fries. What do we do in the morning? Papa reads his paper while he drinks his coffee, Maman drinks her coffee while she leafs through catalogues, Colombe drinks her coffee while she listens to France Inter and I drink hot chocolate while reading manga. Just now I'm reading Taniguchi manga; he's a genius, and he's teaching me a lot about people.

But yesterday I asked Maman if I could drink some tea. My grandmother drinks black tea at breakfast, flavoured with bergamot. Even though I don't find it particularly good, it seems less aggressive than coffee, which is a nasty person's drink. But at the restaurant last night Maman ordered some jasmine tea and she let me taste it. I thought it was so good, so 'me', that this morning I said that from now on I want to have tea at breakfast. Maman shot me a strange look (her 'poorly-purged-sleeping-tablet' look) then she said, Yes yes sweetheart you're old enough now.

Tea and manga instead of coffee and newspapers: something elegant and enchanting, instead of adult power-struggles and their sad aggressiveness.

12. Phantom Comedy

After Manuela has left, I attend to all manner of captivating activities: I do the housework, use the mop in the hallway, take the rubbish bins out into the street, pick up the leaflets, water the flowers, prepare the cat's repast (including a slice of ham with a fat edge of rind), make my own meal – cold Chinese noodles with tomato, basil and Parmesan – read the newspaper, take a moment's retreat in my den to read a very fine Danish novel, and handle the crisis in the foyer where Lotte, the Arthens's granddaughter, Clémence's eldest, is crying outside my lodge because Grandpa doesn't want to see her.

At nine in the evening at last I have finished everything and I suddenly feel old and very depressed. Death does not frighten me, least of all that of Pierre Arthens, but it is the waiting that is unbearable, this suspension of time when something has not yet happened and where we feel how very useless it is to struggle. I sit on in the kitchen, in silence, in the half-light, a bitter taste of absurdity in my mouth. My mind drifts slowly. Pierre Arthens . . . A brutal despot, hungry for glory and accolades and yet, torn to the very end between an aspiration for art and a thirst for power, he endeavoured to use language in pursuit of an illusion. Which way lies truth, in the end? In power, or in Art? Is it not the power of well-crafted discourse which enables us not only to sing the praises of mankind's creations but also to denounce as a crime of illusory vanity the urge to dominate, which moves us all – yes, *all*, even a wretched concierge in her cramped lodge who, although she may have renounced any visible power, nevertheless pursues those dreams of power in her mind?

Indeed, what constitutes life? Day after day, we put up the brave struggle to play our role in this phantom comedy. We are good primates, so we spend most of our time maintaining and defending our territory, so that it will protect and gratify us; climbing – or trying not to slide down – the tribe's hierarchical ladder, and fornicating in every manner imaginable – even mere phantasms – as much for the pleasure of it as for the promised offspring. Thus we use up a considerable amount of our energy in intimidation and seduction, and these two strategies alone ensure the quest for territory, hierarchy and sex that gives life to our conatus. But none of this touches our consciousness. We talk about love, about good and evil, philosophy and civilisation, and we cling to these respectable icons the way a tick clings to its nice, big, warm dog.

There are times, however, when life becomes a phantom comedy. As if aroused from a dream, we watch ourselves in action and, shocked at the realisation of how much vitality is required simply to support our primitive requirements, we wonder, bewildered, where Art fits in. All our frenzied nudging and posturing suddenly become utterly insignificant; our cosy little nest is reduced to some futile barbarian custom, and our position in society, hard-won and eternally precarious, is but a crude vanity. As for our progeny, we view them now with new eyes, and we are horrified, because without the cloak of altruism, the reproductive act seems extraordinarily out of place. All that is left is sexual pleasure, but if it is relegated to a mere manifestation of primal abjection, it will fail in proportion, because a loveless session of gymnastics is not what we have struggled so hard to master.

Eternity eludes us.

At times like this, all the romantic, political, intellectual, metaphysical and moral beliefs that years of instruction and education have tried to inculcate in us seem to be foundering on the altar of our true nature, and society, a territorial field mined with the powerful charges of hierarchy, is sinking into the nothingness of Meaning. Exeunt rich and poor, thinkers, researchers, decision-makers, slaves, the good and the evil, the creative and the conscientious, trade unionists and individualists, progressives and conservatives; all that's left are primitive hominoids whose nudging and posturing, mannerisms and finery, language and codes are all located on the genetic map of an average primate, and all add up to no more than this: hold your rank, or die.

At times like this you desperately need Art. You seek to reconnect with your spiritual illusions, and you wish fervently that something might rescue you from your biological destiny, so that all poetry and grandeur will not be cast out from the world.

Thus, to withdraw as far away as you can from the jousting and combat that are the appanages of our warrior species, you drink a cup of tea, or maybe you watch a film by Ozu, and place upon this sorry theatre the seal of Art and its greatest treasures.

13. Eternity

At nine in the evening, I put a cassette into the video player, a film by Ozu, *The Munekata Sisters*. This is my tenth Ozu film this month. Why? Because Ozu is a genius who can rescue me from biological destiny.

It all started one day when I told Angèle, our little librarian, that I was very fond of early Wim Wenders films, and she said, Oh, have you seen *Tokyo-Ga*? And when you've seen *Tokyo-Ga*, which is an extraordinary documentary devoted to Ozu, then obviously you want to find out more about Ozu. So I found out more about Ozu and, for the first time in my life, the Art of the cinema made me laugh and cry as real entertainment should.

I press the start button, sip my jasmine tea. From time to time I rewind, thanks to this secular rosary known as the remote control.

And here is an extraordinary scene.

The father, played by Chishu Ryu, one of Ozu's preferred actors and a vital lead through all his work, an extraordinary man who radiates warmth and humility – this father, therefore, is about to die, and is conversing with his daughter Setsuko about the stroll they have just taken through Kyoto. They are drinking sake.

THE FATHER
And the Moss Temple! The light made the moss even more splendid.

SETSUKO

And the camellia on the moss, too.

THE FATHER

Oh, did you notice? How beautiful it was! *(Pause.)* There are beautiful things in old Japan. *(Pause.)* Insisting that it's all bad . . . I find that outrageous.

The film continues and, right at the end, comes this last scene, in a park, where Setsuko, the eldest, is talking with Mariko, her capricious younger sister.

SETSUKO, *her face radiant*

Tell me, Mariko, why are the mountains of Kyoto violet?

MARIKO, *mischievously*

It's true. They look like aduki bean paste.

SETSUKO, *smiling*

It's such a lovely colour.

The film is about disappointed love, arranged marriages, parents and children, brotherhood, the death of the father, the old and new faces of Japan, as well as alcohol and the violence of men.

But above all it is about something that is unattainable to Western sensibilities, and that only Japanese culture can elucidate. Why do these two short, unexplained scenes, not driven by anything in the plot, arouse in us such a powerful emotion, containing the entire film between their ineffable parentheses?

Here is the key to the film.

SETSUKO

True novelty is that which does not grow old, despite the passage of time.

The camellia against the moss of the temple, the violet hues of the Kyoto mountains, a blue porcelain cup – this sudden flowering of pure beauty at the heart of ephemeral passion: is this not something we all aspire to? And something that, in our Western civilisation, we do not know how to attain?

The contemplation of eternity within the very movement of life.

Go on, catch up with her!

When I think there are people who don't have television! How do they manage? I could spend hours watching. I turn the sound off and watch. I feel as if I'm watching things with an X-ray. If you turn the sound off, in fact, you're removing the wrapping paper, the pretty tissue paper enveloping some two-bit piece of rubbish. If you watch the television news reports in this way, you'll see: the images have no connection to each other, the only thing that does link them is the commentary, which wants you to take a chronological succession of images for a real succession of events.

Anyway, I love television. And this afternoon I saw an interesting movement of the world: a diving contest. Several contests, in fact. It was a retrospective of all the world championships in this particular sport. There were individual dives, with compulsory figures and freestyle, men and women, but above all, what caught my interest was the synchronised diving. In addition to their individual prowess with all these twists, somersaults and flips, the two divers have to be synchronised. Not just more or less together, no: perfectly together, to the very thousandth of a second.

The funniest thing is when the divers have very different builds: a stocky little person with a long slim one. You tell yourself, this will never work; from a physical point of view, they cannot take off and arrive at the same time, but they do – work that one out. Object lesson: in the world, everything is compensation. When you can't go as fast, you push harder. But here's where I found subject matter for my journal: two young Chinese women got up on the springboard. Two long slim goddesses with shining black plaits, who could have been twins, they looked so alike, but the commentator made a point of saying they weren't even sisters. In short, they went out on the springboard and at that point I think we must have all been doing the same thing: holding our breath.

Following a few graceful bounces, they jumped. The first microseconds were perfect. I felt that perfection in my body; it would seem it's a question of 'mirror neurons': when you watch someone doing something, the same neurons that they activate in order to do something become active in your brain, without you doing a thing. An acrobatic dive without budging from the sofa and while eating crisps: that's why we like watching sports on television. Anyway, the two graces jump and, right at the beginning, it's ecstasy. And then, catastrophe! All at once you get the impression that they are very, very slightly out of synch. You stare at the screen, a knot in your stomach: no doubt about it, they are out of synch. I know it seems crazy to describe it like this when the jump itself cannot last more than maybe three seconds in all but, precisely because it doesn't last more than three seconds, you look at every phase as if it lasted a century. And now it has become clear, you can no longer hide from the truth: they are out of synch! One of them is going to reach the water before the other! It's horrible!

I sat there shouting at the television: go on, catch up with her, go on! I felt incredibly angry with the one who had dawdled. I sank deeper into the sofa, disgusted. What is this? Is that the movement of the world? An infinitesimal lapse that has just succeeded in ruining the possibility of perfection forever? I spent at least half an hour in a foul mood. And then suddenly I wondered: but why did I want so desperately for her to catch up? Why does it feel so rotten when the movement is not in synch? It's not very hard to come up with an answer: all those things that pass before us, which we miss by a hair and which are botched for eternity . . . All the words we should have said, gestures we should have made, the fleeting moments of *kairos* that were there one day and that we did not know how to grasp and that were buried forever in the void . . . Failure, by a hair's breadth . . . But then another idea surfaced thanks to these mirror neurons. A disturbing idea, moreover, and vaguely Proustian, no doubt (which annoys me). What if literature were a television we gaze into in order to activate our mirror neurons and give ourselves some action-packed cheap thrills? And even worse: what if literature were a television showing us all the things we have missed?

So much for the movement of the world! It could have been perfection and it was a disaster. It should be experienced in reality and it is pleasure by proxy, as always.

And so I ask you: why stay in such a world?

14. When of a Sudden, Old Japan

The next morning, Chabrot rings at my lodge. He seems to have mastered his emotions, his voice no longer trembles, his nose is dry and suntanned. But he makes me think of a ghost.

'Pierre has died,' he says, in a flat voice.

'I am sorry.'

I truly am sorry for him, for even if Pierre Arthens is no longer in pain, Chabrot will have to learn to live, however dead he may feel. 'The undertakers will be arriving,' adds Chabrot in his spectral voice. 'I'd be very grateful if you'd show them up to the apartment.'

'Of course.'

'I'll be back in two hours, to take care of Anna.'

He looks at me for a moment in silence.

'Thank you,' he says, for the second time in twenty years.

I am tempted to reply in keeping with the ancestral traditions of concierges but, I scarcely know why, the words will not come out. Perhaps it is because Chabrot will not be coming here any more, because the strongest barriers break down in the presence of death, because I am thinking about Lucien, and because decency, after all, precludes any sort of wariness that might offend the deceased.

So I do not say, Don't mention it, but rather: 'You know . . . everything comes at its appointed time.'

That might sound like a platitude, although it is also something similar to what Marshal Kutuzov says to Prince

Andrei in *War and Peace*: *I have been much blamed, both for war, and for peace . . . But everything comes at its appointed time . . . Tout vient à son heure pour qui sait attendre.*

I would give anything to be able to read it in Russian. What I have always liked about this passage are the pauses, the balance between war, and peace, the ebb and flow of his thoughts, like the tide on the shore carrying the riches of the ocean, in, and out. Was this merely a whim on the part of the translator, embroidering something that might have been very simple in the original – *I have been much blamed, both for war, and for peace* – thus consigning my maritime ruminations to the chapter of unfounded extravagance, or is this the very essence of a superb text which, even today, still moves me, however I resist, to tears of joy?

Chabrot nods his head slowly, then departs.

The rest of the morning is dreary. I have no posthumous affection for Pierre Arthens, but I find myself wandering about like a lost soul, unable even to read. The camellia and the moss had offered me a brief but happy interlude from the coarseness of the world: now that is over, leaving no hope, and my heart is bitter, tormented by the darkness of all these unhappy events.

When all of a sudden old Japan intervenes: from one of the apartments wafts a melody, clearly, joyfully distinct. Someone is playing a classical piece on the piano. Ah, sweet, impromptu moment, lifting the veil of melancholy . . . In a split second of eternity, everything is changed, transfigured. A few bars of music, rising from an unfamiliar piece, a touch of perfection in the flow of human dealings – I lean my head slowly to one side, reflect on the camellia on the moss of the temple, reflect on a cup of tea, while outside the wind is rustling the foliage, the forward rush of life is crystallised in a brilliant jewel of a moment that knows neither plans nor future, human destiny is rescued from the pale succession of days, glows with light at last and, surpassing time, warms my tranquil heart.

15. The Rich Man's Burden

Civilisation is the mastery of violence, the triumph, constantly challenged, over the aggressive nature of the primate. For primates we have been and primates we shall remain, however often we learn to find joy in a camellia on moss. This is the very purpose of education. What does education imply? One must offer camellias on moss, tirelessly, in order to escape the natural impulses of our species, because those impulses do not change, and continually threaten the fragile equilibrium of survival.

I am a very camellia-on-moss sort of person. If I really think about it, there is nothing else that can quite explain my withdrawal into this bleak lodge of mine. As I was convinced very early on of the pointlessness of my existence, I could have chosen to rebel, and taking God as my witness that I had been cruelly used by fate, I could have resorted to the violence inherent in our condition. But school made of me a soul whose unpromising destiny led only to abnegation and confinement. The wonder of my second birth had shown me the way to master my impulses: since it was school that had given birth to me, I had to show my allegiance, and thus I complied with my instructors' intentions by tamely becoming a most civilised human being. In fact, when the struggle to dominate our primate aggressiveness takes up arms as powerful as books and words, the undertaking is an easy one, and that is how I became an educated person, finding in written symbols the strength to resist my own nature.

Thus I was utterly astonished by my own reaction when Antoine Pallières rang imperiously at the lodge three times, and without a greeting began reproachfully haranguing me for the disappearance of his chrome scooter: I slammed the door in his face, and at the same time very nearly amputated my cat's tail as he was slipping out of the door.

Not so very camellia-on-moss after all, I thought.

And as I had to allow Leo re-entry into his quarters, I immediately opened the door again after I had slammed it.

'Pardon me,' I said, 'a draught.'

Antoine Pallières looked at me with the expression of someone who wonders if he has really seen what he thinks he has seen. But as he has been conditioned to imagine that only what must happen does happen, in the way that rich people convince themselves that their lives run along a heavenly track that the power of money has quite naturally laid for them, Antoine decided to believe me. I find this a fascinating phenomenon: the ability we have to manipulate ourselves so that the foundation of our beliefs is never shaken.

'Yes, well, anyway I was mainly coming to give you this from my mother,' he said.

And he handed me a white envelope.

'Thank you,' I said, and shut the door in his face for the second time.

And here I am in my kitchen with the envelope in my hand.

'What is wrong with me this morning?' I say to Leo.

The death of Pierre Arthens has been wilting my camellias.

I open the envelope and read this little note written on a business card whose surface is so glossy that the ink, to the dismay of the defeated blotter, has bled slightly underneath each letter.

Madame Michel,
Would you be so kind as, to sign for the packages

from the dry cleaner's this afternoon?
I'll pick them up from your lodge this evening.
Scribbled signature

I was not prepared for such an underhand attack. I collapse in shock on the nearest chair. I even begin to wonder if I am not going mad. Does this have the same effect on you, when this sort of thing happens?

Let me explain:

The cat is sleeping.

You've just read a harmless little sentence, and it has not caused you any pain or sudden fits of suffering, has it? Fair enough.

Now read again:

The cat, is sleeping.

Let me repeat it, so that there is no cause for ambiguity:

The cat comma is sleeping.

The cat, is sleeping.

Would you be so kind as, to sign for.

On the one hand we have an example of a prodigious use of the comma that takes great liberties with language, as said commas have been inserted quite unnecessarily, but to great effect:

'*I have been much blamed, both for war, and for peace . . .*'

And on the other hand, we have this dribbling scribbling on vellum, courtesy of Sabine Pallières, this comma slicing the sentence in half with all the trenchancy of a knife blade:

Would you be so kind as, to sign for the packages from the dry cleaner's?

If Sabine Pallières had been a Portuguese maid born under a fig tree in Faro, or a concierge who'd just arrived from the high-rise banlieues of Paris, or if she were the mentally challenged member of a tolerant family who had taken her in out of the goodness of their hearts, I might have whole-heartedly

105

forgiven such guilty nonchalance. But Sabine Pallières is wealthy. Sabine Pallières is the wife of a bigwig in the arms industry, Sabine Pallières is the mother of a cretin in a conifer-green duffel coat who, once he has his requisite diplomas and has obtained his Political Science degree, will in all likelihood go on to disseminate the mediocrity of his paltry ideas in a right-wing ministerial cabinet, and Sabine Pallières is, more-over, the daughter of a nasty woman in a fur coat who sits on the selection committee of a very prestigious publishing house and who is always so overloaded with jewels that there are days when I fear she will collapse from the sheer weight of them.

For all of these reasons, Sabine Pallières has no excuse. The gifts of fate come with a price. For those who have been favoured by life's indulgence, rigorous respect in matters of beauty is a non-negotiable requirement. Language is a bountiful gift and its usage, an elaboration of community and society, is a sacred work. Language and usage evolve over time: elements change, are forgotten or reborn, and while there are instances where transgression can become the source of an even greater wealth, this does not alter the fact that to be entitled to the liberties of playfulness or enlightened misuse of language, one must first and foremost have sworn one's total allegiance. Society's elect, those whom fate has spared from the servitude that is the lot of the poor, must, consequently, shoulder the double burden of worshipping and respecting the splendours of language. Finally, Sabine Pallières's misuse of punctuation constitutes an instance of blasphemy that is all the more insidious when one considers that there are marvellous poets born in stinking caravans or high-rise slums who *do* have for beauty the sacred respect that it is so rightfully owed.

To the rich, therefore, falls the burden of Beauty. And if they cannot assume it, then they deserve to die.

At this critical moment in my indignant ruminations someone rings at my lodge.

Profound Thought No. 7

To build
You live
You die
These are
Consequences

The more time goes by, the more determined I become to set this place on fire. Not to mention committing suicide. The need becomes painfully obvious: I got told off by Papa because I corrected one of his guests who'd said something untrue. In fact it was Tibère's father. Tibère is my sister's boyfriend. He's at the École Normale Supérieure with her, but doing mathematics. And they call these people the elite . . . The only difference I can see between Colombe, Tibère, their friends and a gang of 'working-class' kids is that my sister and her chums are more stupid. They drink and smoke and talk as if they were from some housing estate and toss phrases around like 'Hollande really done Fabius with his referendum, get a load of that, the dude's a total killer' (I swear to you), or: 'All the supervisors appointed over the last two years are total nazis, yes, the far right has got us under lockdown, better not mess with them' (heard only yesterday). At a lower level, you get: 'Right, the blonde that J.B. is stalking, she does English, a blonde, right' (idem) and slightly above: 'Marian's lecture, that was like, excellent, when he said that existence isn't the first attribute of God' (idem, just after closing the file on the blonde English student). What am I supposed to think? And here's the icing on the cake (give or take a word): 'Being an atheist doesn't mean you can't see the power of metaphysical ontology. Yeah, what matters is the conceptual power, not truth. And that filthy priest Marian, he's badass, you get me? Chills you out.'

The white pearls
Fallen on my sleeves with heart still full
We parted
I take them with me
As a memory of you

(Kokinshu)

I put some of Maman's yellow foam earplugs in my ears and read haikus from Papa's *Anthology of Classical Japanese Poetry* so that I couldn't hear their degenerate conversation. Afterwards, Colombe and Tibère stayed by themselves and started making unspeakable sounds, knowing perfectly well that I could hear them. The worst of it was that Tibère was staying for dinner because Maman had invited his parents. Tibère's father is a film producer, and his mother has an art gallery on the Quai de Seine. Colombe absolutely adores Tibère's parents, she's going with them to Venice next weekend, good riddance, for three days I'll have some peace.

So, at dinner, Tibère's father said: 'What, haven't you heard of go, the fantastic Japanese game? I'm in the middle of producing a film version of Shan Sa's novel, *The Girl Who Played Go*, it's a fa-bu-lous game, the Japanese equivalent of chess. Yet another invention we owe to the Japanese, it is fa-bu-lous, I promise you!' And he began to explain the rules of go. He had it all wrong. To start with, it's the Chinese who invented go. I know because I read a cult manga on go. It's called *Hikaru No Go*. Secondly, it is not a Japanese equivalent to chess. Other than the fact that it's a board game and that two adversaries confront each other over black and white pieces, it's as different from chess as cats are from dogs. In chess, you have to kill to win. In go, you have to build to live. And thirdly, some of the rules that Mister I'm-the-father-of-an-idiot described were wrong. The aim of the game is not to eat your opponent but to build the

108

biggest territory. The rule regarding taking stones says that you can 'commit suicide' if it is to take your adversary's stones and not that you're strictly forbidden to go anywhere you might be automatically taken. And so on.

So when Mister I-have-engendered-a-pustule said, 'The ranking system of players starts at one *kyu* and then it goes up to thirty *kyu* and after that you go to *dan:* first *dan,* then second, and so on,' I couldn't restrain myself. I said, 'No, it's in the opposite order: you begin with thirty *kyu* and go up to one.'

But Mister Forgive-me-I-knew-not-what-I-was-doing was obstinate and said grumpily, 'No, dear child, I do believe I am right.' I shook my head; Papa was frowning and looking at me. The worst of it is that it was Tibère who saved me. 'Yes, Papa, she's right, first *kyu* is strongest.' Tibère is a maths student, he plays chess and go. I hate the idea. Beautiful things should belong to beautiful souls. But in any event it's Tibère's father who was wrong and Papa, after dinner, told me off: 'If you're only going to open your mouth to make my guests look ridiculous, then please don't.' What should I have done? Open my mouth like Colombe to say, 'To be perfectly honest, I don't know what to think of this season's productions at the Théâtre des Amandiers,' when she's utterly incapable of reciting a single line from Racine, never mind appreciating the beauty of it. Open my mouth like Maman to say, 'Apparently the Biennale last year was very disappointing,' when she would kill for her house plants and let all of Vermeer go up in flames? Open my mouth like Papa to say, 'The French cultural exception is a subtle paradox,' which is virtually word for word exactly what he has said at the last sixteen dinner parties? Open my mouth like Tibère's mother to say, 'These days you can scarcely find a single decent cheese-maker in all of Paris.' At least she's not at odds with her Auvergne shopkeeper roots.

When I think of go . . . Any game where the goal is to build territory has to be beautiful. There may be phases of combat, but they are only the means to an end, to allow your territory to survive. One of the most extraordinary aspects of the game of go is that it has been proven that in order to win, you must live, but you must also allow the other player to live. Players who are too greedy will lose: it is a subtle game of equilibrium, where you have to get ahead without crushing the other player. In the end, life and death are only the consequences of how well or how poorly you have made your construction. This is what one of Taniguchi's characters says: you live, you die, these are consequences. It's a proverb for playing go, and for life.

Live, or die: mere consequences of what you have built. What matters is building well. So here we are, I've assigned myself a new obligation. I'm going to stop undoing, deconstructing, I'm going to start building. Even with Colombe I'll try to do something positive. What matters is what you are doing when you die, and when the sixteenth of June comes around, I want to be building.

16. Constitution's Spleen

The someone ringing at my door turns out to be the charming Olympe Saint-Nice, the daughter of the diplomat on the second floor. I like Olympe Saint-Nice. I think that one must have considerable strength of character to survive such a ridiculous first name, especially when one knows it must have destined the unfortunate girl to peals of laughter and 'Hey, Olympe, can I climb on your mount?' all through what must have seemed an interminable adolescence. Moreover, Olympe Saint-Nice apparently does not wish to claim her birthright: she aspires neither to a rich marriage, nor to the corridors of power, nor to diplomacy, and least of all to any sort of celebrity. Olympe Saint-Nice wants to become a veterinary surgeon.

'A country vet,' she confided to me one day when we were talking cats on my doormat. 'In Paris all you get are house pets. I want cows and pigs, too.'

Olympe is not one for affected charades, the way some people in the building are, to prove that because she is a well-brought-up-child-of-leftists-without-prejudices she is conversing with the concierge. Olympe talks to me because I have a cat, and that brings us into a community of interests; I greatly admire her ability to circumvent all the barriers that society puts up along our laughable way through life.

'I've got to tell you what happened to Constitution,' she says when I open the door.

'Please come in then, do you have five minutes?'

Not only does she have five minutes, she is so delighted to find someone with whom she can talk cats and little cat woes that she stays for an hour and drinks five cups of tea one after the other.

Yes, I really do like Olympe Saint-Nice.

Constitution is a lovely little female with caramel-coloured fur, a rosebud-pink nose, white whiskers and lilac pads: she belongs to the Josses, and like all the pets in the building, she is taken to see Olympe the moment she even farts in the wrong direction. Thus, this useless but enchanting creature, three years of age, recently meowed all night long, depriving her owners of their sleep.

'Why, then?' I ask at the right moment, because we are absorbed by the complicity of acting out a tale and each of us wishes to play her role to perfection.

'A urinary tract infection!' says Olympe. 'A urinary tract infection!'

Olympe is only nineteen and is waiting with frenzied impatience to start veterinary college. In the meantime she works relentlessly and both bewails and enjoys the afflictions that befall the fauna of our building, the only beasts upon which she can practise.

That is why she has announced Constitution's urinary tract infection to me as if she had found a seam rich with diamonds.

'Urinary tract infection!' I chime enthusiastically.

'Yes,' she sighs, her eyes shining. 'Poor sweetie, she was peeing all over the place and –' Olympe takes a breath before reaching the best part of the story – 'she displayed mildly haemorrhagic urine!'

Dear God, this is good. If she had said, There was blood in her pee, the story would have been over in no time. But Olympe, cloaking her cat doctor's uniform with emotion, has also adopted the terminology. I have always found great delight in hearing people speak like this. 'Mildly haemorrhagic urine' is, to me, a form of light entertainment: it has a nice ring to it and evokes a singular world, a brief refreshing change from literature. For the very same reason, I enjoy reading the leaflets that come with medication, the respite provided by the precision of each technical term, which conveys the illusion of meticulousness and a frisson of simplicity, and elicits a spatio-temporal dimension free of any striving for Beauty, creative angst or the never-ending and hopeless aspiration to attain the sublime.

'There are two possible aetiologies for urinary tract infections,' continues Olympe. 'Either an infectious germ, or renal dysfunction. I felt her bladder to start with, to be sure she didn't have distension.'

'Distension?!'

'In cases of renal dysfunction where the cat cannot urinate, the bladder fills up and gets terribly distended, to the point where you can feel it if you palpate the abdomen,' explains Olympe. 'But this wasn't the case. And she didn't seem to be in pain when I was examining her. But she was still peeing everywhere.'

I spare a thought for Solange Josse's living room, transformed into a giant litter box with trendy ketchup-coloured accents. But for Olympe that is mere collateral damage.

'So did Solange have urine tests done?'

'Yes, but there was nothing wrong with Constitution. No kidney stones, no insidious germs lurking in her peanut-sized bladder, no infiltrations of enemy bacteriological agents. And yet, for all the anti-inflammatory, antispasmodic and antibiotic medication administered, Constitution remains obdurate.'

'So what is wrong with her?' I ask.

'You won't believe this,' says Olympe. 'She has interstitial idiopathic cystitis.'

'Good Lord, what's that?' I ask, eager for the next development.

'Well, you might say, Constitution is a nervous wreck,' replies Olympe with a peal of laughter. 'Interstitial is whatever has to do with an inflammation of the walls of the bladder and idiopathic means no identified medical cause. In short, when she's stressed, she gets inflammatory cystitis. Just like women.'

'But why on earth would she be stressed?' I am thinking out loud, for if Constitution, whose daily life as a fat decorative lazybones is disturbed by nothing worse than kindly veterinary examinations consisting of having one's bladder rubbed, has reason to be stressed out, the rest of the animal kingdom is bound to succumb to serious panic attacks.

'The vet said: only the cat knows why.'

And Olympe pouts with frustration.

'Not long ago Paul [Josse] told her she was fat. There's no way of knowing. It could be anything.'

'And how do you treat it?'

'As you do with humans,' laughs Olympe. 'You prescribe Prozac.'

'Are you serious?'

'Absolutely.'

What did I tell you. Animals we are, animals we shall remain. The fact that a rich person's cat suffers from the same afflictions as a civilised woman is hardly a reason to call this cruel and inhuman treatment of felines or the contamination by mankind of an innocent domestic animal; rather, on the contrary, one should point to the deep-rooted solidarity under-lying the fate of all animal species. We share the same appetites, we endure the same afflictions.

'In any event,' says Olympe, 'this will give me pause when I treat animals I don't know.'

She gets up and bids a friendly goodbye.

'Thank you, Madame Michel, you're the only one I can talk to about things like this.'

'Oh, you're most welcome, Olympe, it was my pleasure.'

And I am about to close the door when she says,

'Oh, by the way, Anna Arthens is going to sell the apartment. I hope the new owners will have cats, too.'

17. A Partridge's Arse

Anna Arthens is selling her place!

'Anna Arthens is selling her place!' I say to Leo.

'Well I never,' he replies – or at least that is my impression.

I've been living here for twenty-seven years and no apartment has ever been sold out of the family. Old Madame Meurisse left her place to young Madame Meurisse, and the same thing happened, more or less, for the Badoises, the Josses, and the Rosens. The Arthens arrived at the same time we did; in a way, we grew old together. As for the de Broglies, they'd already been here for a very long time, and still occupy the premises. I don't know how old the Councillor is, but as a young man he already seemed old, which means that now that he is truly very old, he still seems young.

Anna Arthens, consequently, is the very first, under my mandate as concierge, to sell property that will change hands and name. Oddly enough, the thought of it terrifies me. Am I therefore so used to the eternal repetition of the same old things that the prospect of a change that is as yet hypothetical plunging me once again into the river of time serves to remind me of that river's currents? We live each day as if it were merely a rehearsal for the next, and the cosy existence at 7, Rue de Grenelle, with its daily proof of continuity, suddenly seems like an island battered by storms.

Considerably upset, I get out my shopping trolley and, leaving Leo behind snoring gently in his chair, I head with an

115

unsteady step for the market. At the corner of Rue de Grenelle and Rue du Bac I encounter Gégène, the imperturbable inhabitant of his cardboard boxes, and as I approach he watches me like a trapdoor spider sizing up his prey.

'Hey, Ma'ame Michel, you gone and lost yer cat again?' he shouts, and laughs.

Here is one thing at least that never changes. Gégène is a tramp who spends his winters here and has done so for years: he sleeps in squalid cardboard boxes, and wears an old great-coat which, like its owner, has somehow miraculously made it this far and, like him, is redolent of a turn-of-the-century Russian merchant.

'You should go to the shelter,' I tell him, as I always do, 'it's going to get cold tonight.'

'Ha, ha,' he squeals, 'that shelter, I'd like to see *you* there. I'm better off here.'

I go on my way, then feeling guilty, turn back.

'I thought I'd let you know . . . Monsieur Arthens died last night.'

'The food critic?' asks Gégène, with a glint in his eye, and his nose raised like a hunting dog sniffing out a partridge's arse.

'Yes, the food critic. His heart suddenly gave out.'

'My, my!' Gégène is clearly moved.

'Did you know him?' I ask, for the sake of saying something.

'My, my!' says the tramp again. 'Why do the good ones have to go first?'

'He had a good life,' I say hesitantly, surprised at the turn the conversation is taking.

'Ma'ame Michel,' says Gégène, 'people like him, they don't make 'em any more. My, my, I'm going to miss the old fellow.'

'Did he give you something, I don't know, some money at Christmas?'

Gégène looks at me, then spits at his feet.

116

'Nothing – in ten years not a single coin, what do you expect? No two ways about it, he was quite a character. Don't make 'em like that any more, no they don't.'

This little exchange is disturbing, and while I thread my way up and down the aisles of the market, I let my thoughts wander back to Gégène. I've never given poor people credit for having noble souls, on the pretext that they are poor and only too well acquainted with life's injustices. But I have always assumed that they would be united in their hatred of the propertied classes. Gégène has set the record straight on that score and taught me this: if there is one thing that poor people despise, it is other poor people.

Basically, that does make sense.

I wander up and down, distractedly, and find myself in the cheese section, where I buy a chunk of Parmesan and a fine piece of Soumaintrain.

18. Ryabinin

When something is bothering me, I seek refuge. No need to travel far; a trip to the realm of literary memory will suffice. For where can one find more noble distraction, more entertaining company, more delightful enchantment than in literature?

Quite suddenly I find myself by the olives, thinking about Ryabinin. Why Ryabinin? Because Gégène wears that old greatcoat, embellished in the back with buttons at the waist, and it reminds me of Ryabinin's greatcoat. In *Anna Karenina,* Ryabinin, a greatcoat-wearing timber merchant, comes to see Levin, a country aristocrat, about a sale with Stepan Oblonsky, a Moscow aristocrat. The merchant swears on all the icons and all the saints that Oblonsky will profit from the sale, but Levin accuses him of cheating his friend out of a small forest that is worth three times what Ryabinin has offered. This scene is preceded by a dialogue where Levin asks Oblonsky if he has counted the trees in his forest.

'How, count the trees?' exclaims the gentleman. 'You may as well count the sand in the sea!'

'You may be certain that Ryabinin has counted them,' retorts Levin.

I am particularly fond of this scene, first of all because it takes place in Pokrovskoye, in the Russian countryside. Ah, the Russian countryside . . . there is a very special charm about such a place – it is wild and yet still bound to mankind through the land, mother to us all . . . The most beautiful scene in *Anna*

Karenina is set at Pokrovskoye. Levin, dark and melancholy, is trying to forget Kitty. It is springtime, he goes off with the peasants to mow the fields. In the beginning the task seems too arduous for him. He is about to give up when the old peasant leading the row calls for a rest. Then they begin again with their scythes. Once again Levin is about to collapse from exhaustion, once again the old man raises his scythe. Rest. And then the row moves forward again, forty hands scything swathes and moving steadily towards the river as the sun rises. It is getting hotter and hotter, Levin's arms and shoulders are soaked in sweat, but with each successive pause and start, his awkward, painful gestures become more fluid. A welcome breeze suddenly caresses his back. A summer rain. Gradually, his movements are freed from the shackles of his will, and he goes into a light trance which gives his gestures the perfection of conscious, automatic motion, without thought or calculation, and the scythe seems to move of its own accord. Levin delights in the forgetfulness that movement brings, where the pleasure of doing is marvellously foreign to the striving of the will.

This is eminently true of many happy moments in life. Freed from the demands of decision and intention, adrift on some inner sea, we observe our various movements as if they belonged to someone else, and yet we admire their involuntary excellence. What other reason might I have for writing this – ridiculous journal of an ageing concierge – if the writing did not have something of the art of scything about it? The lines gradually become their own demiurges and, like some witless yet miraculous participant, I witness the birth on paper of sentences that have eluded my will and appear in spite of me on the sheet, teaching me something that I neither knew nor thought I might want to know. This painless birth, like an unsolicited proof, gives me untold pleasure, and with neither toil nor certainty but the joy of frank astonishment I follow the pen that is guiding and supporting me.

119

In this way, in the full proof and texture of my self, I accede to a self-forgetfulness that borders on ecstasy, to savour the blissful calm of my watching consciousness.

Finally, climbing back into the cart, Ryabinin complains openly to his clerk about the mannerisms of these fine gentlemen.

'And with regard to the purchase, Mikhail Ignatich?' asks the lad.

'Well, well! . . .' replies the merchant.

As we may rapidly conclude, from a human being's appearance and position, to their intelligence . . . Ryabinin, accountant of the sand in the sea, wily actor and brilliant manipulator, has no time for whatever negative opinions his person might inspire. He was born intelligent, and a pariah, but he has no dreams of glory; the only thing that compels him to action is the promise of profit, the prospect of politely fleecing the overlords of an imbecilic system that has nothing but scorn for him but does not know how to stop him. Thus am I, poor concierge, resigned to a total lack of luxury – but I am an anomaly in the system, living proof of how grotesque it is, and every day I mock it gently, deep within my impenetrable self.

Profound Thought No. 8

If you forget the future
You lose
The present

Today we went to Chatou to see Mamie Josse, Papa's mother, who moved to an old people's home two weeks ago. Papa went with her when she settled in and this time we all went together to see her. Mamie can't live all alone any more in her big house in Chatou: she's almost blind, she has arthritis, and she can hardly walk or hold anything in her hands and the minute you leave her alone she gets frightened. Her children (Papa, my uncle François and my aunt Laure) tried to manage things for her with a private nurse but she couldn't stay there 24/7 either; besides, all of Mamie's friends were already in old people's homes, so it seemed like a good solution.

Mamie's old people's home is something else. I wonder how much it costs a month, a luxury home like this? Mamie's room is big, and light, with lovely furniture and lovely curtains, a little adjoining living room and a bathroom with a marble bathtub. Maman and Colombe went into raptures over the marble bathtub, as if Mamie could care less that her tub is marble when her fingers are concrete . . . Besides, marble is ugly. Papa didn't say much. I know he feels guilty that his mother is in a home. 'Well, you don't expect us to take her in?' said Maman when they both thought I was out of earshot (but I hear everything, especially things I'm not supposed to hear). 'No, Solange, of course not . . .' replied Papa, in a tone that implied, 'Let's pretend I think the opposite, all the while saying "No, no" with a weary and resigned air about me, like a good husband who goes along with her – that way I come out of it as the good guy.'

I'm very well acquainted with that tone of Papa's. It means: 'I know I'm a coward but don't anyone try to tell me as much.' Obviously, it couldn't fail: 'You really are a coward,' said Maman, furiously flinging a dishcloth into the sink. The minute she gets angry, it's really weird, she has to throw something. Once she even threw Constitution. 'You don't want it any more than I do,' she continued, picking up the dishcloth again and waving it in front of Papa's face. 'In any event, it's done,' said Papa – which are the words of a coward to the power of ten.

As far as I'm concerned, I'm glad Mamie is not coming to live with us. Although in four thousand square feet it wouldn't really be a problem. I do, however, think that old people deserve some respect. And in a home, you get no more respect, that's for sure. When you go there, it means: 'I'm done for, I'm nobody, everyone, myself included, is just waiting for one thing: death, a dreary end to all this boredom.' No, the reason I don't want Mamie to come and live with us is that I don't like her. She's a nasty old woman and before that she was a nasty young woman. I think this too is profoundly unjust: take a very old man, who was once a heating engineer, a kindly man, who never showed anything but kindness to those around him, a man who knew how to create love and give it and receive it, who connected with people in a human and sensitive way. His wife is dead, his children don't have two pennies to rub together and, moreover, they have their own kids – and lots of them – to feed and raise. And they live right at the other end of the country. So you put this nice old man in an old people's home near the village where he was born, where his children can only come to see him twice a year – a home for poor people, where he has to share a room, where the food's revolting and the staff are fighting off their own certainty of ending up in the same place some day by mistreating the inmates. Is this the price you pay for love, to end your life in sordid promiscuity? Now take my grandmother, who has never contributed to anything in life beyond a long series of receptions, fixed smiles, intrigues and futile expenses, and consider the fact that she is entitled to a charming room, with a private living room, and *Coquilles Saint-Jacques* for lunch. Is that the reward for emotional anorexia – a marble bathtub in a ruinously expensive bijou residence?

So I don't like Mamie and she doesn't like me very much either. She adores Colombe, however, who returns her feelings in kind, which means she has her eye on her inheritance – with the utterly genuine detachment of the girl-who-doesn't-have-her-eye-on-her-inheritance. So I thought the day in Chatou would be an unbelievable ordeal, and bingo: Maman and Colombe go into raptures about the bathtub, Papa looks as if he's just swallowed his umbrella, and old dried-out bedridden invalids are being wheeled around the corridors with all their drip bags, a madwoman ('Alzheimer's,' said Colombe with a learned air – no, really!) calls me 'Pretty Clara' and shouts two seconds later that she wants her dog right away, practically poking my eye out with her huge diamond ring, and to boot, someone even tried to escape! The residents who are still healthy have electronic bracelets around their wrists: when they try to go outside the walls of the residence it beeps at the reception desk and the staff rush out after the fugitives who, obviously, get caught after a hundred hard-earned yards and who protest vigorously that this is not supposed to be the Gulag, and they ask to speak to the director and make all sorts of weird gestures until they are shoved into their wheelchairs. This lady who attempted her final sprint had changed her clothes after lunch: she had put on her escape outfit, a dress with polka dots and ruffles all over, very practical for climbing over fences. In short, at 2 p.m., after the bathtub, the *Coquilles Saint-Jacques* sauce and the spectacular escape of Edmond Dantès, I was ripe for despair.

Then suddenly I remembered that I had decided to build and not destroy. I looked all around me for something positive, careful not to look at Colombe. I couldn't find anything. All these people looking for death, not knowing what to do . . . And then, oh miracle, Colombe herself provided me with a solution, yes, Colombe. When we left, after we'd kissed Mamie and promised to come back soon, my sister said, 'OK, it looks like Mamie is nicely settled in. But as for everything else . . . we have to hurry up and forget about it, and quickly.' Let's not quibble about the 'hurry up quickly', because that would be petty, let's just concentrate on the idea: to forget about it quickly.

On the contrary, we absolutely mustn't forget it. We mustn't forget old people with their rotten bodies, old people who are so close to death, something that young people don't want to think about (so it is to homes that they entrust the care of accompanying their parents to the threshold, with no fuss or bother). And where's the joy in these final hours that they ought to be making the most of? They're spent in boredom and bitterness, endlessly revisiting memories. We mustn't forget that our bodies decline, friends die, everyone forgets about us, and the end is solitude. Nor must we forget that these old people were young once, that a lifespan is pathetically short, that one day you're twenty and the next day you're eighty. Colombe thinks you can 'hurry up and forget' because it all seems so very far away to her, the prospect of old age, as if it were never going to happen to her. But just by observing the adults around me I understood very early on that life goes by in no time at all, yet they're always in such a hurry, so stressed out by deadlines, so eager for now so they needn't think about tomorrow . . . But if you dread tomorrow, it's because you don't know how to build the present, and when you don't know how to build the present, you tell yourself you can deal with it tomorrow, and it's a lost cause anyway because tomorrow always ends up becoming today, don't you see?

So, we mustn't forget any of this, absolutely not. We have to live with the certainty that we'll get old and that it won't look nice or be good or feel happy. And tell ourselves that it's now that matters: to build something, now, at any price, using all our strength. Always remember that there's an old people's home waiting somewhere and so we have to surpass ourselves every day, make every day undying. Climb our own personal Everest and do it in such a way that every step is a little bit of eternity.

That's what the future is for: to build the present, with real plans, made by living people.

ON GRAMMAR

1. Infinitesimal

This morning Jacinthe Rosen introduced me to the new owner of the Arthens apartment.

His name is Kakuro Something. I failed to understand properly because Madame Rosen always talks as if she has a cockroach in her mouth and because the lift door opened at that very moment to let Monsieur Pallières senior out, all cloaked in haughtiness. He greeted us cursorily and hurried off with the jerky stride of a busy captain of industry.

The newcomer is a gentleman in his sixties, very presentable and very Japanese. He is rather small and slim, his face is wrinkled but his features are sharp. His entire person emanates kindliness, but I also sense decisiveness, joviality and a strong will.

At the moment he is enduring Jacinthe Rosen's pithiatic prattling. She brings to mind a hen at the foot of a mountain of grain.

'Bonjour, Madame' were his first and only words, in unaccented French.

I am wearing my semi-retarded concierge uniform. We are dealing with a new resident here, and force of habit has not yet compelled him to assume that I am inept, so I must make a special pedagogical effort. I limit myself therefore to a refrain of asthenic yeses in response to Jacinthe Rosen's hysterical salvoes.

'You will show Monsieur Something [Shou?] the outbuildings?'

'Will you explain the mail to Monsieur Something [Pshoo?]?'

'The decorators are coming on Friday. Could you keep an eye out for Monsieur Something [Opshoo?], between ten and half past ten?'

And so on.

Monsieur Something betrays no signs of impatience, and waits politely, looking at me with a kindly smile. Everything is going very well, I feel. All we need do is wait for Madame Rosen to tire and I shall be able to repair to my den.

And then.

'The doormat that was outside the Arthens's door hasn't been cleaned. Can you bring it to the cleaner's?' asks the hen.

Why must the comedy always turn to tragedy? To be sure, I also misuse language on occasion, although I tend to use such abuses as weapons.

'Some kinda heart attack, eh,' is what I had said to Chabrot, to put him off the scent that my outlandish manners have laid.

I am therefore not so sensitive that a minor misuse will cause me to lose my reason. One must concede to others what one tolerates in oneself; besides, Jacinthe Rosen and the cockroach in her mouth were born in the dreary banlieue of Bondy in a row of buildings with grimy stairwells: consequently, I am more indulgent in her case than I would be for Madame Would-you-be-so-kind-as-comma-to.

And yet, there is an element of tragedy: I flinched when she said *bring* and at that very moment Monsieur Something also flinched, and our eyes met. And since that infinitesimal nanosecond when – of this I am sure – we were joined in linguistic solidarity by the shared pain that made our bodies shudder, Monsieur Something has been observing me with a very different gaze.

A watchful gaze.

And now he is speaking to me.

130

'Were you acquainted with the Arthens? I have heard they were quite an extraordinary family,' he says.

'No,' I reply, on my guard, 'I didn't really know them, they were just another family here.'

'Yes, a happy family,' says Madame Rosen, who, visibly, is getting impatient.

'You know, all happy families are alike,' I mutter, to have done with this business, 'there's nothing more to it.'

' "Every unhappy family is unhappy in its own way," ' he says, giving me an odd look and all of a sudden, even if it's not for the first time, I shudder.

Yes, I assure you. I shudder – but quite involuntarily. It just happened, there was nothing I could do, I was overwhelmed.

As misfortunes never travel alone, Leo decides it is time to slip between our legs, rubbing against Monsieur Something on his way.

'I have two cats,' he says. 'May I ask your cat's name?'

'Leo,' replies Jacinthe Rosen in my stead, then, breaking off our conversation, she hooks her arm under Monsieur Something's and, saying thank you without looking at me, begins to steer him towards the lift. With infinite tact, he places his hand on her forearm and gently brings her to a halt.

'Thank you, Madame,' he says to me, then allows himself to be led away by his possessive fowl.

2. In a Moment of Grace

Do you know what an involuntary act signifies? Psychoanalysts say that it reflects the insidious manoeuvring of one's hidden unconscious. What a pointless theory, in fact. When we do something involuntarily, this is the most visible sign of the power of our conscious will; for our will, when opposed by emotion, makes use of all its wiles to attain its ends.

'I suppose this means I want to be found out,' I say to Leo, who has just re-entered his quarters and – I could swear upon it – has been conspiring with the universe to fulfil my desire.

All happy families are alike; every unhappy family is unhappy in its own way is the first line in *Anna Karenina* and, like any self-respecting concierge, I am not supposed to have read it; nor ought I to have jumped at the second part of the sentence when Monsieur Something, in that moment of grace, pronounced it as if I had not known that Tolstoy was its author – for although common people may be sensitive to great works though they do not read them, literature, in their presence, cannot aspire to the lofty peaks where the educated elite place it.

I spend the day trying to convince myself that I am getting into a panic over nothing, and that Monsieur Something, who has at his disposal a wallet so well stuffed that he was able to buy the entire fourth floor, has other more pressing concerns than the Parkinsonian shudderings of a feeble-minded concierge.

And then, at around seven in the evening, a young man rings at my lodge.

'Good evening, Madame,' he says, articulating to perfection, 'my name is Paul Nguyen, I am Monsieur Ozu's private secretary.'

He hands me his business card.

'Here is my mobile phone number. Contractors will be coming to work for Monsieur Ozu and we would not like this to cause you any additional work. So if there is the slightest problem, please call me, I will come right away.'

You will note at this juncture in our little mystery that the current vignette is barren of dialogue, an element that one ordinarily notices by virtue of a succession of quotation marks running vertically down the page as the speakers each take their turn.

By rights, there should have been something like:

'Delighted to meet you.'

And then:

'Very well, I shall call you if need be.'

But there appears to be nothing of the sort.

The fact of the matter is that with absolutely no effort on my part I am mute. I am fully conscious that my mouth is open but not a sound comes out, and I greatly pity this handsome young man who is obliged to contemplate a one-hundred-and-fifty-pound toad named Renée.

Generally, at this point in an encounter, the protagonist will enquire, 'Do you speak French?'

But Paul Nguyen merely smiles and waits.

With a Herculean effort I manage to say something.

Actually, it initially comes out as something like: 'Grmbill.'

But he continues to wait with the same magnificent abnegation.

'Monsieur Ozu?' I finally say with considerable difficulty, in a voice worthy of Yul Brynner.

'Yes, Monsieur Ozu,' he says. 'You didn't know his name?'

'No,' I say with effort, 'I had not understood it very well. How do you spell it?'

'O-z-u,' he says.

'Ah, I see. It is Japanese?'

'Quite, Madame. Monsieur Ozu is Japanese.'

He takes his leave, very affable, while my Good Night seems to travel through a throat afflicted with triple bronchitis. I close the door and collapse onto a chair, squashing Leo in the process.

Monsieur Ozu. Could it be that I am in the middle of some insane dream, crafted with suspenseful, Machiavellian twists of plot, a flood of coincidences and a denouement where the heroine in her nightgown awakes in the morning with an obese cat on her feet and the static of the morning radio in her ears?

But we all know perfectly well that, in essence, dreams and waking hours do not have the same texture and, upon careful examination of all my sensory perception, I am able to determine with certainty that I am awake.

Monsieur Ozu! Could he be the filmmaker's son? Nephew? Distant cousin?

Well I never.

Profound Thought No. 9

If you offer a lady enemy
Macaroons from Ladurée
Don't go thinking
You'll be able
To see beyond

The gentleman who has bought the Arthens apartment is Japanese! His name is Kakuro Ozu! That's just great; something like this *would* happen right before I die. Twelve and a half years in a cultural desert and now when it's time to go and pack it in a Japanese gentleman arrives . . . It really is too unfair.

But I want to see the positive side of things: at least he is here, and really here, and what's more we had a very interesting conversation yesterday. First of all, there's the fact that everyone in the building is absolutely crazy about Monsieur Ozu. My mother speaks of nothing else, my father listens to her for once, whereas usually his mind is elsewhere when she starts to rant about the goings-on in the building; Colombe pinched my Japanese textbook and, in an unprecedented event in the annals of 7, Rue de Grenelle, Madame de Broglie came for tea. We live on the fifth floor, directly above the former Arthens apartment and lately there has been all this building work going on – a massive amount of work! It was clear that Monsieur Ozu had decided to change everything, and everyone was drooling with desire to see what he had changed. In a world full of fossils, the slightest movement of a pebble on the slope of the cliff is nearly enough to bring on a whole series of heart attacks – so you can imagine what happens when someone dynamites the whole mountain! In short, Madame de Broglie was dying to have a look at the fourth floor, so when she ran into Maman last week in the hall she wheedled an invitation out of her. And you know what her pretext was? It's really funny. Madame de Broglie is the wife of Monsieur de Broglie, the State Councillor who lives on the first floor and who joined the Council under Giscard d'Estaing – he's so conservative that he won't say hello to divorced people. Colombe calls him 'the old fascist' because she's never read a thing about the French right wing, and Papa holds him up as a perfect example of the ossification of political ideas. His wife fits the image: posh suit, string of pearls, pinched lips and loads of grandchildren called Grégoire or Marie. Until now she would scarcely say hello to Maman (who is a socialist, dyes her hair and wears pointed shoes). But last week she jumped on us as if her life depended on it. We were in the hall, we had just come back from shopping and Maman was in a very good mood because she had found a duck-egg blue linen tablecloth for two hundred and forty euros. And I swear I thought I was having auditory hallucinations. After the customary 'Bonjour, Madame,' Madame de Broglie said to Maman, 'I have something to ask you,' which must already have really hurt her to say. 'Please, do go right ahead,' said Maman with a smile (thanks to the tablecloth and her anti-depressants). 'Well, my little daughter-in-law, Étienne's wife, is not very well these days and I think she'll have to consider therapy.' 'Oh?' said Maman with an even bigger smile. 'Yes, um, you see, some sort of psychoanalysis.' Madame de Broglie looked like a snail lost in the Sahara but she stood fast all the same. 'Yes, I see,' said Maman, 'and how may I be of assistance, Madame de Broglie?' 'Well, the thought occurred to me that you might have an idea . . . of well . . . how to go about it . . . so I would like to discuss it with you, that's all.' Maman could not get over her good fortune: a duck-egg blue linen tablecloth, the prospect of spouting all her knowledge about psychoanalysis and Madame de Broglie dancing the dance of the seven veils – oh yes, a good day indeed! And she couldn't resist because she knew perfectly well what the other woman's actual intention was. My mother may be a bit of a bumpkin where intellectual subtlety is concerned, but you still can't fool her completely. She knows perfectly well that the day the de Broglies are genuinely interested in psychoanalysis, the Gaullists will start singing the *Internationale* – clearly, the name of her sudden success was 'the fifth-floor landing lies directly above the fourth-floor landing'. Still, she decided to act magnanimously, to prove to Madame de Broglie how kind and open-minded socialists can be – but not without a little ragging to begin with. 'By all means, Madame de Broglie. Would you like me to come to your home one evening to discuss it?' she asked. The other woman looked constipated, she wasn't expecting such a suggestion, but she gathered herself very quickly and, as a woman of the world, she said, 'No, no, please, I don't want you to have to come down, I will come up to see you.' Maman had already had her little moment of satisfaction so she didn't insist. 'Well, I'm in this afternoon,' she said, 'why don't you come and have a cup of tea at about five o'clock?'

The tea party was perfect. Maman did things just as one should: she used the tea service that Mamie had given her, gold leaf and butterflies and roses; she offered macaroons from Ladurée, and, all the same, brown sugar (a leftie indulgence). Madame de Broglie, who had just spent a good quarter of an hour on the landing below, looked a bit embarrassed but satisfied nonetheless. And a bit surprised. I think our place was not how she had imagined. Maman pulled out all the stops regarding good manners and worldly conversation, including an expert commentary on where to buy good coffee, before leaning her head to one side and saying, 'So, Madame de Broglie, you are concerned about your daughter-in-law?' 'Hmm, ah, yes,' said the other woman, who had almost forgotten her pretext and was now struggling to find something to say. 'Well yes, she's depressed,' is all she came out with. So Maman shifted into the next gear. After all this generosity it was time to hand her neighbour the bill. Madame de Broglie was treated to an entire course on Freud, including several titillating anecdotes on the sexual mores of the Messiah and his apostles (including a lurid aside on Melanie Klein), and punctuated with references to women's lib and secularism in French schools. The works. Madame de Broglie took it like a good Christian. She endured the onslaught with admirable stoicism, convincing herself all the while that this was a small price to pay to expiate her sin of curiosity. When they parted, both ladies were perfectly satisfied, but for different reasons, and at dinner that evening Maman said, 'Madame de Broglie may be sanctimonious, but she does know how to be charming.'

In short, everyone is excited about Monsieur Ozu. Olympe Saint-Nice told Colombe (who despises her and calls her 'Our Holy Lady of the Pigs') that he has two cats and that she is dying to see them. Jacinthe Rosen waffles on and on about the comings and goings on the fourth floor and she goes into a trance every time. As for me, I'm excited too, but not for the same reasons. Here's what happened.

I was in the lift with Monsieur Ozu and it got stuck between the second and third floors for ten minutes because some dolt had not closed the gate properly before deciding to walk down after all. When this happens you have to wait for someone to realise or, if it's taking too long, you have to shout your head off to alert the neighbours, but of course you must remain digni-fied, which isn't always easy. We didn't shout. So we had time to introduce ourselves and get acquainted. All the ladies in the building would have sold their souls to be in my place. I was just really happy because my considerable Japanese side was obviously delighted to speak to an authentic Japanese gentle-man. But what I really liked, above all, was the content of our conversation. First of all, he said, 'Your mother told me you were studying Japanese at school. What is your level?' I casually took note of the fact that Maman has been gossiping again to draw attention to herself, and then I replied in

Japanese, 'Yes, sir, I know a little Japanese but not very well.' And he replied in Japanese, 'Do you want me to correct your accent?' and then translated right away into French. Well, I appreciated that for a start. Lots of people would have said, 'Oh, you speak so well! Bravo!' whereas I'm sure I must sound like some cow from Outer Mongolia. So I answered in Japanese, 'Please do, sir,' and he corrected one inflection and then said, still in Japanese, 'Call me Kakuro.' I replied in Japanese, 'Yes, Kakuro-san,' and we laughed. And that is when the conversation (in French) got really interesting. He said, right out, 'I'm very intrigued by our concierge, Madame Michel. I would like your opinion.' I know plenty of people who would try to worm the information out of me, acting all innocent. But he was upfront. 'I think . . . that she's not what we think,' he added.

I've had my own suspicions on the matter for a while now too. From a distance, she's a real concierge. Close up . . . well, close up . . . there's something weird going on. Colombe hates her and thinks she's the dregs of humanity. Colombe, in any case, thinks that anyone who doesn't meet her cultural standard is the dregs of humanity, and for Colombe the cultural standard is social power and shirts from agnès b. As for Madame Michel . . . how can we tell? She radiates intelligence. And yet she really makes an effort, like, you can tell she is doing everything she possibly can to act like a concierge and come across as stupid. But I've been watching her, when she used to talk with Jean Arthens or when she talks to Neptune when Diane has her back turned, or when she looks at the ladies in the building who walk right by her without saying hello. Madame Michel has the elegance of the hedgehog: on the outside, she's covered in quills, a real fortress, but my gut feeling is that on the inside, she has the same simple refinement as the hedgehog: a deceptively indolent little creature, fiercely solitary – and terribly elegant.

Well, having said that, I admit it: I'm not a clairvoyant. If nothing out of the ordinary had happened, I would still be seeing

139

the same thing everyone sees: a concierge who, most of the time, is grumpy. But something did happen not long ago and it's odd that Monsieur Ozu's question came along just when it did. Two weeks ago, Antoine Pallières knocked over Madame Michel's shopping bag just as she was opening her door. Antoine Pallières is the son of Monsieur Pallières, the industrialist on the sixth floor who lectures Papa on how France ought to be run and sells arms to international criminals. The son is less dangerous because he's a real moron, but you never know: the capacity to do harm is often an item of family capital. Anyway, Antoine Pallières knocked over Madame Michel's shopping bag. Beets, noodles, bouillon cubes and soap all fell out and as I walked past I glimpsed a book amidst all the things on the ground. I say glimpsed because Madame Michel rushed over to pick everything up, looking angrily at Antoine (he was obviously not inclined to lift his little finger), but she also looked worried. He didn't notice but I had all the time I needed to figure out what the book in Madame Michel's shopping bag was – or rather what kind of book, because there have been loads of the same type on Colombe's desk since she started philosophy. It was a book from a publisher called Vrin – ultra-specialised in philosophy books for university. What is a concierge doing with a Vrin book in her shopping bag? is the question that, unlike Antoine Pallières, I asked myself.

'I think you're right,' I said to Monsieur Ozu and we immediately progressed from being neighbours to something more, conspirators. We exchanged our impressions of Madame Michel, and Monsieur Ozu said he was willing to bet that she was a clandestine erudite princess, and we said goodbye promising to investigate this further.

So here is my profound thought for the day: this is the first time I have met someone who seeks out people and who sees beyond. That may seem trivial but I think it is profound all the same. We never look beyond our assumptions and, what's worse, we have given up trying to meet others; we just meet ourselves. We don't recognise each other because other people have become our permanent mirrors. If we actually realised this, if we were to become aware of the fact that we are only ever looking at ourselves in the other person, that we are alone in the wilderness, we would go crazy. When my mother offers macaroons from Ladurée to Madame de Broglie, she is telling herself her own life story and just nibbling at her own flavour; when Papa drinks his coffee and reads his paper, he is contemplating his own reflection in the mirror, as if practising the Coué method or something; when Colombe talks about Marian's lectures, she is ranting about her own reflection; and when people walk by the concierge, all they see is a void, because she is not from their world.

As for me, I implore fate to give me the chance to see beyond myself and truly meet someone.

3. Beneath the Skin

A few days go by.

As on every Tuesday, Manuela comes to my lodge. I just have time, before she closes the door behind her, to hear Jacinthe Rosen talking with young Madame Meurisse next to the lift, which is taking its own sweet time to arrive.

'My son says that the Chinese are very difficult to deal with.'

Madame Rosen's resident cockroach affects her pronunciation: she does not say Chinese, but Chanese.

I've always dreamt of visiting Chana. It's more interesting than China, after all.

'He dismissed the baroness,' says Manuela. Her cheeks are pink and her eyes are shining. 'And everyone else along with her.'

I adopt the very air of innocence.

'Who did?'

'Monsieur Ozu, of course!' Manuela looks at me reproachfully.

For over a fortnight now all the talk in the building is of Monsieur Ozu moving into the apartment of the late Pierre Arthens. In this frozen place, this glacial prison of power and idleness, the arrival of a new resident and the unbelievable things that, under his orders, a whole host of professional contractors have been getting up to – their numbers so impressive that even Neptune has given up on trying to sniff each and every one – this arrival, therefore, has brought with it a wave of excitement and panic all at the same time. For the conventional aspiration to see tradition maintained and the contingent disapproval of anything that might remotely evoke newly acquired wealth – ostentatious interior decoration, the installation of stereo equipment, excessive use of meals delivered from the traiteur – were in open competition with a deeper hunger, deep in the guts of all these benighted souls blinded by boredom: the hunger for novelty. Thus, for two weeks or more 7, Rue de Grenelle throbbed to the rhythm of the comings and goings of painters, carpenters, plumbers, cabinet-makers and delivery men, carrying furniture, carpets and electronic equipment, until the grand finale, the actual removal company; and all these people had clearly been hired to transform the fourth floor from top to bottom. So, needless to say, all the residents of the building were dying to see that transformation for themselves. The Josses and the Pallières no longer took the lift: discovering new well-springs of vigour, they would wander at all hours across the landing of the fourth floor, which naturally they could not avoid if they were to leave and then return to their own apartments. They now attracted the envious gazes of all the other residents: Bernadette de Broglie plotted to take tea with Solange Josse – never mind that she is a socialist; and Jacinthe Rosen volunteered to drop off the package for Sabine Pallières that had just been delivered to my lodge – I was only too pleased myself to entrust her with the task, making a great hypocritical fuss over it in the process.

Because I alone, of everyone in the building, have been careful to avoid Monsieur Ozu. We met twice in the hallway but he was always accompanied and merely greeted me politely, and I did likewise. Nothing in his behaviour betrayed anything other than courtesy and indifferent kindliness. But just as children can sense that beneath the skin of conventional behaviour lies the true stuff of which human beings are made, my internal radar, suddenly on high alert, told me that Monsieur Ozu was watching me closely, biding his time.

It was his secretary who saw to all the tasks requiring any contact with me. I am also willing to wager that Paul Nguyen has something to do with the fascination Monsieur Ozu's coming has been exerting on the residents. He is a strikingly handsome young man. From Asia and his Vietnamese father, he has acquired distinguished manners and a mysterious serenity. From Europe and his mother (a White Russian), he has inherited height and Slavic cheekbones, as well as the light shade of his slightly almond-shaped eyes. He is both manly and delicate, a perfect synthesis of masculine good looks and Asian gentleness.

I learned about his background one afternoon when there was a great commotion all around, and I could see he was very busy: he rang at my lodge to apprise me of the arrival early the next morning of a new crew of delivery men, and I offered him a cup of tea; he accepted without more ado. We conversed in an exquisitely nonchalant manner. Who would ever have imagined that such a handsome and competent young man – for he was most competent, I'd swear by all the gods, we all could tell by the way he organised the work and never seemed overwhelmed or tired, getting everything done in a calm manner – would also be so utterly devoid of any form of snobbery? When he took his leave, thanking me warmly, I realised that in his presence I had forgotten even the very notion of trying to hide who I was.

But back to the news of the day.

'He dismissed the baroness, and everyone else.'

Manuela is elated, and cannot hide it. Anna Arthens, upon leaving Paris, had solemnly promised Violette Grelier that she would commend her to the new owner. Monsieur Ozu, wishing to honour the request of the widow from whom he was buying the property (and consequently breaking her heart),

144

had agreed to receive her former servants and talk to them. The Greliers, with Anna Arthens as their sponsor, could have found a desirable position in any good household, but Violette was nurturing the insane hope that she might be able to stay on in the same place where, in her own words, she had spent the best years of her life.

'Leaving here would be like dying,' she had said to Manuela. 'Well, I'm not talking about you, my dear. You'll just have to get used to the idea.'

'Get used to the idea, fiddle-dee-dee,' says Manuela who, since she followed my advice and watched *Gone with the Wind*, has been taking herself for the Scarlett of Argenteuil. 'She's leaving, and I'm staying!'

'Monsieur Ozu is hiring you?'

'You'll never guess, he's taken me on for twelve hours, and I'll be paid like a princess!'

'Twelve hours! How will you manage?'

'I'm going to drop Madame Pallières,' she replies, on the verge of ecstasy, 'I'm going to drop Madame Pallières.'

And because one really should over-indulge in things that are this good:

'Yes,' she says again, 'I'm going to drop Madame Pallières.'

We savour a moment of silence to honour this profusion of blessings.

'I'll make the tea,' I say, interrupting our state of bliss. 'White tea, to celebrate.'

'Oh, I forgot, I brought something.'

She removes a little pouch in ivory tissue paper from her shopping bag.

I set about untying the blue velvet ribbon. Inside, dark chocolate Florentines glisten like black diamonds.

'He's going to pay me twenty-two euros an hour,' says Manuela, putting the cups on the table then sitting down again, after courteously enjoining Leo to set off and discover

145

the world. 'Twenty-two euros! Can you believe it? The others pay me eight, ten, eleven! That *pretensiosa* Pallières woman, she pays me eight euros and leaves her filthy pants under the bed.'

'Perhaps Monsieur Ozu will leave his filthy pants under the bed,' I say, smiling.

'Oh, he's not the type!' She grows thoughtful. 'I hope I'll know what to do, in any case. Because he has a lot of strange stuff up there, you know. And he's got all these *bonzes* to water and spray.'

Manuela means Monsieur Ozu's bonsai. These are tall and slender ones, and do not have the typical tortured shape that can often leave a forbidding impression; to me, on their way through the hall to their new home, they evoked another era, and the faint whisper of their foliage suggested the fugitive vision of a distant forest.

'Who would have thought the decorators would do all this,' continues Manuela. 'Knock everything down and redo it!'

For Manuela, a decorator is an ethereal being who places cushions on expensive sofas and takes a step back to admire the effect.

'They're knocking the walls down with sledgehammers,' she had told me a week earlier, breathless after trying to climb the stairs four at a time with a huge broom in her hand. Now she continued, 'You know . . . it's really lovely now. I wish you could see it.'

'What are his cats called?' I ask, to distract her and remove this dangerous, hare-brained idea from her mind.

'Oh, they're gorgeous!' she says, looking at Leo with consternation. 'They're ever so thin and move around without a sound, like this.'

With her hand she draws strange undulations in the air.

'Do you know their names?' I ask again.

'The female is Kitty, but I didn't catch the male's name.'

A bead of cold sweat races down my spine.

'Levin?' I venture.

'Yes, that's it. Levin. How did you know?' She frowns. 'Not that revolutionary guy, is it?'

'No, the revolutionary was Lenin. Levin is the hero of a great Russian novel. Kitty is the woman he is in love with.'

'He has had all the doors changed.' Manuela is only moderately interested in Russian novels. 'They slide now. And would you believe it, it's much more practical. I wonder why we don't do the same. You save a lot of room, and it's not as noisy.'

How true. Once again, Manuela brilliantly sums up the situation, and earns my admiration. But her innocent remark also brings on a delicious sensation for other reasons.

4. Break and Continuity

Two reasons, to be exact, both related to Ozu's films.

The first has to do with the sliding doors themselves. From the very first film I saw, *Flavour of Green Tea over Rice*, I was fascinated by the way the Japanese use space in their lives, and by these doors that slide and move quietly along invisible rails, refusing to offend space. For when we push open a door, we transform a place in a very insidious way. We offend its full extension, and introduce a disruptive and poorly proportioned obstacle. If you think about it carefully, there is nothing uglier than an open door. An open door introduces a break in the room, a sort of provincial interference, destroying the unity of space. In the adjoining room it creates a depression, an absolutely pointless gaping hole adrift in a section of wall that would have preferred to remain whole. In either case a door disrupts continuity, without offering anything in exchange other than freedom of movement, which could easily be ensured by another means. Sliding doors avoid such pitfalls and enhance space. Without affecting the balance of the room, they allow it to be transformed. When a sliding door is open, two areas communicate without offending each other. When it is closed, each regains its integrity. Sharing and reunion can occur without intrusion. Life becomes a quiet stroll – whereas our life, in the homes we have, seems like nothing so much as a long series of intrusions.

'How true,' I say to Manuela, 'it's more practical and less abrupt.'

The second reason has to do with an association of ideas which led me from sliding doors to women's feet. In Ozu's films, I don't know how many shots I have seen where the actors slide open the front door, come into the hall and remove their shoes. The women, above all, are particularly gifted at this sequence of gestures. They come in, slide the door along the wall, and take two quick steps that lead them to the foot of the raised area where the family rooms are located; without bending over they remove their laceless shoes from their feet and with a supple, gracious motion of their legs pivot around as they climb, back first, onto the platform. Their skirts puff out slightly; the way they bend their knees in order to climb up is energetic and precise, and their bodies easily follow the slight pirouette of their feet, which leads to a curiously broken and casual series of steps, as if their ankles were hobbled. But while such hindrance in one's gestures generally evokes some sort of constraint, the lively little steps with their incomprehensible fits and starts confer onto the feet of these walking women the seal of a work of art.

When we Westerners walk, our culture dictates that we must, through the continuity of a movement we envision as smooth and seamless, try to restore what we take to be the very essence of life: efficiency without obstacles, a fluid performance that, being free of interruption, will represent the vital élan thanks to which all will be realised. For us the standard is the cheetah in action: all his movements fuse together harmoniously, one cannot be distinguished from the next, and the swift passage of the great wild animal seems like one long continuous movement symbolising the deep perfection of life. When a Japanese woman disrupts the powerful sequence of natural movement with her jerky little steps, we ought to experience the disquiet that troubles our soul whenever nature is violated in this way, but in fact we are filled with an unfamiliar blissfulness, as if disruption could lead to a sort of ecstasy, and a grain of sand to beauty. What we discover in this affront to the sacred rhythm of life, this defiant movement of little feet, this excellence born of constraint, is a paradigm of Art.

When movement has been banished from a nature that seeks its continuity, when it becomes renegade and remarkable by virtue of its very discontinuity, it attains the level of aesthetic creation.

Because Art is life, playing to other rhythms.

Profound Thought No. 10

Grammar
A stratum of consciousness
Leading to beauty

I n the morning, as a rule, I always take a moment to listen to music in my room. Music plays a huge role in my life. It is music that helps me to endure . . . well . . . everything there is to endure: my sister, my mother, school, Achille Grand-Fernet, and so on. Music is not merely a pleasure to the ears the way that gastronomy is to the palate or painting to the eyes. There's nothing terribly original about the fact that I put music on in the morning, just that it sets the tone for the rest of the day. It's very simple but also sort of complicated to explain: I believe that we can choose our moods, because we are aware that there are several mood-strata and we have the means to gain access to them. For example, to write a profound thought, I have to put myself onto a very special stratum, otherwise the ideas and words just don't come. I have to forget myself and at the same time be superconcentrated. But it's not a question of 'the will', it's a mechanism I can set in motion or not, like scratching my nose or doing a backwards somersault. And to activate the mechanism there's nothing better than a little music. For example, to relax, I put on something that takes me into a sort of faraway mood, where things can't really reach me, where I can look at them as if I were watching a film: a 'detached' stratum of consciousness. In general, for that particular stratum, I resort to jazz or, more effective overall but longer to take effect, Dire Straits (long live my MP3 player).

So, this morning I listened to Glenn Miller before leaving for school. I guess it didn't last long enough. When the incident occurred, I lost all my detachment. It was during French with Madame Fine (who is a living antonym because she has a repository of spare tyres around her midriff). What's more, she wears pink. I love pink, I think it's a colour that gets a bad press, it's made out to be a thing for babies or women who wear too much make-up, but pink is really a subtle and delicate colour, and it figures a lot in Japanese poetry. But pink and Madame Fine are a bit like jam and pigs. Anyway, this morning I had French with her. That in itself is already a chore. French with Madame Fine is reduced to a long series of technical exercises, whether we're doing grammar or reading texts. With her it's as if a text was written so that we can identify the characters, the narrator, the setting, the plot, the time of the story and so on. I don't think it has ever occurred to her that a text is written above all to be read and to arouse emotions in the reader. Can you imagine, she has never even asked us the question: 'Did you like this text / this book?' And yet that is the only question that could give meaning to the narrative points of view or the construction of the story . . . Never mind the fact that the minds of younger kids are, I think, more open to literature than, say, the minds of secondary school pupils or students. Let me explain: at my age, all you need is to talk to us about something with some passion, pluck the right strings (love, rebellion, thirst for novelty, etc.) and you have every chance of succeeding. Our history teacher, Monsieur Lermit, had us hooked by the end of the second lesson by showing us photos of these people who'd had their hand or their lips cut off under Sharia law, because they'd been stealing or smoking. But he didn't do it as if he were showing us a gory film or something. It was enthralling, and we listened attentively throughout the lesson, the point of which was to warn us against the foolishness of mankind, and not Islam specifically. So if Madame Fine had taken the trouble to read a few verses of Racine to us, with a tremor in her voice (*Que le jour recommence et que le jour finisse / Sans que jamais Titus puisse voir Bérénice*) she would have discovered that the average adolescent is fully ripe for the tragedy of love. By secondary school it's harder: adulthood is around the corner, kids already have an intuitive idea of how grown-ups behave, and they begin to wonder what role and what place they are going to inherit on life's stage, and anyway by then something has been spoiled, and the goldfish bowl is no longer very far away.

It is bad enough to have to put up with the usual grind of a literature lesson without literature and a language lesson without cognisance of language, so this morning when I felt something snap inside me, I just couldn't contain myself. Madame Fine was making a point about the use of qualifying adjectives as epithets, on the pretext that our compositions were completely barren of said grammatical grace notes, 'Whereas really, it's the sort of thing you learn in year four.' She went on: 'Am I to honestly believe there are students who are this incompetent at grammar,' and she looked straight at Achille Grand-Fernet. I don't like Achille Grand-Fernet but in this case I agreed with him when he asked his question. I feel it was long overdue. More-over, when a literature teacher uses a split infinitive like that, I'm really shocked. It's like someone sweeping the floor and for-getting the dust under the furniture. 'What's the point of grammar?' asked Achille Grand-Fernet. 'You ought to know by now,' replied Madame Never-mind-that-I-am-paid-to-teach-you. 'Well, I don't,' replied Achille, sincerely for once, 'no one ever bothered to explain it to us.' Madame Fine let out a long sigh, of the 'do I really have to put up with such stupid questions' variety, and said, 'The point is to make us speak and write well.'

I thought I would have a heart attack there and then. I have never heard anything so grossly inept. And by that, I don't mean it's *wrong*, just that it is *grossly inept*. To tell a group of adolescents who already know how to speak and write that that is the purpose of grammar is like telling someone that they need

153

to read a history of toilets through the ages in order to pee and poo. It is utterly devoid of meaning! If she had shown us some concrete examples of things we need to know about language in order to use it properly, well, OK, that would be a start. She could tell us, for example, that knowing how to conjugate a verb in all its tenses helps you avoid making the kind of major mistakes that would put you to shame at a dinner party ('I would of came to the party earlier but I tooked the wrong road'). Or, for example, that to write a proper invitation in English to a little *divertissement* at the Chateau of Versailles, knowing the rules governing spelling and the use of apostrophes in *la langue de Shakespeare* can come in very useful: it would save you from embarrassment such as: 'Deer freind, may we have the plesure of you're company at Versaille's this evening? The Marquise de Grand-Fernet.' But if Madame Fine thinks that's all grammar is for . . . We already knew how to use and conjugate a verb long before we knew it was a verb. And even if knowing can help, I still don't think it's something decisive.

Personally I think that grammar is a way to attain Beauty. When you speak, or read, or write, you can tell if you've said or read or written a fine sentence. You can recognise a well-turned phrase or an elegant style. But when you are applying the rules of grammar skilfully, you ascend to another level of the beauty of language. When you use grammar you peel back the layers, to see how it is all put together, see it quite naked, in a way. And that's where it becomes wonderful, because you say to yourself, 'Look how well made this is, how well constructed it is!' 'How solid and ingenious, rich and subtle!' I get completely carried away just knowing there are words of all different natures, and that you have to know them in order to be able to infer their potential usage and compatibility. I find there is nothing more beautiful, for example, than the very basic components of language, nouns and verbs. When you've grasped this, you've grasped the core of any statement. It's magnificent, don't you think? Nouns, verbs . . .

Perhaps, to gain access to all the beauty of the language that grammar unveils, you have to place yourself in a special state of awareness. I have the impression that I do that anyway without any special effort. I think that it was at the age of two, when I first heard grown-ups speak, that I understood once and for all how language is made. Grammar lessons have always seemed to me a sort of synthesis after the fact and, perhaps, a source of supplemental details concerning terminology. Can you teach children to speak and write correctly through grammar if they haven't had the illumination that I had? Who knows. In the meanwhile, all the Madame Fines on the planet ought rather to ask themselves what would be the right piece of music to play to make their pupils go into a grammatical trance.

So I said to Madame Fine: 'Not at all! That is completely reductivist!' There was great silence in the classroom because as a rule I never open my mouth and because I had contradicted the teacher. She looked at me with surprise then she put on one of those stern looks that all teachers use when they feel that the wind is veering to the north and their cosy little punctuation lesson might turn into a tribunal of their pedagogical methods. 'And what do you know about it, Mademoiselle Josse?' she asked acidly. Everyone was holding their breath. When the star pupil is displeased, it's bad for the teaching body, particularly when that body is well fed, so this morning it was like a thriller and a circus act all rolled into one: everyone was waiting to see what the outcome of the battle would be, and they were hoping it would be a bloody one.

'Well,' I said, 'when you've read Jakobson, it becomes obvious that grammar is an end in itself and not simply a means: it provides access to the structure and beauty of language, it's not just some trick to help people get by in society.'

'Some trick! Some trick!' she scoffed, her eyes popping out of her head. 'For Mademoiselle Josse grammar is a trick!'

If she had listened carefully to what I said, she would have understood that, precisely, for me grammar is *not* a trick. But I think the reference to Jakobson caused her to lose it completely, never mind that everyone was giggling, including Cannelle Martin, even though they didn't get what I had said at all, but they could tell a little cloud from Siberia was hovering over the head of our fat French teacher. In reality, I've never read a thing by Jakobson, obviously not. Though I may be superbright, I'd still rather read manga or literature. But Maman has a friend (who's a university lecturer) who was talking about Jakobson yesterday (while they were indulging in a hunk of Camembert and a bottle of red wine at five in the afternoon). So, in class this morning I remembered what she had said.

At that moment, when I could sense that the rabble were growling and showing their teeth, I felt pity. I felt sorry for Madame Fine. And I don't like a lynching. It never shows anyone in a good light. Never mind that I don't want anybody to go digging into my knowledge of Jakobson and begin to doubt the reality of my IQ.

So I backed off and didn't say anything. I got two hours of detention and Madame Fine saved her professorial skin. But when I left the classroom, I could feel her worried little gaze following me out of the door.

And on the way home I thought: pity the poor in spirit who know neither the enchantment nor the beauty of language.

5. A Pleasant Impression

But Manuela, not terribly sensitive to the little steps of Japanese women, is already steering us towards another territory.

'That Rosen woman is in a real state because Monsieur Ozu hasn't got two lamps that are the same.'

'Really?' I say, taken aback.

'Yes, really. And why is that? The Rosens have two of everything, because they're afraid they'll end up missing something. You know Madame Rosen's favourite story?'

'No,' I reply, already enthralled to think where this conversation might lead.

'During the war her grandfather, who had tons of stuff stored in his cellar, saved his family by doing a favour for a German who was looking for a reel of thread to sew a button back onto his uniform. If her grandfather hadn't had the thread, he would have been done for, and everyone else along with him. So believe it or not, in her cupboards and in the cellar she has two of everything. And does that make her any happier? And can you see any better in a room just because you have two lamps exactly the same?'

'I've never thought about it. But it's true that we tend to decorate our interiors with superfluous things.'

'Super what things?'

'Things we don't really need, like at the Arthens's. The same lamps and two identical vases on the mantelpiece, the same identical armchairs on either side of the sofa, two matching bedside tables, rows of identical jars in the kitchen . . .'

'Now you make me think about it, it's not just about the lamps. In fact, there aren't two of anything in Monsieur Ozu's apartment. Well, I must say it makes a pleasant impression.'

'Pleasant in what way?'

She thinks for a moment, wrinkling her brow.

'Pleasant like after Christmas, when you've had too much to eat. I think about the way it feels when everyone has left . . . My husband and I, we go to the kitchen, I make up a little bouillon with fresh vegetables, I slice some mushrooms really finely and we have our bouillon with those mushrooms in it. You get the feeling you've just come through a storm, and it's all calm again.'

'No more fear of being short of anything. You're happy with the present moment.'

'You feel it's natural – and that's the way it should be, when you eat.'

'You enjoy what you have, there's no competition. One sensation after the other.'

'Yes, you have less but you enjoy it more.'

'Who can manage to eat several things at once?'

'Not even poor Monsieur Arthens.'

'I have two matching bedside tables with two identical lamps,' I say, suddenly remembering.

'Me too,' replies Manuela.

She nods.

'Maybe we're all sick, with this too much of everything.'

She gets up, kisses me on the cheek and heads back to her toil as a modern-day slave at the Pallières's. After she has left I remain seated with my empty tea cup. There is one chocolate Florentine left, which I nibble out of greediness, with my front teeth, like a mouse. If you change the way you crunch into something, it is like trying something new.

And I sit meditating, savouring the unexpected and incongruous nature of our conversation. Who has ever heard of a

158

maid and a concierge making use of their afternoon break to ponder the cultural significance of interior decoration? You would be surprised by what ordinary little people come out with. They may prefer stories to theories, anecdotes to concepts, images to ideas – that doesn't stop them from philosophising. So: have our civilisations become so destitute that we can only live in our fear of want? Can we only enjoy our possessions or our senses when we are certain that we shall always be able to enjoy them? Perhaps the Japanese have learned that you can only savour a pleasure when you know it is ephemeral and unique; armed with this knowledge, they are yet able to weave their lives.

I am weary. Dull and never-ending repetition has come to tear me from my thoughts once again – boredom was born on a day of uniformity. Someone is ringing at my lodge.

6. Wabi

A t the door stands a courier, chewing what must be a piece of gum for elephants, given the vigour and range of mandibular activity to which he is compelled.

'Madame Michel?' he asks.

He thrusts a package into my hands.

'Nothing to sign?' I ask.

But he has already vanished.

It is a rectangular package wrapped in sturdy brown paper and tied with string, of the type used to close sacks of potatoes, or which you might attach to a cork and subsequently drag around the apartment for the entertainment of a cat that must be tricked into getting the only exercise to which he will consent. In fact, this package tied up with string makes me think of Manuela's tissue-paper wrapping because, although the paper is more rustic than refined, there is something similar in the care given to the authenticity of the wrapping, something deeply consonant. You might note that the most noble concepts often emerge from the most coarse and commonplace things. *Beauty is consonance* is a sublime thought, handed to me by a ruminating courier.

If you think about it at all seriously, aesthetics are really nothing more than an initiation to the Way of Consonance, a sort of Way of the Samurai applied to the intuition of authentic forms. We all have a knowledge of harmony, anchored deep within. It is this knowledge that enables us, at every instant, to apprehend quality in our lives and, on the rare occasions when everything is in perfect harmony, to appreciate it with the apposite intensity. And I am not referring to the sort of beauty that is the exclusive preserve of Art. Those who feel inspired, as I do, by the greatness of small things will pursue them to the very heart of the inessential where, cloaked in everyday attire, this greatness will emerge from within a certain ordering of ordinary things and from the certainty that *all is as it should be*, the conviction that *it is fine this way*.

I untie the string and tear the paper. It's a book, a fine edition bound in navy-blue leather of a coarse texture that is very *wabi*. In Japanese *wabi* means 'an understated form of beauty, a quality of refinement masked by rustic simplicity'. I'm not really sure what this means but this binding is most definitely *wabi*.

I put on my glasses and decipher the title.

Profound Thought No. 11

Birch trees
Teach me that I am nothing
And that I am deserving of life

Maman announced at the dinner table last night, as if it were a pretext to let the champagne flow freely, that it was exactly ten years ago that she started her 'anaaalysis'. Everyone will agree that this is absolutely maaarvellous. As far as I can see, only psychoanalysis can compete with Christians in their love of drawn-out suffering. What my mother didn't say is that it's also been exactly ten years since she started taking anti-depressants. But apparently she doesn't see the connection. Personally I don't think she's taking the anti-depressants to ease her anxiety but rather to endure the analysis. When she describes her sessions, it's enough to make you want to bang your head against the wall. The guy says 'hmmm' at regular intervals, and repeats the end of her sentences ('And I went to Lenôtre's with my mother': 'Hmmm, your mother?' 'I do so like chocolate': 'Hmmm, chocolate?'). If this is how it is, I can set up shop as a psychoanalyst tomorrow. He gives her copies of lectures from the 'Freudian Cause' which, contrary to what you might think, aren't just some sort of rebus but are actually supposed to mean something. Fascination with intelligence is in itself fascinating, but I don't think it's a value in itself. There are tons of intelligent people out there, and there are a lot of morons too but there are also plenty of well-functioning brains. I'm going to say something really banal, but intelligence, in itself, is neither valuable nor interesting. Very intelligent people have devoted their lives to the question of the sex of angels, for example. But

162

many intelligent people have a sort of bug: they think intelligence is an end in itself. They have one idea in mind: to be intelligent, which is really stupid. And when intelligence takes itself for its own goal, it operates very strangely: the proof that it exists is not to be found in the ingenuity or simplicity of what it produces, but in how obscurely it is expressed. If you could see all the bumf Maman brings home from her 'sessions' . . . Full of the Symbolic, and foreclusion, and subsuming the Real, with the help of a whole lot of mathematical formulae and dubious syntax. It's complete rubbish! Even the texts that Colombe is reading (she's working on William of Ockham, a fourteenth-century Franciscan monk) are not nearly as ludicrous. Conclusion: better to be a thinking monk than a post-modern thinker.

In addition, it was a Freudian day. That afternoon I was eating chocolate. I really like chocolate and it is probably the only thing I have in common with Maman and my sister. While I was biting into a bar with hazelnuts, I felt one of my teeth crack. I went to look at myself in the mirror and saw that I had indeed lost a little chip off my incisor. This summer in Quimper at the market I tripped on a rope and fell over and already broke half of this tooth and since then tiny pieces have been crumbling off from time to time. Anyway, I lost that little piece of incisor and it made me laugh because I remember what Maman said about a dream she's been having often lately: she is losing her teeth, they go all black and fall out one after the other. And so this is what her analyst said about the dream: 'Chère Madame, a Freudian would tell you that it is a dream about death.' That's funny, isn't it? It's not even the naivety of his interpretation (falling teeth = death, umbrella = penis, etc.), as if culture did not have huge powers of suggestion that have nothing to do with reality. He thinks that in this way he will establish his intellectual superiority ('a Freudian would say') over mere erudition (he wants you to

163

know he is distancing himself from Freud) – but you're left with the impression that it's a parrot who is speaking.

Fortunately, to get over all of this, I went to Kakuro's today to drink tea and eat coconut biscuits that were very good and very refined. He came to our door to invite me and said to Maman, 'We met in the lift and we were in the middle of a very interesting discussion.' 'Oh, really?' said Maman, surprised. 'Well, you are very lucky indeed, my daughter hardly speaks to us.' Turning to me, he said, 'Would you like to come and have a cup of tea and let me introduce you to my cats?' and of course Maman, enticed by where this could lead, accepted eagerly on my behalf. She already had her modern-geisha-invited-to-rich-Japanese-man's-house plan in her head. One of the reasons that everyone is so fascinated with Monsieur Ozu is that he really is very rich (so they say). In short, I went to have tea at his place and meet his cats. On that point I'm really not any more convinced by his cats than by mine but at least Kakuro's cats are truly decorative. I explained my point of view on the matter, and he replied that he believed in the radiance and sensitivity of an oak tree, and all the more so where cats are concerned. We went on to discuss the definition of intelligence and he asked me if he could write down my formula in his moleskine notebook: 'It is not a sacred gift, it is a primate's only weapon.'

And then we got to talking about Madame Michel again. He thinks her cat is named Leo for Leo Tolstoy and we agreed that a concierge who reads Tolstoy and books published by Vrin may not be your average concierge. He even has some very pertinent reasons for thinking that she must really like *Anna Karenina* and he has decided to send her a copy. 'We'll see how she reacts,' he said.

But that is not my profound thought for the day. It comes from something that Kakuro said. We were talking about Russian literature, which I haven't read at all. Kakuro was explaining that what he loves in Tolstoy's novels is that they are 'whole-world novels' and moreover they take place in Russia, a country where there are birch trees wherever you look, and during the Napoleonic wars the aristocracy had to learn to speak Russian all over again because before that they only ever spoke French. Well, that's just grown-up chitchat but what is great about Kakuro is that he is so polite in everything he does. It's really pleasant to listen to him talking, even if you don't care about what he's saying, because he is truly talking to you, he is addressing himself to you. This is the first time I have met someone who cares about me when he is talking: he's not looking for approval or disagreement, he looks at me as if to say, 'Who are you? Do you want to talk to me? How nice it is to be here with you!' That is what I meant by saying he is polite – this attitude that gives the other person the impression of really being there. Anyway, basically, this Russia of the great Russians, I really couldn't care less. They spoke French? Big deal! So do I, and I don't exploit the muzhiks. But on the other hand, and I can't really understand why, I do care about the birch trees. Kakuro was talking about the Russian campaign, and all the swaying, rustling birch trees, and I felt light, so light . . .

After I'd had a chance to think about it for a while I began to understand why I felt this sudden joy when Kakuro was talking about the birch trees. I get the same feeling when anyone talks about trees, any trees: the linden tree in the farmyard, the oak behind the old barn, the stately elms that have all disappeared now, the pine trees along windswept coasts, etc. There's so much humanity in a love of trees, so much nostalgia for our first sense of wonder, so much power in just feeling our own insignificance when we are surrounded by nature . . . yes, that's it: just thinking about trees and their indifferent majesty and our love for them teaches us how ridiculous we are – vile parasites squirming *on the surface* of the earth – and at the same time how deserving of life we can be, when we can honour this beauty that owes us nothing.

Kakuro was talking about birch trees and, forgetting all those psychoanalysts and intelligent people who don't know what to do with their intelligence, I suddenly felt my spirit expand, for I was capable of grasping the utter beauty of the trees.

SUMMER RAIN

1. Clandestine

S o I put on my glasses and decipher the title.
Leo Tolstoy, *Anna Karenina.*
With a card:

To Madame Michel,
In honour of your cat.
With my warmest regards,
Kakuro Ozu

It is always reassuring to be disabused of one's own paranoia.

My hunch was right. I have been found out.

A wave of panic rolls over me.

I stand up, like a robot, then sit back down. I read the card again.

Something moves house inside me – yes, how else to describe it, I have the preposterous feeling that one existing inner living space has been replaced by another. Does that never happen to you? You feel things shifting around inside you, and you are quite incapable of describing just what has changed, but it is both mental and spatial, the way moving house is.

In honour of your cat.

Genuinely incredulous, I hear a little laugh, a sort of giggle, coming from my own throat.

It is worrying, but it is also funny.

A dangerous impulse – all impulses are dangerous for those

169

who lead a clandestine existence – compels me to fetch a sheet of paper, an envelope and a biro (orange), to write:

Thank you, you shouldn't have.
The concierge.

I go out into the hall with the stealth of a Sioux – ah, no one – and slip my missive into Monsieur Ozu's letter box.

I return to the lodge with furtive steps – since there's not a soul around – and, exhausted, collapse into the armchair, with the satisfaction of having done my duty.

A powerful feeling of utter dismay at what I have done submerges me.

Utter dismay.

Such a stupid impulse: far from putting an end to the pursuit, this will encourage it a hundred-fold. A major strategic error. These wretched involuntary acts are beginning to get on my nerves.

A simple *I'm afraid I don't understand*, signed, *the concierge*, would have conveyed the proper meaning.

Or even: *You've made a mistake, I'm returning your package.*

No fuss, short and concise: *Delivered to the wrong address.*

Clever and definitive: *I don't know how to read.*

More devious: *My cat doesn't know how to read.*

Subtle: *Thank you, but Christmas boxes are given in January.*

Or even, administrative: *Please confirm receipt.*

What have I done, instead, but simper as if we were at a literary salon?

Thank you, you shouldn't have.

I propel myself out of my armchair and rush to the door.

Woe and damnation.

Through the window I can see Paul Nguyen heading for the lift, the contents of the letter box in his hand.

I am undone.

There is only one thing for it: to lie low.

Come what may, I'm not here, I know nothing, I don't respond, I don't write, I take no initiative.

Three days go by, on tenterhooks. I have persuaded myself that the very thing that I decided not to think about does not exist, but I can't stop thinking about it, to the point of once forgetting to feed Leo, who is now the incarnation of mute feline reproach.

Then, at around ten o'clock, there is a ring at my door.

2. The Great Work of Making Meaning

I open the door.

Monsieur Ozu is standing there.

'Dear lady,' he says, 'I am glad that you were not displeased with my little gift.'

In shock, I cannot understand a word.

'Yes, I was,' I reply, aware that I am sweating like an ox. 'Um, um, no.' I am pathetically slow to correct my stumbling reply. 'Well, thank you, thank you very much indeed.'

He gives me a kindly smile.

'Madame Michel, I haven't come here so that you can thank me.'

'No?' I say, adding my own brilliant rendition of 'let your words die upon your lips,' the art of which I share with Phaedra, Bérénice and poor Dido.

'I have come to ask you to have dinner with me tomorrow evening,' he says. 'That way we shall have the opportunity to talk about our shared interests.'

'Umm . . .' A relatively brief reply.

'A neighbourly dinner, a very simple affair.'

'Between neighbours? But I'm the concierge,' I plead, although whatever may be inside my head is in a state of utter confusion.

'It is possible to be both at once,' he replies.

Holy Mary Mother of God, what am I to do?

There is always the easy way out, although I am loath to use it. I have no children, I do not watch television and I do not believe in God – all paths taken by mortals to make their lives *easier.* Children help us to defer the painful task of confronting ourselves, and grandchildren take over from them. Television distracts us from the onerous necessity of finding projects to construct in the vacuity of our frivolous lives: by beguiling our eyes, television releases our mind from the great work of making meaning. Finally, God appeases our animal fears and the unbearable prospect that some day all our pleasures will cease. Thus, as I have neither future nor progeny nor pixels to deaden the cosmic awareness of absurdity, and in the certainty of the end and the anticipation of the void, I believe I can affirm that I have not chosen the easy path.

And yet I am quite tempted.

No thank you, I'm already busy, would be the most appropriate route.

There are several polite variations.

That's very kind of you but I have a schedule as full as a government minister's (hardly credible).

What a pity, I'm leaving for Megève tomorrow (pure fantasy).

I am sorry, I've got family coming round (blatant lie).

My cat is ailing, I can't leave him alone (sentimental).

I'm sick, I'd better keep to my room (shameless).

Ultimately, I steel myself to say: thank you but I have people coming over this week, when suddenly the serene affability with which Monsieur Ozu stands before me opens a meteoric breach in time.

3. Beyond Time

Snowflakes falling inside the globe.

Before memory's eyes, on Mademoiselle's desk – she was my teacher until I reached the older children's class, with Monsieur Servant – is the little glass globe. When we had been good pupils we were allowed to turn it upside down and hold it in the palm of our hand until the very last snowflake had fallen at the foot of the chromium-plated Eiffel Tower. I was not yet seven years old, but I already knew that the measured drift of the little cottony particles foreshadowed what the heart would feel in moments of great joy. Time slowing, expanding, a lingering graceful ballet, and when the last snowflake has come to rest, we know we have experienced a suspension of time that is the sign of a great illumination. As a child I often wondered whether I would be allowed to live such moments – to inhabit the slow, majestic ballet of the snowflakes, to be released at last from the dreary frenzy of time.

Is that what it means to feel naked? All one's clothes are gone, yet one's mind is overladen with finery. Monsieur Ozu's invitation has made me feel completely naked, soul-naked, each glistening snowflake alighting on my heart with a delicious burning tingle.

I look at him.

And throw myself into the deep, dark, icy, exquisite waters beyond time.

4. Spiders' Webs

'Why, oh why on earth, for the love of God?' I ask Manuela, that very afternoon.

'What do you mean?' she says, setting out the tea things. 'It sounds lovely!'

'You must be joking,' I moan.

'You must think practically, now,' she says. 'You can't go like that. Your hair is all wrong,' she asserts, looking at me with the eye of an expert.

Do you have any idea of Manuela's notions on the subject of hairdressing? She may be an aristocrat of the heart but she is a true proletarian when it comes to hairstyling. Teased, twisted, puffed out then sprayed with a wicked concoction of chemical spiders' webs: a woman's hair, according to Manuela, must be architectural or nothing at all.

'I'll go to the hairdresser's,' I say, trying to act unprecipitately.

Manuela looks at me doubtfully.

'What are you going to wear?'

Other than my everyday dresses, my concierge dresses, all I have is a sort of white nuptial meringue buried beneath layers of mothballs, or a lugubrious black pinafore which I use for the rare funerals to which I am invited.

'I'll wear my black dress.'

'The funeral dress?' Manuela is dismayed.

'That's all I have.'

'Well, you'll have to buy something.'

'It's only a dinner.'

'That's as may be,' answers the duenna lurking inside Manuela. 'But don't you dress up when you go for dinner with other people?'

5. Of Lace and Frills and Flounces

Now things start to get difficult: where am I to buy a dress? Ordinarily, I order clothes by post, even socks, underwear and vests. The idea of trying something on in front of an anorexic virgin – something which, on me, will look like a sack of potatoes – has always deterred me from going into boutiques. It is most unfortunate that it is now too late to order anything by post and have it delivered in time.

If you have but one friend, make sure you choose her well.

The very next morning Manuela bursts into my lodge.

She is carrying a clothes-bag, and hands it to me with a triumphant smile.

Manuela is a good six inches taller than I am, and weighs at least twenty pounds less. I can think of only one woman in her family whose figure might be comparable to mine: her mother-in-law, the formidable Amalia, who has a real penchant for frills and furbelows, although she does not strike one as being the sort to indulge in fantasy. Portuguese-style passementerie has something rococo about it: nothing imaginative or light, just a delirious accumulation, where a dress ends up looking like a straitjacket made of lace, and even a simple blouse like an entry in a seamstresses' ruffles and frills competition.

So you may imagine how worried I am. The dinner is already promising to be an ordeal; this could also turn it into a farce.

'You will look like a film star!' says Manuela, as I feared. Then suddenly feeling sorry for me: 'I'm joking,' as she pulls out of the bag a beige dress that seems to have been spared where flounces are concerned.

'Where did you get it?' I ask, examining the dress.

At first glance, it's the right size. It also appears to be a pricey dress, in wool gabardine, with a very simple cut, a shirt collar and buttons down the front. Very sober; very chic. The kind of dress Madame de Broglie would wear.

'I went to see Maria last night,' replies Manuela, pleased as punch.

Maria is a Portuguese seamstress who lives next door to my saviour. But to Manuela she's more than a mere compatriot. The two of them grew up together in Faro, each of them married one of the seven Lopes brothers and came with them to France, where they managed to have their children at almost exactly the same intervals, only a few weeks apart. They even share a cat, and similar tastes in refined patisserie.

'You mean it's someone else's dress?'

'Mmm,' answers Manuela, pouting slightly. 'But you know, she won't come to collect it. The lady died last week. And by the time it takes them to realise she left a dress at the seamstress's . . . you'll have time to have ten dinners with Monsieur Ozu.'

'This dress belongs to a dead woman?' I say, horrified. 'I can't do that.'

'Why not?' asks Manuela, frowning. 'It's better than if she were alive. Just think, if you got a spot on it – you'd have to rush off to the dry cleaner's, make up some sort of excuse and what a hassle that would be.'

'Morally . . . I can't do it,' I protest.

'Morally?' says Manuela, pronouncing the word as if it were something disgusting. 'What does that have to do with it? Are you stealing? Are you harming anyone?'

'But it is someone else's property, I can't just appropriate it for myself.'

178

'But she's dead! And you're not stealing, you're just borrowing it for the evening.'

When Manuela begins to embellish on semantic differences, there's not much point putting up a struggle.

'Maria told me she was a very nice lady. She gave her dresses, and a very nice palpaga coat. She couldn't wear them any more because she'd put on weight, so she said to Maria, "Could these be of any use to you?" You see, she was a very nice lady.'

Palpaga is a type of llama with a highly valued wool fleece and a head adorned with a papaya.

'I don't know . . .' I say half-heartedly. 'I just get the feeling I'm stealing from a dead person.'

Manuela looks at me from the height of her exasperation.

'You are borrowing, not stealing. And what is she going to do with that dress, poor woman?'

There is nothing to be said to that.

'Time for Madame Pallières,' says Manuela with delight, changing the subject.

'I'll savour the moment with you.'

'I'm on my way, then.' She heads for the door. 'In the meanwhile, try on the dress, go to the hairdresser's, and I'll be back later to have a look.'

I look at the dress for a moment, doubtfully. In addition to my reticence to clothe myself in the garments of the deceased, I am greatly afraid that the dress will look utterly incongruous on my person. Violette Grelier is to dishcloths what Pierre Arthens was to silk, and what I am to a shapeless purple or navy-blue overall.

I shall wait until I get back to try it on.

And I did not even thank Manuela.

A choir is a beautiful thing

Yesterday afternoon was my school's choir performance. In my posh neighbourhood school, there is a choir: nobody thinks it's uncool and everyone competes to join but it's very exclusive: Monsieur Trianon, the music teacher, hand-picks his choristers. The reason the choir is so successful is because of Monsieur Trianon himself. He is young and handsome and he has the choir sing not only the old jazz standards but also the latest hits, with very classy orchestration. Everyone gets all dressed up and the choir performs for the other students. Only the choir members' parents are invited because otherwise there'd be too many people. The gymnasium is always packed fit to burst as it is and there's an incredible atmosphere.

So yesterday off I headed to the gymnasium at a trot, led by Madame Fine because as usual on Tuesday afternoon first period we have French. 'Led by' is saying a lot: she did what she could to keep up the pace, wheezing like an old whale. Eventually we got to the gym, everybody found a place as best they could. I was forced to listen to the most asinine conversations coming at me from below, behind, on every side, all around (in the tiered seats), and in stereo (mobile, fashion, mobile, who's going out with whom, mobile, rubbish teachers, mobile, Cannelle's party) and then finally the choir arrived to thunderous applause, dressed in red and white with bow ties for the boys and long dresses with shoulder straps for the girls. Monsieur Trianon sat down on a high stool, his back to the audience, then raised a sort of baton with a little flashing red light at the end, silence fell and the performance began.

Every time, it's a miracle. Here are all these people, full of heartache or hatred or desire, and we all have our troubles and the school year is filled with vulgarity and triviality and consequence, and there are all these teachers and kids of every shape and size, and there's this life we're struggling through full of shouting and tears and laughter and fights and break-ups and dashed hopes and unexpected luck – it all disappears, just like that, when the choir begins to sing. Everyday life vanishes into song, you are suddenly overcome with a feeling of brotherhood, of deep solidarity, even love, and it diffuses the ugliness of everyday life into a spirit of perfect communion. Even the singers' faces are transformed: it's no longer Achille Grand-Fernet that I'm looking at (he is a very fine tenor), or Déborah Lemeur or Ségolène Rachet or Charles Saint-Sauveur. I see human beings, surrendering to music.

Every time, it's the same thing, I feel like crying, my throat goes all tight and I do the best I can to control myself but sometimes I come close: I can hardly keep myself from sobbing. So when they sing a canon I look down at the ground because it's just too much emotion at once: it's too beautiful, and everyone singing together, this marvellous sharing. I'm no longer myself, I am just one part of a sublime whole, to which the others also belong, and I always wonder at such moments why this cannot be the rule of everyday life, instead of being an exceptional moment, during a choir performance.

When the music stops, everyone applauds, their faces all lit up, the choir radiant. It is so beautiful.

In the end, I wonder if the true movement of the world might not be a voice raised in song.

6. Just a Trim

Will you believe me if I tell you that I have never been to the hairdresser's? When I came to the city from the country, I discovered that there are two equally absurd professions, each of which accomplishes a task one ought to be able to take care of on one's own. To this very day I still find it difficult to believe that florists and hairdressers are not parasites, the former living off nature, which belongs to everyone, the latter performing with an outlandish amount of play-acting and smelly products a task which I can expedite in my own bathroom with a pair of well-sharpened scissors.

'Who cut your hair like this?' asked the hairdresser indignantly once I had, with a Dantean effort, entrusted to her the mission of transforming my head of hair into a domesticated work of art.

She is pulling and shaking two strands of an immeasurable dimension on either side of my ears.

'Well, perhaps I shouldn't ask,' she continues disgustedly, sparing me the shame of having to inform on myself. 'People have no respect for anything any more, you see it all the time.'

'I'd just like a trim,' I say.

I am unsure what is meant by that but it's a classic line from early-afternoon TV series, which are filled with young women caked in make-up, and who invariably spend their time at the gym or the hairdresser's.

'Trim? There's nothing to trim! We have to start from scratch, Madame!'

She examines my scalp with a critical eye, and lets out a whistling sigh.

'You have really good hair, that's a start. We should be able to do something with it.'

In the end, my hairdresser turns out to be a good sort. Once her outrage, the legitimacy of which is actually there to confirm her own professional legitimacy, has abated – and because it is always good to read from the social script to which we owe our allegiance – she looks after me with grace and good humour.

What is to be done with a thick mass of hair other than cut it every which way when it begins to expand? This had been my lifelong credo in matters of hairstyling. Henceforth, to attempt to sculpt the resulting unruly mass into a shape shall be my abiding cutting-edge capillary concept.

'You really do have beautiful hair,' she concludes, observing her labours, visibly satisfied. 'It is thick and silky. You shouldn't be letting just anyone cut it.'

Can a hairstyle change a person to such a degree? I cannot believe my own reflection in the mirror. Now that they are no longer confined by a black helmet, my features – which I have already qualified as anything but attractive – are framed by a light and playful wave, and are decidedly more appealing. It makes me look . . . respectable. I even think I look like an aspiring Roman matron.

'It's . . . fantastic,' I say, wondering how I will ever hide this ill-considered folly from the stares of the residents.

It is inconceivable that all these years in pursuit of invisibility have run aground on the shoals of a matronly hairstyle.

I go home, hugging the walls. With incredible luck, I do not run into anyone. But I do fancy that Leo is giving me strange looks. I go up to him and he puts his ears back, a sure sign of anger or confusion.

'Oh come on then, don't you like it?' And then I realise that he is sniffing the air around me.

The shampoo. I reek of avocado and almond.

I stick a kerchief on my head and attend to sundry fascinating chores, the high point being the conscientious polishing of the brass knobs on the lift cage.

It is now ten to two in the afternoon.

In ten minutes Manuela will emerge from the darkness of the stairwell to come and inspect the finished product.

I do not really have time for meditation. I remove my kerchief, undress hastily, slip on the beige gabardine dress that belongs to a dead woman and there comes the knock at the door.

7. The Vestal Virgin in Her Finery

'Wow . . . holy moly!' says Manuela.

Onomatopoeia and a slang expression coming from the mouth of Manuela, whom I've never known to say a single trivial word, is rather like the Pope forgetting himself and shouting to the cardinals, *Where the devil is that bloody mitre?*

'Don't tease me.'

'Tease you? But Renée, you look wonderful!'

Full of emotion, she sits down.

'A real lady,' she adds.

That is what I'm worried about.

'I'm going to look ridiculous going to dinner like this – like some vestal virgin in her finery,' I say, making the tea.

'Not at all, it's natural, you're going to dinner, people get dressed up. Everyone thinks that's perfectly normal.'

'And what about this?' I ask, raising my hand to my scalp and getting a shock as I touch this light, airy thing.

'You went and put something on your head afterwards, it's all flat at the back,' says Manuela, frowning, reaching in her bag for a little pouch of red tissue paper.

'Nuns' farts,' she adds.

Yes, do let us talk about something else.

'Well?' I ask.

'Oh, if only you had seen her!' she sighs. 'I thought she was going to have a heart attack. I said: "Madame Pallières, I'm sorry but I can't come any more." She looked at me, she didn't

185

get it. I had to tell her two more times! Then she sat down and said, "How am I going to manage?" '

Manuela pauses, annoyed.

'If she had said, "How am I going to manage *without you?*" She's lucky I was able to get Rosie for her. Otherwise I would have said, "Madame Pallières, you can do what you like, I don't give a d—" '

Damn mitre, says the Pope.

Rosie is one of Manuela's many nieces. I know what this means. Manuela may be thinking about going back to Portugal, but a seam as lucrative as 7, Rue de Grenelle has to stay in the family – so she's been introducing Rosie in her place as part of getting ready for the big day.

Dear God, what am I going to do without Manuela?

'How am I going to manage without you?' I say with a smile.

Suddenly we both have tears in our eyes.

'You know what I think?' asks Manuela, wiping her cheeks with a very large red handkerchief fit for a toreador. 'The fact I've quit Madame Pallières, it's a sign. There are going to be some good changes.'

'Did she ask you why?'

'That's the best bit,' says Manuela. 'She didn't dare. Being so well brought up, sometimes it's a problem.'

'But she'll find out soon enough.'

'Yes,' whispers Manuela, jubilantly. 'But you know what? In a month's time she'll say, "Your little Rosie is a gem, Manuela. You did the right thing, passing the job on to her." Oh these rich people . . . What the hell!'

Fucking mitre, says the Pope impatiently.

'Come what may,' I say, 'we are friends.'

We exchange a smile.

'Yes,' says Manuela. 'Come what may.'

Profound Thought No. 12

This time a question
On destiny
And its scripture
Early for some
And not for others

I don't know what to do: if I set fire to the apartment, it could spread to Kakuro's. To complicate the existence of the only adult person thus far who seems worthy of respect is not the right way to go about things. But all the same setting fire to the place still means a lot to me. Today I had a fascinating encounter. I went to Kakuro's for tea. Paul was there, his secretary. Kakuro had invited Marguerite and me when he met us in the hallway with Maman. Marguerite is my best friend. We've been in the same class for two years and it was love at first sight, right from the start. I don't know if you have any idea what a secondary school in Paris is like in this day and age in the posh neighbourhoods – but quite honestly, the slum areas of Marseille have nothing on ours. In fact it may even be worse here, because where you have money, you have drugs – and not just a little bit and not just one kind. My mother's ex-militants from May '68 make me laugh with their oh-so-daring memories of joints and bongs. At school (it is a state school, after all, my father was a Minister of the Republic), you can buy everything: acid, Ecstasy, coke, speed, etc. When I think of the days when kids used to sniff glue in the toilets, they seem really corny and innocent. My classmates get high on Ecstasy the way we pig out on chocolate truffles and the worst of it is that where there are drugs, there's sex. Don't act surprised: nowadays kids sleep together really young. There are kids in year seven (not a lot, but a few all the same) who've already had sexual relations. It's depressing. First of all, I think that sex, like love, is a sacred thing. My last name isn't de Broglie, but if I were going to live beyond puberty, it would be really important to me to keep sex as a sort of marvellous sacrament. And secondly, a teenager who pretends to be an adult is still a teenager. If you imagine that getting high at a party and sleeping around is going to propel you into a state of full adulthood, that's like thinking that dressing up as an Indian is going to make you an Indian. And thirdly, it's a really weird way of looking at life to want to become an adult by imitating everything that is most catastrophic about adulthood . . . Where I'm concerned, just seeing my mother shooting up with her anti-depressants and sleeping tablets has been enough to inoculate me for life against that sort of substance abuse. Lastly, teenagers think they're adults when in fact they're imitating adults who never really made it into adulthood and who are running away from life. It's pathetic. Mind you, if I were Cannelle Martin, the class pin-up, I would wonder what else I could do with my days besides take drugs. Her destiny is already scrawled across her forehead. In fifteen years, after she's made a wealthy marriage just for the sake of making a wealthy marriage, her husband will cheat on her, going to other women for the thing that his perfect, cold and futile wife has always been utterly incapable of giving him – let's just say human, and sexual, warmth. So she'll transfer all her energy onto her houses and her children and, through some sort of unconscious revenge, she'll end up making the kids clones of herself. She'll doll her daughters up like high-class courtesans, toss them out into the arms of the first financier to come along, and she'll order her sons to go out and conquer the world like their father did, and to cheat on their wives with pointless young women. You think I'm off my head? When I look at Cannelle Martin, with her long gossamer blonde hair, her big blue eyes, her tartan miniskirts, her ultra-clingy T-shirts and her perfect belly-button, I swear to you I can see it as clearly as if it had all already happened. For the time being, all the boys in the class

188

begin to drool whenever they see her, and she is under the illusion that these pubescent males are paying tribute to her feminine charms when in fact they are merely idealising the consumer product she represents. You think I'm being catty? Not at all, it really makes me unhappy to see this, it hurts me for her sake, it really does. So when I met Marguerite for the first time . . . Marguerite is of African descent, and if she's called Marguerite, it's not because she lives in a posh banlieue like Auteuil, it's because it's the name of a flower. Her mother is French and her dad is Nigerian. He works at the Ministry of Foreign Affairs but he doesn't look like any of the other diplo-mats we know. He is straightforward. He seems to like what he does. He's not at all cynical. And his daughter is as lovely as the day is long: Marguerite is pure beauty, her skin, her smile, her incredible hair. And she smiles all the time. When Achille Grand-Fernet (the class show-off) sang to her, on the very first day, 'Melissa the mulatto from Majorca scarcely wears any clothes at all,' Marguerite sang right back, straight off and with a big smile: 'Hey mama dear, it hurts, why'd you go and make me so u-ugly.' That's something I really admire in Marguerite: she's no whizz on the conceptual or logical side but she has an unbelievable gift for repartee. It really is a talent. I'm intellectually gifted, she is a champion of precision response. I'd give anything to be like that; I only ever find the right answer five minutes too late and I trot out the whole dialogue in my head. The first time Marguerite ever came over, Colombe said, 'Marguerite, that's a pretty name but it's the sort of thing they named women of our grandmothers' generation.' And she answered right back: 'And is *your* other name Christophe?' Colombe stood there with her mouth wide open; it was a sight to see! She must have mulled it over for hours, the subtlety of Marguerite's response, telling herself that it happened by chance, no doubt – but she was upset, all the same! Same thing when Jacinthe Rosen, Maman's great friend, said, 'It must be hard to style hair like yours' (Marguerite has the wild mane of a lion of the savannah), Marguerite replied, 'I don' understan' what she say dat white lady.'

With Marguerite, our favourite topic of conversation is love. What is love? How will we love? Who will it be? When? Why? Our opinions differ. Oddly enough, Marguerite has an intellectual vision of love, whereas I'm an incorrigible romantic. She sees love as the fruit of a rational choice (of the www.sharedtastes.com variety) whereas I think it springs from a delicious impulse. There is one thing we do agree on, however: love mustn't be a means, it must be an end.

Our other favourite topic of conversation is fate, and people's prospects in life. Cannelle Martin: ignored, cheated on by her husband, marries off her daughter to a financier, encourages her son to cheat on his wife, ends her life in Chatou in a room costing eight thousand euros a month. Achille Grand-Fernet: becomes a heroin addict, goes into rehab at the age of twenty, takes over his father's plastic bag business, marries a bleached blonde, engenders a schizophrenic son and an anorexic daughter, becomes an alcoholic, dies of liver cancer at the age of forty-five. And so on. And if you want my opinion, the most awful thing is not that we're playing this game, but that it isn't a game.

Anyway, when Kakuro ran into Maman and Marguerite and me in the hall, he said, 'My great-niece is coming to visit me this afternoon, would you like to join us?' Maman said, 'Oh yes, of course,' before you could say Jack Robinson; she's hoping this will lead to her own invitation some day soon. And so we both went down. Kakuro's great-niece is called Yoko, she's the daughter of his niece Élise who is the daughter of his sister Mariko. She is five. She's the prettiest little girl on earth! And adorable, too. She chirps and babbles and clucks and looks at people with the same kindly, open gaze as her great-uncle. We played hide and seek, and when Marguerite found her in a cupboard in the kitchen, Yoko laughed so hard she did a wee in her pants. And then we ate some chocolate cake while we talked with Kakuro, and she listened and gazed at us sweetly with her big eyes (and with chocolate up to her eyebrows).

Looking at her, I wondered, Is she going to end up just like all the others, too? I tried to picture her ten years older, blasé, with high-rise boots and a cigarette dangling from her mouth, and then another ten years later in a sanitised decor waiting for her kids to come home while she plays the good Japanese wife and mummy. But it didn't work.

And I felt extraordinarily happy. It's the first time in my life that I've met someone whose fate is not predictable, someone whose paths in life still remain open, someone who is fresh and full of possibility. I said to myself, Oh, yes, I would like to see Yoko grow up, and I knew that this wasn't just an illusion connected with her young age, because none of my parents' friends' little kids have ever made that sort of impression on me. I also said to myself that Kakuro must have been like that himself when he was little, and I wondered if anyone back then had looked at him the way I was looking at Yoko, with delight and curiosity, just waiting to see the butterfly emerge from its cocoon, not knowing, yet trusting, the purpose of its wings.

And so I asked myself a first question: Why? Why these people and not the others?

And yet another: What about me? Is my fate already written all over my face? If I want to die, it's because I believe it must be.

But if, in our world, there is any chance of becoming the person you haven't yet become . . . will I know how to seize that chance, turn my life into a garden that will be completely different from that of my forebears?

8. Saints Alive

A t seven o'clock, more dead than alive, I head for the fourth floor, praying fit to burst that I shall not run into anyone.

The hallway is deserted.

The stairs are deserted.

The landing outside Monsieur Ozu's apartment is deserted.

This silent desert, which should have filled me with joy, weighs upon my heart with a dark foreboding and I am overcome with an irrepressible desire to flee. My gloomy lodge suddenly seems a cosy, shining refuge, and I feel a wave of nostalgia thinking of Leo sprawled in front of a television, which no longer seems so iniquitous. After all, what is there to lose? All I have to do is turn on my heel and go back down the stairs and into my lodge. Nothing could be simpler. It is an entirely reasonable proposition, unlike this dinner, which borders on absurdity.

A sound from the fifth floor, just above my head, interrupts my thoughts. I begin instantly to sweat with fear – how very elegant – and, not fully understanding my own gesture, press frantically on the doorbell.

Not even time for my heart to start pounding: the door opens.

Monsieur Ozu greets me with a big smile.

'Good evening, Madame Michel!' he trumpets with what seems like genuine good humour.

Saints alive, the sound on the fifth floor is becoming more distinct: someone closing a door.

'Yes, good evening,' I say, and very nearly shove past my host to get through the door.

'Let me take your things,' says Monsieur Ozu, still smiling profusely.

I hand him my handbag and take in the immense hallway before me.

Something draws my gaze.

9. Dull Gold

Directly opposite the entrance, in a ray of light, hangs a painting.

This is the situation: here am I, Renée, fifty-four years of age, with bunions on my feet, born in a bog and bound to remain there; here am I going to dinner at the home of a wealthy Japanese man – whose concierge I happen to be – solely because I was startled by a quotation from *Anna Karenina*; here am I, Renée, intimidated and frightened to my innermost core, and so acutely aware of the inappropriateness and blasphemous nature of my presence here that I could faint – here, in this place which, although it may be physically accessible to the likes of me, is nevertheless representative of a world to which I do not belong, a world that wants nothing to do with concierges; as I was saying, here am I, Renée, somewhat carelessly allowing my gaze to wander beyond Monsieur Ozu and into a ray of light that is striking a little painting in a dark frame.

Only the splendours of Art can explain why the awareness of my unworthiness has suddenly been eclipsed by an aesthetic blackout. I no longer know who I am. I walk around Monsieur Ozu, captured by the vision.

It is a still life, representing a table laid for a light meal of bread and oysters. In the foreground, on a silver plate, are a half-bared lemon and a knife with a chiselled handle. In the background are two closed oysters, a shard of shell, gleaming mother-of-pearl, and a pewter saucer which probably contains pepper. In between the two are a goblet lying on its side, a roll showing its doughy white interior and, on the left, half-filled with a pale golden liquid, is a large goblet, balloon-shaped like an upside-down dome, with a large cylindrical stem decorated with glass lozenges. The colours range from yellow to ebony. The background is dull gold, slightly dusty.

I am a fervent admirer of still lifes. I have borrowed all the books on painting from the library and pored over them in search of still-life paintings. I have been to the Louvre, the Musée d'Orsay, the Musée d'Art Moderne and I saw – a dazzling revelation – the Chardin exhibition at the Petit Palais in 1979. But Chardin's entire oeuvre does not equal one single master work of Dutch painting from the seventeenth century. The still lifes of Pieter Claesz, Willem Claesz-Heda, Willem Kalf and Osias Beert are masterpieces of the genre – masterpieces full stop, for which, without a moment's hesitation, I would trade the entire Italian Quattrocento.

And this picture, without a moment's hesitation either, is unquestionably a Pieter Claesz.

'It's a copy,' says Monsieur Ozu behind me; I had totally forgotten about him.

Must this man forever startle me?

I am startled.

Taking hold of myself, I am about to say something like:

'It's very pretty,' a statement that is to Art as using 'bring' when you mean 'take' is to the beauty of language.

Having regained my self-control, I am about to resume my role as obtuse caretaker by uttering something like:

'Amazing the things they can do nowadays!' (In response to: it's a copy.)

And I also very nearly deliver the fatal blow, from which Monsieur Ozu's suspicions would never recover and which would establish the proof of my unworthiness forever:

'Those glasses are weird.'

195

I turn around.

The words, 'A copy of what?' which I abruptly decide are the most appropriate, remain stuck in my throat.

And instead, I say, 'It's so beautiful.'

10. What Congruence?

Whence comes the sense of wonder we perceive when we encounter certain works of art? Admiration is born with our first gaze and if subsequently we should discover, in the patient obstinacy we apply to flushing out the causes thereof, that all this beauty is the fruit of a virtuosity that can only be detected through close scrutiny of a brush that has been able to tame shadow and light and restore shape and texture, by magnifying them – the transparent jewel of the glass, the tumultuous texture of the shells, the clear velvet of the lemon – this neither dissipates nor explains the mystery of one's initial dazzled gaze.

The enigma is constantly renewed: great works are the visual forms which attain in us the certainty of timeless consonance. The confirmation that certain forms, in the particular aspect that their creators have given them, return again and again throughout the history of art and, in the filigree of individual genius, constitute nonetheless facets of a universal genius is something deeply unsettling. What congruence links a Claesz, a Raphael, a Rubens and a Hopper? Despite the diversity of subject matter, supports and techniques, despite the insignificance and ephemeral nature of lives always doomed to belong to one era and one culture alone, and despite the singular nature of a gaze that can only ever see what its constitution will allow and that is tainted by the poverty of its individuality, the genius of great artists penetrates to the heart of the mystery and exhumes, under various guises, the same sublime form that we seek in all artistic production. What congruence links a Claesz, a Raphael, a Rubens and a Hopper? We need not search, our eye locates the form that will elicit a feeling of consonance, the one particular thing in which everyone can find the very essence of Beauty, without variations or reservations, context or effort. In the still life with a lemon, for example, this essence cannot merely be reduced to the mastery of execution; it clearly does inspire a feeling of consonance, a feeling that *this is exactly the way it ought to have been arranged.* This in turn allows us to feel the power of objects and of the way they interact, to hold in our gaze the way they work together and the magnetic fields that attract and repel them, the ineffable ties that bind them and engender a *force*, a secret and inexplicable wave born of both the tension and the balance of the configuration – this is what inspires the feeling of consonance. The disposition of the objects and the dishes achieves the universal in the singular: the timeless nature of the consonant form.

11. Existence without Duration

Whatis the purpose of Art? To give us the brief, dazzling illusion of the camellia; to carve from time an emotional aperture that cannot be reduced to animal logic. How is Art born? It is begotten in the mind's ability to sculpt the sensorial domain. What does Art do for us? It *gives shape* to our emotions, makes them visible and, in so doing, places a seal of eternity upon them, a seal representing all those works that, by means of a particular form, have incarnated the universal nature of human emotions.

The seal of eternity . . . What absent world does our heart intuit when we see these dishes and cups, these carpets and glasses? Beyond the frame of the painting there is, no doubt, the tumult and boredom of everyday life – itself an unceasing and futile pursuit, consumed by plans; but within the frame lies the plenitude of a suspended moment, stolen from time, rescued from human longing. Human longing! We cannot cease desiring, and this is our glory, and our doom. Desire! It carries us and crucifies us, delivers us every new day to a battlefield where, on the eve, the battle was lost; but in sunlight does it not look like a territory ripe for conquest, a place where – even though tomorrow we will die – we can build empires doomed to fade to dust, as if the knowledge we have of their imminent fall had absolutely no effect on our eagerness to build them now? We are filled with the energy of constantly wanting that which we cannot have, we are abandoned at dawn on a field littered with corpses, we are transported until our death by projects that are no sooner completed than they must be renewed. Yet how exhausting it is to be constantly desiring . . . We soon aspire to pleasures without the quest, to a blissful state without beginning or end, where beauty would no longer be an aim or a project but the very proof of our nature. And that state is Art. This table – did I have to set it? Must I covet this repast in order to see it? Somewhere, *elsewhere*, someone wanted that meal, someone aspired to that mineral transparency and sought the pleasure offered by the salt, silky caress of a lemony oyster on his tongue. This was but one project of a hundred as yet unhatched, leading to a thousand more, the intention to prepare and savour a banquet of shellfish – someone else's plan, in fact, that existed in order for the painting to come to life.

But when we gaze at a still life, when – even though we did not pursue it – we delight in its beauty, a beauty borne away by the magnified and immobile figuration of things, we find pleasure in the fact that there was no need for longing, we may contemplate something we need not want, may cherish something we need not desire. So this still life, because it embodies a beauty that speaks to our desire but was given birth by someone else's desire, because it cossets our pleasure without in any way being part of our own plans, because it is offered to us without requiring the effort of desiring on our part: this still life incarnates the quintessence of Art, the certainty of timelessness. In the scene before our eyes – silent, without life or motion – a time exempt of plans for the future is incarnated, perfection purloined from duration and its weary greed – pleasure without desire, existence without duration, beauty without will.

For Art is emotion without desire.

Will he move, or won't he

Today Maman took me to see her shrink. Reason: I hide. Here's what Maman said to me: 'Sweetheart, you know very well that it is driving us mad the way you go off and hide. I think it would be a good idea for you to come and talk about it with Dr Theid, especially after what you said the other time.' In the first place, Dr Theid is only a doctor in my mother's perturbed little mind. He's no more a doctor or author of a doctoral dissertation than I am, but obviously it gives Maman great satisfaction to be able to say 'Doctor', something to do with his apparent ambition to treat her, and take his time (ten years) about it. He is after all an old leftie who converted to psychoanalysis after a few years of not terribly violent studies in Nanterre and a lucky encounter with a big noise in the Freudian Cause. And in the second place, I don't see what the problem is. That I 'hide' is not true, anyway; I go off to be alone in a place where no one can find me. I just want to be able to write my Profound Thoughts and my Journal of the Movement of the World in peace and, before that, I just wanted to be able to think quietly in my head without being disturbed by the inanities my sister says or listens to on the radio or her music system, or without Maman coming to bother me, whispering, 'Mamie's here, sweetheart, come and give her a kiss,' which is one of the least enticing injunctions I know.

When Papa, putting on his angry look, asks me, 'Well, why on earth are you hiding?' in general, I don't reply. What could I say? 'Because you all get on my nerves and I have a work of great significance to produce before I die?' Obviously, I can't. So, last time I tried to be funny, just so they'd stop over-dramatising things. I put on a sort of lost look, I stared at Papa and, with the voice of someone on their deathbed, said, 'It's because of all these voices in my head.' Egad! Red alert throughout the house! Papa's eyes were popping out of his head, Maman and Colombe came running at full tilt when he called out for them and everybody was talking to me at the same time: 'Sweetheart, it's not serious, we'll get you out of there' (Papa), 'I'll call Dr Theid right away' (Maman), 'How many voices have you heard?' (Colombe), and so on. Maman put on the expression she keeps for special occasions, somewhere between worry and excitement: and what if my daughter were a Case for Science? How awful, but how glorious! So, seeing them get all carried away like this I said, 'No, I'm just kidding!' but I had to say it several times before they heard me and then another few times before they believed me. And even then I'm not sure I convinced them. In the end, Maman made an appoint-ment for me to see Doc T., and we went there this morning.

First we sat in a very elegant waiting room with magazines dating from various periods: a few *National Geographics* from ten years ago and the latest *Elle* clearly displayed on top of the pile. And then Dr Theid came in. Looking just like his photograph (in a magazine that Maman had shown to everyone), but in the flesh, in living colour and odour: that is, brown and pipe tobacco. A dashing fiftysomething, carefully groomed; but, above all, everything was brown: his hair, neatly trimmed beard, com-plexion (newly minted Seychelles), pullover, trousers, shoes and watch strap – all in the same chestnut tones. Or, like dead leaves. With, moreover, a high-class pipe aroma (light tobacco: honey and dried fruit). Anyway, I said to myself, let's go and have a nice autumnal chat by the fireplace among people from good families – a refined conversation, constructive and perhaps even a bit silken (I love that adjective).

Maman came in with me, we sat down on the two chairs facing his desk and he sat behind the desk, in a big swivel armchair with strange wings, *Star Trek* style. He crossed his hands in front of his belly, looked at us and said, 'How are you two ladies today?'

Well, that was a very bad start. It instantly got my hackles up. The kind of sentence that a supermarket employee uses to sell two-sided toothbrushes to Madame and her daughter hiding behind their shopping trolley is not exactly what you expect from a shrink now, is it? But my anger stopped short when I became aware of something that would be fascinating for my Journal of the Movement of the World. I looked carefully, concentrating as hard as I could, and I thought, No, it's not possible. Yes, yes, it is! It is possible! Incredible! I was enthralled, to such a degree that I hardly heard Maman telling him all her little woes (my daughter hides, my daughter frightens us, tells us she hears voices, my daughter doesn't speak to us, we are worried about my daughter) saying 'my daughter' two hundred times while I was sitting there five inches away and, as a result, when he spoke to me, I almost jumped.

Let me explain. I knew that Dr T. was alive because he had walked ahead of me, sat down and talked. But for all the rest, he may as well have been dead: he did not move. Once he was wedged into his spaceship armchair, not another movement; just his lips trembling, but with great restraint. And the rest of him: immobile, perfectly immobile. Usually when you speak you don't just move your lips, you naturally bring other things into play: facial muscles, tiny little gestures of the hands, neck, shoulders; and when you're speaking, it's still very difficult to stay absolutely motionless, there's always a little trembling somewhere, an eyelid blinking, an imperceptible wiggling of the foot, etc.

But here: nothing! Nada! Wallou! A living statue! Can you imagine! 'So, young lady,' he said, making me jump, 'what do you have to say about all this?' I had trouble getting my thoughts together because I was completely absorbed by his immobility and so it took me a while to come up with an answer. Maman was writhing on her chair as if she had haemorrhoids but the Doc was staring at me without blinking. I said to myself: I have to make him move, there must be something that will get him to move. So I said, 'I will only speak in the presence of my lawyer,' hoping that that would do it. Total flop: he didn't budge. Maman sighed like a martyred Madonna but our man stayed perfectly immobile. 'Your lawyer . . . hmm . . .' he said, without moving. By now I was completely absorbed by the challenge. Will he move, or won't he? I decided to muster all my forces into battle. 'You're not on trial here,' he added, 'you know that, hmm.' And I was thinking, if I manage to make him move, it will all be worth it, really, I won't have wasted my day! 'Well,' said the statue, 'my dear Solange, I'd like to have a little tête-à-tête with this young lady.' My dear Solange got up, flashed him the look of a tearful cocker spaniel, and left the room, making a lot of useless movements (to compensate, no doubt).

'Your mother is very worried about you,' he attacked, managing this time not to move even his lower lip. I thought for a moment, and decided that provocation was not the best tactic if I were to succeed. If you want to reinforce your psycho-analyst's belief in his own mastery, provoke him the way kids provoke their parents. So I decided to say something with a lot of gravitas: 'Do you think it has something to do with the foreclosure of the Name of the Father?' Do you think that made him move? Not a fraction. He remained immobile and impassive. But I seemed to detect something in his eyes, like a flicker. I decided to exploit the lead further. 'Hmm?' he went, 'I don't think you understand what you are saying.' 'Oh yes, yes, I do,' I said, 'but there is one thing I don't understand in Lacan, it is the exact nature of his relation to structuralism.' He opened his mouth slightly to say something but I was quicker. 'Oh, yeah, and the mathemes, too. All those knots, it's a bit muddled. Do you understand any of it, this topology stuff? Everybody has known for quite a while that it's a scam, haven't they?' Here I detected some progress. He hadn't had time to close his mouth and, in the end, it stayed open. Then he took hold of himself and on his motionless face came a motionless expression of the You-want-to-play-games-with-me-little-girl? sort. Well, yes, I do want to play games with you, you big fat *marron glacé*. So I waited. 'You are a very intelligent young lady, that I know,' he said (price of this information conveyed by my dear Solange: sixty euros for half an hour). 'But a person can be very intelligent and at the same time quite destitute, you know, very lucid and very unhappy.' No kidding. Did you find that in *Pif Gadget*? I almost asked. And then suddenly I felt like upping the ante. I was, after all, sitting across from the guy who has been costing my family close to six hundred euros a month for nearly a decade, the results of which we are already familiar with: three hours a day of squirting house plants and an impressive consumption of state-subsidised substances. I felt my anger flaring up, nice and nasty. I leaned towards the desk and said in a very deep voice: 'Listen carefully, Monsieur Permafrost Psychologist, you and I are going to strike a little bargain. You're going to leave me alone and in exchange I won't wreck your little trade in human suffering by spreading nasty rumours about you among the Parisian political and business elite. And believe me – at least if you say you can tell just how intelligent I am – I am fully capable of doing this.' I didn't really think this would work. I couldn't believe it. You really have to be out to lunch to believe such a load of nonsense. And yet, however incredible, victory: a shadow of disquiet passed over the face of the good Doctor Theid. I think he believed me. It's extraordinary: if there is one thing I'll never do, it's spread untrue rumours to harm someone. My father with his Republican soul has inoculated me with the virus of deontology, and I may find that as absurd as all the rest but I stick to it, strictly. But the good doctor, who has only had my mother on whom to base his opinions of our family, has apparently decided that the threat is real. And there, oh miracle! He moved! He clicked his tongue, uncrossed his arms, stretched one hand out towards the desk and slapped his palm against the kid-leather blotter. A gesture of exasperation but also intimidation. Then he stood up, all gentle kindness vanished, and went to the door, and called Maman back in, and gave her some patter about my good mental health and that everything would be fine and sent us expeditiously away from his autumnal fireside.

At first I was really pleased with myself. I had managed to make him move. But as the day went on I started to feel more and more depressed. Because what happened when he moved was something not very nice, not very decent. So what if I know there are adults who wear masks that are all sweetness and light but who are very hard and ugly underneath, and so what if I know that all you have to do is see right through them for their masks to fall; when it happens with this sort of violence, it hurts. When he slapped the blotter, what it meant was, 'Fine, you see me as I am, no point carrying on with this useless farce, it's a done deal, your pathetic little bargain, now get the hell out of here, and fast.' Well, that hurt, yes, it hurt. I may know that the world is an ugly place, I still don't want to see it.

Yes, it's time to leave a world where something that moves can reveal something so ugly.

12. A Wave of Hope

I am a fine one to reproach those phenomenologists for their catless autism: I have devoted my life to the quest of timelessness.

But those who seek eternity find solitude.

'Yes,' he says as he takes my bag, 'I agree. It is one of the sparest paintings, yet it contains a great deal of harmony.'

Monsieur Ozu's place is very grand and very beautiful. Manuela's stories had led me to expect a Japanese interior, but although there are sliding doors and bonsai and a thick black carpet edged with grey and objects that are clearly Asian – a coffee table in dark lacquer or, all along an impressive row of windows, bamboo blinds drawn at various levels, giving the room its Eastern atmosphere – there are also armchairs and a sofa, consoles, lamps and bookshelves, all clearly European. It is very . . . elegant. Just as Manuela and Jacinthe Rosen had noted, however, there is nothing superfluous. Nor is it spartan, or empty, as I had imagined, transposing the decors from Ozu's films to a level that would be more luxurious yet identical in its sobriety, so characteristic of this strange civilisation.

'Come,' says Monsieur Ozu, 'let's not stay here, it's too formal. We're going to have dinner in the kitchen. Anyway, I'm the one who's cooking.'

I see that he is wearing an apple-green apron over a chestnut-coloured crew-neck sweater and beige linen trousers. On his feet are black leather slippers.

I trot along behind him to the kitchen. Oh gracious me. In

such a setting I would cook every day, even for Leo. Nothing could turn out ordinary; even opening a can of Whiskas would be a real treat.

'I am very proud of my kitchen,' says Monsieur Ozu with simplicity.

'And so you should be,' I reply, without a trace of sarcasm.

Everything is white and pale wood, with long worktops and tall dressers filled with blue, black and white dishes and bowls. In the centre is the range with oven and hotplates, a sink with three bowls, and a bar seating area with comfortable stools, where I take a seat facing Monsieur Ozu, who is busy at the stove. He has set a small bottle of sake down before me, with two beautiful little cups in crazed blue porcelain.

'I don't know if you are familiar with Japanese cuisine?'

'Not very.'

A wave of hope lifts me up. It may have become apparent thus far that we have hardly exchanged a dozen words, and all the while I am acting as if I were an old friend of Monsieur Ozu's, while he stands there cooking in his apple-green apron, after a hypnotic Dutch episode that elicited no commentary and is now filed in the chapter of forgotten things.

Perhaps this evening will simply be an initiation into Japanese cuisine. A plague on Tolstoy and all my doubts: Monsieur Ozu, a new resident who is as yet ill-acquainted with hierarchy, has invited his concierge for an exotic dinner. They will converse about sashimi and soy noodles.

Could there be a more innocent occasion?

And then, catastrophe.

13. Tiny Bladder

To begin with, I must confess that I do have a small bladder. How else can I explain that the least little cup of tea sends me running to the ladies' and a whole teapot will have me repeating the operation in proportion to its contents? Manuela is a regular camel: she holds what she drinks for hours on end, happily nibbling away at her Florentines without ever moving from her chair, while I find myself making endless pathetic tos and fros to the bathroom. But that is when I am at home: in the space of my six hundred square feet the toilet is never very far away, easily located in a familiar place.

And here I am now and my tiny bladder has just reminded me of its existence. Painfully aware that I have imbibed litres of tea that very afternoon, I cannot ignore its message: reduced autonomy.

How does one deal with this situation in polite society?

Where is the loo? does not strike me as the most fitting option.

On the other hand:

Would you kindly tell me where the place is?, however tactful my efforts not to name the place, could be easily misunderstood and, consequently, merely exacerbate my embarrassment.

I need to pee, while sober and informative, is not something you say at the table to someone you do not know.

Where is the toilet? is problematic. It's a cold request, with something of the musty provincial restaurant about it.

This is not bad:

Where is the bathroom? This I like, because the terminology has something innocent and welcoming about it, conjuring images of lavender-scented bubbles. But it nevertheless has ineffable connotations evoking bodily functions.

At that point I am struck by a flash of genius.

'Ramen is prepared using noodles and bouillon, it's Chinese in origin, but in Japan it is eaten regularly at lunchtime,' says Monsieur Ozu, lifting up an impressive quantity of noodles which he has just dipped into cold water.

'Excuse me, where is the lavatory?' is the only reply I can find to give him.

I will grant you that this is somewhat abrupt.

'Oh, forgive me, I forgot to show you,' says Monsieur Ozu, perfectly naturally. 'The door behind you, then the second on the right in the hallway.'

Can't everything always be this simple?

It would seem not.

Knickers or Van Gogh?

T oday I went with Maman to the sales on Rue Saint-Honoré. Hell on earth. There were queues outside some of the boutiques. And I think you can picture what sort of boutiques you have on Rue Saint-Honoré: that people can throw themselves so tenaciously into getting a reduced scarf or pair of gloves that even with the markdown will still cost as much as a Van Gogh just floors me. But these ladies go at it with an enraged passion. And even with a certain lack of elegance.

But all the same my day wasn't a total loss, because I was able to observe a very interesting movement – although, alas, it was anything but aesthetic. Very intense, however – indeed it was! And funny, too. Or tragic, I'm not really sure. Since I started this journal, I guess I've lowered my sights, in fact. My original idea was to discover the harmony in the movement of the world and here I am about to describe well-bred ladies squabbling over a pair of lace knickers. But anyway . . . I think that in any event I didn't fully believe in it. So while I'm at it, I may as well just have some fun . . .

Here's what happened: Maman and I went into a boutique of fine lingerie. Fine lingerie is already an interesting name. What else would it be – coarse lingerie? Anyway, what it means, in fact, is sexy lingerie; you won't find your grandmother's sturdy old cotton drawers in a place like this. But since it's Rue Saint-Honoré, obviously, it's sexy chic, with hand-stitched lace underwear, silk thongs and cashmere nightgowns. We didn't have to queue to get in, but it would have been better if we had because inside the boutique we were crammed shoulder to shoulder. It was like being inside a mangle. Icing on the cake: Maman immediately went into ecstasies when she started digging through a pile of underwear in really dodgy colours (red and black, or petrol blue). I wondered where I could hide and find shelter while she was looking for (faint hope) some flannelette pyjamas, and I threaded my way towards the back of the changing rooms. I wasn't alone: there was a man, the only man, and he looked as dejected as Neptune when he's missed a shot at Athena's hindquarters. That's the downside of 'I love you dear'. The poor bloke gets dragged off to a steamy session of trying on chic underwear and finds himself in enemy territory, with thirty females in a trance who step on his feet and look daggers at him whenever he tries to park his cumbersome male carcass somewhere. As for his lovely lady friend, she has been metamorphosed into a vengeful fury, ready to kill for a fuchsia tanga.

I shot him a glance full of sympathy, to which he responded with the expression of a hunted beast. From where I stood I had an unrestricted view of the entire shop and of Maman who was drooling over some sort of teeny-tiny bra made of white lace (at least there was some lace) and huge purple flowers. My mother is forty-five, a few pounds overweight, but the big purple flower doesn't frighten her off; the sobriety and chic of a uniform beige, on the other hand, would leave her paralysed with terror. Anyway, there's Maman painstakingly extirpating this mini floral bra from the rack, and she thinks it's her size, and she reaches for the matching knickers, three racks lower down. She is tugging on them with determination but suddenly she frowns: at the other end of the knickers there is another lady, who is also tugging on the knickers and frowning. They look at each other, look at the rack, and realise that these knickers are the last survivors of a long morning of sales: they prepare to do battle, each armed with her most ingratiating smile.

212

And now the stage is set for an interesting movement: a pair of knickers at one hundred and thirty euros does not amount to much more than a few centimetres of ultra fine lace. So you have to smile at the other woman, hold firmly onto the knickers, and pull them towards you but without tearing them. I'll tell you straight out: if in our world the laws of physics are constant, this will not be possible. After a few seconds of unsuccessful endeavour, the two ladies say amen to Newton but don't give up. The war will have to be fought using other means – diplomacy (one of Papa's favourite words). And this results in the following interesting movement: pretend to be unaware of pulling firmly on the knickers, while asking for them with faux courtesy. So here are Maman and the other lady and all of a sudden it's as though they have each lost their right hand, which is in fact clinging to the knickers. It's as if the knickers did not exist, as if Maman and the lady were chatting quite calmly about a pair of knickers that were still on the rack, that neither one would ever dream of trying to expropriate by force. Where has my right hand gone? Poof! Vanished! Disappeared! Time for diplomacy!

As everybody knows, diplomacy always fails when there is an imbalance of power. No one's ever seen the stronger party accept the other party's diplomatic proposals. As a result, the negotiations which began in unanimity with, 'Oh, I think I was quicker than you, chère Madame,' don't get you very far. When I went up to Maman, they had reached the point of, 'I won't let go of them,' and it's easy enough to believe both warring factions.

And of course Maman lost: when I came up to her, she remembered that she was a respectable mother and that it would not be possible for her, unless she wanted to sacrifice all dignity before my eyes, to send her left fist smack into the other woman's face. So she regained the use of her right hand, and let go of the knickers. End result: one left with the knickers, the other with the bra. Maman was in a foul mood all through dinner. When Papa asked what was going on she replied, 'You're a member of parliament, you should pay more attention to the degradation of people's attitudes and civil behaviour.'

But let's get back to the interesting movement: two women in full possession of their mental capacities who suddenly become totally unfamiliar with a part of their body. It results in a very odd spectacle: as if there were a break in reality, a black hole opening up in space-time, like in a real sci-fi novel. A negative movement, a sort of hollow gesture, in a way.

So I said to myself, if you can pretend to ignore the fact that you've got a right hand, what else can you pretend to ignore? Can you have a negative heart, a hollow soul?

14. How Much for One Roll?

Phase one of the operation goes smoothly.

I find the second door on the right in the corridor without being tempted to open the seven other doors, as my bladder is so small, and complete phase two with a relief untarnished by embarrassment. It would have been cavalier to question Monsieur Ozu about his bathroom. No mere *bathroom* could be white as snow, from the walls to the toilet bowl, by way of an immaculate toilet seat on which one hardly dares be seated for fear of sullying it. All this whiteness, however, is tempered – so that the whole business does not seem too clinical – by a sun-bright yellow carpet that is thick, deep, silky, satiny and caressing, and that rescues the place from any operating-room atmosphere. From these observations I conceive a great deal of respect for Monsieur Ozu. The clean simplicity of white, with no marble or embellishments – a common weakness among the privileged classes, who seek to make anything trivial seem luxurious – and the gentle softness of a sun-bright carpet are, as far as toilet fixtures go, the very prerequisites of consonance. What are we looking for when we go there? A bit of light, to keep us from thinking of all those dark depths swirling together below us, and something soft on the floor so that we can get our task accomplished without doing penance by freezing our feet, particularly when we go there at night.

The toilet paper, too, is a candidate for sainthood. I find this sign of wealth far more convincing than any Maserati or

Jaguar. What toilet paper does for people's derrières con-
tributes considerably more to the abyss between the classes
than a good many external signs. The paper at Monsieur Ozu's
abode – thick, soft, gentle and delicately perfumed – is there to
lavish respect upon a part of the body that, more than any
other, is partial to such respect. How much for one roll? I
wonder, as I press the middle flush button, which is crossed
with two lotus flowers; my tiny bladder, despite its lack of
autonomy, can hold a fair amount. One lotus flower seems a bit
skimpy, three would be narcissistic.

And then something dreadful happens.

A monstrous racket assails my ears, practically striking me
down on the spot. What is terrifying is that I cannot tell where
it is coming from. It is not the flush, I cannot even hear the
flush, it is coming from above me and right down upon me. My
heart is pounding wildly. You know what the three alternatives
are: in the face of danger, fight, flee or freeze. I freeze. I would
gladly flee but suddenly I am no longer capable of unlocking
the door. A number of hypotheses spring to mind, but offer no
explanation. Did I press the wrong button, misjudging the
amount produced – such presumptuousness, such *pride*,
Renée, two lotus flowers for such a ridiculous contribution –
and consequently am I being punished by the earsplitting
thunder of divine justice? Am I guilty of overindulging – of
luxuriating – in the voluptuousness of the act in a place that
inspires voluptuousness, when we should actually think of it as
impure? Did I succumb to *envy* in coveting this princely bum-
wipe, and have therefore been roundly reminded of my deadly
sin? Have my lumpen manual labourer's fingers, succumbing
to the effect of some unconscious *wrath*, abused the subtle
mechanism of the lotus button, thereby unleashing a cataclysm
in the plumbing that threatens the entire fourth floor with
seismic collapse?

I am still trying with all my strength to flee, but my hands are incapable of obeying orders. I fiddle with the copper latch which, if correctly operated, ought to set me free, but nothing of the sort occurs.

At that very moment, I am convinced I have gone mad, or have arrived in heaven, because the unholy racket, indistinguishable thus far, now becomes clearer and, unthinkably, sounds not unlike Mozart.

Sounds, in fact, like the *Confutatis* from Mozart's *Requiem*. *Confutatis maledictis, Flammis acribus addictis!*

I am hearing beautiful, lyrical voices.

I have gone mad.

'Madame Michel, is everything all right?' asks a voice from behind the door, it is Monsieur Ozu's voice, or, more likely, that of St Peter at the gates of Purgatory.

'I . . . I can't open the door.'

I have been doing everything in my power to convince Monsieur Ozu of my mental deficiency.

And I have succeeded.

'Perhaps you are turning the knob in the wrong direction,' suggests the voice of St Peter, respectfully.

I ponder this information for a moment while it makes its tortuous way to the circuits that will process it.

I turn the knob in the other direction.

The door unlocks.

The *Confutatis* comes to an abrupt end. A delicious wave of silence washes over my grateful body.

'I . . .' I say to Monsieur Ozu, for there is no one else here, 'I . . . well . . . You know, the *Requiem*?'

I should have named my cat Badsyntax.

'Oh, I imagine you were frightened!' he says. 'I should have warned you. This is a Japanese thing . . . my daughter's idea to import it. When you flush, it sets off the music, it's . . . more pleasant, you see?'

What I see, above all, is that we are standing in the hallway outside the toilet, in a situation that is blasting to smithereens all world records for ridiculousness.

'Oh . . .' I say, 'uh . . . I was surprised.' (And I make no mention of all my deadly sins exposed in broad daylight.)

'You are not the first,' says Monsieur Ozu kindly and, if I am not mistaken, with a trace of amusement on his upper lip.

'Mozart's *Requiem* . . . in the bathroom . . . it's rather . . . surprising,' I answer, in order to regain my composure, then I am immediately horrified by the turn I have given the conversation, and in the meanwhile we are still standing in the hallway, facing each other, arms dangling, uncertain what to do next.

Monsieur Ozu looks at me.

I look at him.

Something snaps in my chest, with a decisive little click, like a valve opening and shutting again. Then I notice, helplessly, that my body is trembling slightly and – it never rains but it pours – the same incipient trembling has gained the shoulders of the man standing opposite me.

We look at each other, hesitating.

Then a sort of faint, gentle ooh ooh ooh escapes from Monsieur Ozu's lips.

I realise that the same muffled but irrepressible ooh ooh ooh is rising in my own throat.

Both of us are going ooh ooh ooh very quietly, looking at each other incredulously.

Then Monsieur Ozu's ooh ooh ooh grows more intense.

My own ooh ooh ooh begins to resemble an alarm signal.

We are still looking at each other, exhaling ever more unrestrained ooh ooh oohs from our lungs. Every time they begin to subside, we look at each other and are off on the next round. My guts are paralysed, and tears are streaming down Monsieur Ozu's cheeks.

How long do we stand there laughing convulsively by the

door to the bathroom? I have no idea. But it is long enough to deplete us of all our energy. We exhale a few more exhausted ooh ooh oohs and then, more fatigued than satiated, put on a straight face.

'Let's go back to the living room,' says Monsieur Ozu, quicker than me to regain the use of his respiratory faculties.

15. A Very Civilised Noble Savage

'It's certainly not boring with you around,' is the first thing Monsieur Ozu says to me once we are back in the kitchen and I am comfortably perched on my stool sipping lukewarm sake, which I find fairly bland.

'You are no ordinary person,' he adds, pushing in my direction a small bowl filled with little raviolis which look neither fried nor steamed but somewhere in between. Next to them he places a bowl of soy sauce.

'Gyozas,' he explains.

'On the contrary,' I reply, 'I think I'm a very ordinary person. I'm a concierge. My life is a model of banality.'

'A concierge who reads Tolstoy and listens to Mozart. I did not know this was one of the skills required for your profession.'

And he winks at me. Without further ado he sits down beside me, and applies his chopsticks to his own serving of gyozas.

Never in my life have I felt so at ease. How can I explain? For the first time, I feel utterly trusting, even though I am not alone. Even with Manuela, to whom I would gladly entrust my life, I do not have this feeling of absolute security that comes when one is sure that understanding is mutual. Entrusting one's life is not the same as opening up one's soul, and although I love Manuela like a sister, I cannot share with her the things that constitute the tiny portion of meaning and emotion that my incongruous existence has stolen from the universe.

With my chopsticks I savour the gyozas stuffed with coriander and delicately spiced meat. Aware of a staggering sense of well-being, I chat with Monsieur Ozu as if we have known each other forever.

'One must have some entertainment, after all,' I say. 'I go to the local library and borrow everything I can.'

'Do you like Dutch painting?' he asks and, without waiting for my reply, 'If you were given the choice between Dutch painting and Italian painting, which would you rescue?'

We argue back and forth, a mock heated exchange where I make a passionate defence of Vermeer – but very quickly it becomes apparent that whatever we might say, we still agree with each other.

'You think it's a sacrilege?' I ask.

'Not at all, chère Madame,' he replies, jauntily waving an unfortunate ravioli from left to right above his bowl, 'not at all, do you think I would have copied a Michelangelo to have it hanging in my hallway?'

'You dip the noodles in this sauce,' he adds, placing before me a wicker basket filled with noodles and a sumptuous blue-green bowl that is giving off an aroma of . . . peanuts. 'This is a "zalu ramen", a dish of cold noodles with a slightly sweet sauce. Tell me if you like it.'

And he hands me a heavy linen napkin.

'There might be some collateral damage. Mind your dress.'

'Thank you.'

Goodness knows why, I add:

'It isn't mine.'

I take a deep breath and say,

'You know, I've been living alone for so long and I never go out. I'm afraid I might be something of a noble savage.'

'A very civilised noble savage, in that case,' he says, smiling.

The taste of noodles dipped in peanut sauce is heavenly. I cannot, however, swear to the purity of Maria's dress. It is not very easy to plunge a yard's length of noodle into a semi-liquid sauce and then swallow it without making a bit of a mess. But as Monsieur Ozu is able to manage his own noodles quite adroitly, making a considerable amount of noise all the while, this removes any complex I might have: I proceed merrily to slurp up my long ribbons of noodle.

'Seriously,' says Monsieur Ozu, 'do you not find it amazing? Your cat is called Leo, mine are Kitty and Levin, we both love Tolstoy and Dutch painting and we live in the same place. What are the odds of such a thing happening?'

'You shouldn't have given me that beautiful book,' I say, 'it wasn't necessary.'

'Chère Madame,' replies Monsieur Ozu, 'did it make you happy?'

'Well, of course it made me very happy, but also rather nervous. You know, I would like to remain discreet, I don't want the people here imagining . . .'

'. . . who you are? Why?'

'I don't want any fuss. No one wants a concierge who gives herself airs.'

'Airs? But you don't give yourself . . . airs, you have taste, and qualities, you are enlightened!'

'But I'm the concierge! And anyway, I have no education, I'm not part of that world.'

'Big deal!' says Monsieur Ozu in exactly the same way, would you believe, as Manuela, and this makes me laugh.

He raises an eyebrow, questioning.

'That's my best friend's favourite expression,' I say, by way of an explanation.

'And what does she say, your best friend, about your . . . discretion?'

To be honest, I haven't a clue.

'You know her,' I say, 'it's Manuela.'

'Ah, Madame Lopes? She's your friend?'

222

'She's my only friend.'

'She is a great woman, an aristocrat. You see, you are not the only one who goes against the social norm. What's the harm in that? This is the twenty-first century, for goodness' sake!'

'What did your parents do?' I ask, somewhat ruffled by his lack of discernment.

No doubt Monsieur Ozu thinks that privilege disappeared with Zola.

'My father was a diplomat. I did not know my mother, she died shortly after I was born.'

'I am sorry.'

He makes a gesture with his hand, as if to say, it was long ago.

I forge ahead with my idea.

'You are the son of a diplomat, I am the daughter of impoverished peasants. It is inconceivable for me even to be having dinner here this evening.'

'And yet, you are having dinner here this evening.'

And he adds, with a very sweet smile, 'And I am very honoured.'

The conversation continues in this vein, good-natured and natural. We talk about, in order: Yasujiro Ozu (a distant relation); Tolstoy, and Levin mowing the field with his peasants; exile and the irreducibility of culture; and many other subjects which we debate in succession with the enthusiasm of discovering our shared interest, while enjoying the last of the mountain of noodles and, above all, the disconcerting similarity in the working of our minds.

At one point Monsieur Ozu turns to me and says:

'I would like you to call me Kakuro, it would be so much less awkward. Do you mind if I call you Renée?'

'Not at all,' I reply – and I really do not mind.

Where have I suddenly found this ability to feel such ease in close company?

No answer is required for the time being, for the sake has muddled my brain in a quite delightful way.

'Do you know what aduki beans are?' asks Kakuro.

'The mountains of Kyoto . . .' I say, smiling at my memory of infinity.

'What?'

'The mountains of Kyoto are the colour of aduki bean paste,' I say, trying hard nevertheless to speak clearly.

'That's from a film, isn't it?'

'Yes, in *The Munekata Sisters*, at the very end.'

'Oh, I saw that film a long time ago, but I don't remember it very well.'

'Don't you remember the camellia on the moss of the temple?'

'No, not at all. But you make me want to see it again. Would you like to watch it together some day soon?'

'I have the cassette, I haven't taken it back to the library yet.'

'This weekend, perhaps?'

'Do you have a VCR?'

'Yes,' he says, smiling.

'That's settled, then. But let me make the following suggestion: let's watch the film at tea-time on Sunday, and I'll bring the pastries.'

'Agreed,' says Kakuro.

The evening unfolds while we go on talking with little regard for coherence or the passage of time, endlessly sipping a herbal tea with a strange seaweedy taste. Not surprisingly, I must renew my acquaintance with the snow-coloured toilet bowl and the sun-bright carpet. I select the one-lotus-flower button this time – message received – and weather the assault of the *Confutatis* with all the serenity of a long-standing regular. What is both disconcerting and marvellous about Kakuro Ozu is that he combines a sort of childish enthusiasm and candour with the attentiveness and kindliness of an old sage. I am not accustomed to such a relationship with the world; it seems to me that he views it with indulgence and curiosity, whereas the other human beings I know display either wariness and kindness (Manuela), ingenuity and kindness (Olympe) or arrogance and cruelty (everyone else). Such a combination of eagerness, lucidity and magnanimity is delightfully unusual.

And then I look down at my watch.

It is three o'clock.

I jump to my feet.

'Good Lord, have you seen the time?'

He consults his own watch then looks up with an anxious gaze.

'I had forgotten that you are working early tomorrow. I'm retired, I don't pay any attention to that any more. Will you be all right?'

'Yes, of course, but I have to get some sleep all the same.'

I do not mention the fact that in spite of my advanced age, although everyone knows old people do not sleep a lot, in my case I must sleep like a log for at least eight hours in order to have the slightest discernment in my dealings with the world.

'See you on Sunday,' says Kakuro at his front door.

'Thank you so much, I've had a lovely evening, I'm very grateful to you.'

'It is I who am grateful to you. I haven't laughed like that in a very long time, nor have I had such a pleasant conversation. Would you like me to walk you to your door?'

'No, thank you, there's no need.'

There is always a potential Pallières lurking on the stairs.

'Well then, I'll see you on Sunday,' I say, 'unless we run into each other before then.'

'Thank you, Renée,' he says again, with a broad, childlike grin.

I close my own door behind me, and lean against it; there is Leo snoring away like a trumpet in the TV armchair, and I realise something unthinkable: for the first time in my life, I have made myself a friend.

16. And Then

And then, a summer rain.

17. A New Heart

I remember that summer rain.

Day after day, we pace up and down our life the way we pace up and down a passageway.

Don't forget the lung for the cat . . . have you seen my scooter this is the third time it's been stolen . . . it's raining so hard you'd think it was night . . . we'll just make it, the next showing is at one . . . do you want to take off your raincoat . . . cup of bitter tea . . . silence of the afternoon . . . perhaps we are sick from too much . . . all these *bonzes* to water . . . those giddy young things who run wild . . . look, it's snowing . . . those flowers, what are they called . . . poor sweetie she was peeing all over the place . . . an autumn sky, how sad . . . it gets dark so early now . . . how come the rubbish smells all the way out into the courtyard . . . you know, everything comes at its appointed time . . . no, I didn't know them especially well . . . they were a family like all the others here . . . it is the colour of aduki bean paste . . . my son says the Chanese are very hard to deal with . . . what are his cats called . . . would you sign for the packages from the dry cleaner's . . . all the Christmases, these carols, the shopping, so tiring . . . when you eat a walnut you must use a tablecloth . . . his nose is running what do you know . . . it's already hot it's not even ten yet . . . I slice some mushrooms really finely and we have our bouillon with those mushrooms in it . . . she leaves her filthy pants under the bed . . . we should redo the wallpaper . . .

And then, summer rain . . .

Do you know what a summer rain is?

To start with, pure beauty striking the summer sky, awe-filled respect absconding with your heart, a feeling of insignificance at the very heart of the sublime, so fragile and swollen with the majesty of things, trapped, ravished, amazed by the bounty of the world.

And then, you pace up and down a corridor and suddenly enter a room full of light. Another dimension, a certainty just born. The body is no longer a prison, your spirit roams the clouds, you possess the power of water, happy days are in store, in this new birth.

Just as teardrops, when they are large and round and compassionate, can leave a long strand washed clean of discord, the summer rain as it washes away the motionless dust can bring to a person's soul something like endless breathing.

That is the way a summer rain can take hold in you – like a new heart, beating in time with another's.

18. Gentle Insomnia

After two hours of gentle insomnia, I fall peacefully asleep.

Profound Thought No. 13

Who presumes
To make honey
Without sharing the bee's fate?

Every day I tell myself that my sister cannot possibly sink any further into the slough of disgrace and, every day, I am amazed to see that she does.

This afternoon, after school, there was no one at home. I took some hazelnut chocolate from the kitchen and went to eat it in the living room. I was comfortably settled on the sofa, nibbling on my chocolate and ruminating on my next profound thought. I was thinking that it would be a profound thought about chocolate or the way you nibble it, in particular, with a central question: What is it that is so good about chocolate? The substance itself, or the technique of chewing it?

But however interesting I may have found my subject, I had not factored in the presence of my sister, who had come home earlier than expected and who immediately began to poison my existence by talking to me about Italy. Ever since she went to Venice with Tibère and his parents (staying at the Danieli), that's all she talks about. To make things even worse, on Saturday they went to have dinner at some friends of the Grinpards' who have a huge estate in Tuscany. Colombe now gets ecstatic just saying, *Tuuh*-scany, and Maman chimes in. In case you didn't know, Tuscany is not an ancient land. It exists solely to give people like Colombe, Maman or the Grinpards a frisson of possession. *Tuuh*-scany belongs to them just as Culture and Art do, or anything else you can write with a Capital Letter.

Speaking of *Tuuh*-scany, then, I've already been treated to the donkeys, the olive oil, the light at sunset, the dolce vita and

231

whatever other clichés they could come up with. But because each time I'd managed to slip away quietly, Colombe had not yet been able to try out her favourite story on me. So she made up for it when she saw me on the sofa and she spoiled my tasting session and my nascent profound thought.

On Tibère's parents' friends' estate there are beehives, enough of them to produce a hundred kilos of honey a year. The Tuscans have hired a beekeeper who does all the work so that they can market their honey as 'Flibaggi Estate'. Obviously, they don't do it for the money. But 'Flibaggi Estate' honey is considered to be one of the best in the world, and it adds to the owners' prestige (they live off their private income) because it's used in all the best restaurants by the most illustrious chefs, who make a great fuss about it . . . Colombe, Tibère and Tibère's parents were treated to a tasting session, as if it were wine, and Colombe could go on forever about the difference between thyme honey and rosemary honey. That will really come in handy some day. Up to this point in her story, I was listening distractedly while thinking of my 'crunching into the chocolate' and I figured if her story were to stop at this point I would be getting off lightly.

But you can't ever hope for such a thing from Colombe. Suddenly she put on her superior air and started telling me about the behaviour of bees. Apparently they were given an in-depth account and Colombe's nasty little mind was particularly taken with the passage on the nuptial rites of queens and drones. The incredible organisation of the hive, on the other hand, did not seem to make that much of an impression on her, although I think it's fascinating, especially the fact that these insects have a coded language: all the claims that verbal intelligence is specifically human begin to seem rather relative. But that's not the sort of thing that would ever interest Colombe – she's not working towards a vocational training certificate to become a plumber after all, she's after a master's in philosophy.

232

Nevertheless, she is absolutely titillated by the sexual lives of tiny creatures.

To sum up: the queen bee, when she is ready, takes off on her nuptial flight, pursued by a cloud of drones. The first drone to reach her copulates with her, then dies, because after the act his genital organ remains stuck inside. So he is amputated and this kills him. The second drone to reach the queen, in order to copulate with her, has to remove the genital organ of the previous drone with his feelers and, of course, the same thing will happen to him, and so on and so forth until you end up with ten or fifteen drones who have filled up the queen's sperm pouch and will enable her, in the course of four or five years, to produce two hundred thousand eggs a year.

This is what Colombe is telling me, looking at me with her spiteful air, embellishing her story with saucy comments like, 'She only gets one shot at it, huh, so she uses up fifteen drones!' If I were Tibère, I wouldn't really appreciate my girlfriend going around telling everyone this story. Because, well, you can't help but do a little bit of amateur psychology: when a randy girl goes around saying that it takes fifteen males to satisfy one female and that to thank them she castrates them and kills them – well, you can't help but wonder. Colombe is convinced this makes her look like the liberated-not-at-all-uptight-girl-who-talks-about-sex-perfectly-naturally. And Colombe is forgetting that she's only telling *me* this story in order to shock me and that in addition the content of the story is not at all innocent. In the first place, for someone like me who thinks that people are animals, sexuality is not a salacious subject: it's a scientific matter. It's fascinating. And in the second place, I'd like to remind everyone that Colombe washes her hands three times a day and screams the moment she gets the slightest suspicion that there might be an invisible hair in the shower (visible hairs are more improbable). I don't know why, but I think that all this goes very well with the sexuality of queens.

But above all it is crazy how people think that though they understand nature they can live without it. If Colombe is telling this particular story in this particular way, it's because she thinks it has nothing to do with her. If she's poking fun at the drones' pathetic lovemaking, it's because she is convinced she will never be subjected to anything remotely similar. But I don't see anything shocking or saucy about the nuptial flight of the queens or the fate of the drones, because I feel profoundly similar to all those creatures, even if our behaviour differs. Living, eating, reproducing, fulfilling the task for which we were born, and dying: it has no meaning, true, but that's the way things are. People are so arrogant, thinking they can coerce nature, escape their destiny of little biological things . . . and yet they remain so blind to the cruelty or violence of their own way of living, loving, reproducing and making war on their fellow human beings . . .

Personally I think there is only one thing to do: find the task we have been placed on this earth to do, and accomplish it as best we can, with all our strength, without making things complicated or thinking there's anything divine about our animal nature. This is the only way we will ever feel that we have been doing something constructive when death comes to get us. Freedom, choice, will and so on? Chimeras. We think we can make honey without sharing in the fate of bees, but we are in truth nothing but poor bees, destined to accomplish our task and then die.

PALOMA

1. Terribly Sharp

At 7 a.m. that morning someone rings the bell at my lodge.

It takes me a few seconds to emerge from the void. Two hours of sleep do not leave a person feeling terribly well disposed towards mankind, and the ringing that persists as I hastily throw on my dress and slippers and run my hand through my curiously puffy hair does little to stimulate my altruism.

I open the door and find myself face to face with Colombe Josse.

'Well,' she says, 'were you caught in a traffic jam?'

I cannot believe what I am hearing.

'It is seven in the morning,' I say.

She looks at me.

'Yes, I know,' she says.

'The lodge opens at eight,' I explain, making a great effort at self-control.

'What do you mean, at eight?' she asks, looking shocked. 'There are hours?'

No, a concierge's lodge is a protected sanctuary, oblivious of either social progress or labour laws.

'Yes,' I say, incapable of another word.

'Oh,' she replies in a lazy voice. 'Well, since I'm already here . . .'

'. . . you can come by later.' I slam the door in her face and make a beeline for the kettle.

Through the windowpane I hear her shout, 'Well! That takes the biscuit!' then turn furiously on her heel and press all her rage into the button to call the lift.

Colombe is the elder Josse daughter. Colombe Josse is also a sort of tall blonde leek who dresses like a penniless bohemian. If there is one thing I despise, it's the perverse affectation of rich people who go around dressing as if they were poor, in second-hand clothes that hang on them all crookedly and grey woolly hats, socks full of holes and flowery shirts under threadbare sweaters. Not only is it ugly, it is also insulting: nothing is more despicable than a rich man's scorn for a poor man's longing.

Unfortunately, Colombe Josse also happens to be a brilliant student. This autumn she started philosophy at the École Normale Supérieure.

I make my tea and spread cherry plum jam on *biscottes*, as I try to master the trembling rage afflicting my hands, while an insidious headache worms its way into my brain. I take an exasperated shower, get dressed, bestow an absolutely abject meal upon Leo (brawn and damp leftover cheese rind), go out into the courtyard, take out the rubbish, remove Neptune from the rubbish store and, by eight o'clock, weary of all this toing and froing, I repair to my kitchen, not the least bit calmer for all that.

The Josse family also have a younger daughter, Paloma, who is so discreet and diaphanous that I have the impression I never see her, although she does go out to school every day. But, lo and behold, it is Paloma who, at eight on the dot, shows up as Colombe's envoy.

What a cowardly trick.

The poor child (how old is she? eleven? twelve?) is standing on my doormat, stiff as justice. I take a deep breath – I would not want to transfer the rage inspired by the evil onto the innocent – and try to smile as naturally as possible.

'Good morning, Paloma.'

She fiddles hesitantly with the bottom of her pink cardigan.

'Good morning.' Her voice is reedy.

I look at her carefully. How could I have missed this? Some children have the awkward talent of intimidating adults; nothing in their behaviour corresponds to the standards of their age group. They are too serious, too imperturbable and, at the same time, terribly sharp. Yes, sharp. If I observe Paloma carefully, I detect a trenchant acuity, a chilly wise way about her, which I suppose I had always taken for reserve simply because it was impossible for me to imagine that the flighty Colombe could have a Judge of Humanity for a sister.

'My sister Colombe has sent me to alert you to the fact that she is expecting the delivery of a very important envelope,' says Paloma.

'Very well,' I reply, mindful not to soften my own tone the way adults do when they speak to children – something which, in the end, is as much an indication of scorn as rich people wearing poor people's rags.

'She asks if you can bring it up to our house,' continues Paloma.

'Yes.'

And she goes on standing there.

This is all very interesting.

She goes on standing there, staring at me calmly, without moving, her arms by her side, her lips slightly parted. She has skinny plaits, glasses with pink frames and very large light eyes.

'Would you like a cup of hot chocolate?' I ask, running out of ideas.

She nods, as imperturbable as ever.

'Come in, I was just having some tea.'

And I leave the door to the lodge open, to avert any accusations of child abduction.

'I prefer tea myself, if you don't mind,' she says.

'No, not at all,' I reply, somewhat surprised, observing mentally that a certain amount of data is being stored: the Judge of Humanity, nice turn of phrase, prefers tea.

She sits on a chair and swings her feet in the void, looking at me while I pour out her jasmine tea. I put the cup down before her, and sit down with my own cup.

'Every day I do something so that my sister will think I'm an idiot,' she declares after taking a connoisseur's long swallow. 'My sister spends entire evenings with her friends drinking and smoking and talking as if she were an underprivileged kid from a housing estate, because she thinks her intelligence is beyond question . . .'

Which seems to fit very squarely with the girl's no-fixed-abode sense of style.

'I am here as her envoy because she's a coward and a chicken,' continues Paloma, still staring at me with her big clear eyes.

'Well, it's given us the opportunity to get acquainted,' I say politely.

'May I come back?' she asks, and there is something of an entreaty in her voice.

'Of course,' I say, 'you're more than welcome. But I'm afraid you'll find it boring here, there's not much to do.'

'I just want a place where I can have some peace,' she retorts.

'Can't you have some peace in your own room?'

'No, there's no peace if everyone knows where I am. Before, I used to hide. But now they've found out all my hiding places.'

'You know, people are constantly disturbing me too. I don't know how much peace and quiet you'll find here.'

'I could stay there.' She points to the armchair by the television, which is on with the sound turned off. 'People come to see you, they won't bother me.'

'It's fine with me, but first you will have to ask your mother if she agrees.'

Manuela, who starts work at half past eight, pops her head through the open door. She is about to say something when she sees Paloma with her steaming cup of tea.

'Come in,' I say, 'we were just having some tea and a little chat.'

Manuela raises an eyebrow, which means, in Portuguese at least, What is she doing here? I give a faint shrug. She purses her lips, puzzled.

'Well?' she asks all the same, incapable of waiting.

'Will you come by later?' I ask with a huge smile.

'Ah,' she says, seeing my smile, 'very good, very good, yes, I'll come back, the usual time.'

Then, looking at Paloma:

'Fine, I'll come back later.'

And, politely:

'Goodbye, Mademoiselle.'

'Goodbye,' says Paloma, with her first, faint smile, a poor little out-of-practice smile that breaks my heart.

'You must go on home now,' I say. 'Your family will be getting worried.'

She stands up and heads for the door, dragging her feet.

'It is patently clear,' she says, 'that you are very intelligent.'

And since I am too taken aback to say anything else:

'You have found a good hiding place.'

2. For All Its Invisibility

The envelope that the courier drops off at my lodge for Her Majesty Colombe de la Riffraff is open.

Wide open, without ever having been sealed closed. The adhesive flap still has its white protective strip and the envelope is gaping open like an old shoe, revealing a stack of spiral-bound pages.

Why did no one take the trouble to close it, I wonder, eliminating the hypothesis of trust in the integrity of couriers and concierges, and assuming, rather, a belief that the contents of the envelope could hardly be of interest to them.

I swear by all the saints that this is the first time, and I can only pray that the facts (little sleep, summer rain, Paloma and so on) will be taken into consideration.

Very gently I remove the pages from their envelope.

Colombe Josse, 'The Argument of Potentia dei Absoluta', Master's Thesis under the Direction of Professor Marian, University of Paris I – Sorbonne.

There is a card clipped to the first page:

Dear Colombe Josse,
Here are my notes. Thank you for the courier.
I will see you at the Saulchoir tomorrow.
Regards,
J. Marian

In the introduction I discover that the topic is medieval

philosophy. It is, moreover, a thesis on William of Ockham, a Franciscan monk, philosopher and logician of the fourteenth century. As for the Saulchoir, it is a library of 'religious and philosophical sciences' in the thirteenth arrondissement, run by Dominican monks. The library has a considerable collection of medieval literature including, I'll wager, the complete works of William of Ockham, in Latin, in fifteen volumes. How do I know this? Well, I went there a few years ago. For what purpose? None in particular. I had found this library on a map of Paris and it seemed to be open to the public so I went there as a collector. I wandered up and down between the stacks, which were set far apart and peopled exclusively by very learned old gentlemen or students with pretentious airs about them. I have always been fascinated by the abnegation with which we human beings are capable of devoting a great deal of energy to the quest for nothing and to the rehashing of useless and absurd ideas. I spoke with a young doctoral candidate in Greek patristics and wondered how so much youth could be squandered in the service of nothingness. When you consider that a primate's major preoccupations are sex, territory and hierarchy, spending one's time reflecting on the meaning of prayer for Augustine of Hippo seems a relatively futile exercise. To be sure, there are those who will argue that mankind aspires to meaning beyond mere impulses. But I would counter that while this is certainly true (otherwise, what am I to do with literature?), it is also utterly false: meaning is merely another impulse, an impulse carried to the highest degree of achievement, in that it uses the most effective means – understanding – to attain its goals. For the quest for meaning and beauty is hardly a sign that man has an elevated nature, that by leaving behind his animal impulses he will go on to find the justification of his existence in the enlightenment of the spirit: no, it is a primed weapon in the service of a trivial and material goal. And when the weapon becomes its own subject, this is the simple consequence of the specific neuronal wiring that distinguishes us from other animals; by allowing us to survive, the efficiency of intelligence also offers us the possibility of complexity without foundation, thought without usefulness, and beauty without purpose. It's like a computer bug, a consequence without consequence of the subtlety of our cortex, a superfluous perversion making an utterly wasteful use of the means at its disposal.

But even when the quest does not wander off in this way, it remains a necessity that does not depart from animality. Literature, for example, serves a pragmatic purpose. Like any form of Art, literature's mission is to make the fulfilment of our essential duties more bearable. For a creature such as man, who must forge his destiny by means of thought and reflexivity, the knowledge gained from this will perforce be unbearably lucid. We know that we are beasts who have this weapon for survival, and that we are not gods creating a world with our own thoughts, and something has to make our own wisdom bearable, something has to save us from the woeful eternal fever of biological destiny.

Therefore we have invented Art: our animal selves have devised another way to ensure the survival of our species.

Truth loves nothing better than simplicity of truth: that is the lesson Colombe Josse ought to have learned from her medieval readings. But all she seems to have gleaned from her studies is how to make a conceptual fuss in the service of nothing. It is a sort of endless loop, and also a shameless waste of resources, including the courier and my own self.

I leaf through pages that contain scarcely any comments, although this must be a final version, and am filled with dismay. Granted, the young woman has a fairly efficient way with words, despite her youth. But the fact that the middle classes are working themselves to the bone, using their sweat and taxes to finance such pointless and pretentious research leaves me speechless. Every grey morning, day after gloomy day, secretaries, craftsmen, employees, minor civil servants, taxi drivers and concierges shoulder their burden so that the flower of French youth, duly housed and subsidised, can squander the fruit of all that dreariness upon the altar of ridiculous endeavours.

And yet, at the outset Colombe's thesis has every reason to be enthralling: *Do universals exist, or only singular things?* is the question to which, I gather, William of Ockham devoted most of his life. I am fascinated by his query: is each thing an individual entity – if so, whatever is identical from one thing to another is merely an illusion or an effect of language, proceeding through words and concepts, through generalities designating and embracing several particular things – or *do general forms truly exist*, of which singular things are but a part, and not the mere result of language? When we say 'a table', when we utter the word 'table', when we make the concept of the table, are we still designating only this table or are we *truly* referring to a universal table entity that establishes the reality of all the particular tables that exist? Is the *idea* of the table real, or does it merely belong to the mind? If that is so, then why are certain objects identical? Is it language that is grouping them together artificially into general categories, for the convenience of human understanding, or does a universal form exist to which every specific form belongs?

As far as Will of Ockham is concerned, things are singular, and the realism of universals is erroneous. There are only particular realities, generality is merely in the mind and to presume that generic realities exist is merely to make what is simple complicated. But can we be so sure? Was I not seeking congruence between Raphael and Vermeer only yesterday? The eye recognises a shared form to which both belong, and that is Beauty. And I dare say there must be reality in that form, it cannot be a simple expedient of the human mind classifying

245

in order to understand, and discerning in order to apprehend: for you cannot classify something that is not classifiable, you cannot put things together that cannot be together in a group, or gather those that cannot be gathered. A table can never be a *View of Delft*: the human mind cannot create this dissimilarity, any more than it can invent the deep solidarity connecting a Dutch still life to an Italian Virgin and Child. In every table there is an essence that gives it its form and, similarly, every work of art belongs to a universal form that alone confers its seal upon the work. To be sure, we cannot perceive this universality directly: that is one of the reasons why so many philosophers have baulked at considering essences to be real, for I will only ever see the table that is before me, and not the universal 'table' form; only the painting, and not the very essence of Beauty. And yet . . . and yet it is there, before our eyes: every painting by a Dutch master is an incarnation of Beauty, a dazzling apparition that we can only contemplate through the singular, but that opens a tiny window onto eternity and the timelessness of a sublime form.

Eternity: for all its invisibility, we gaze at it.

3. The Just Crusade

S o, do you think all of this is of any interest to our aspiring candidate for intellectual glory?

'Tis most unlikely.

Colombe Josse, who has no ongoing preoccupation with Beauty or the destiny of tables, is relentless in her exploration of Ockham's philosophical thought, but she ventures only where her utterly uninteresting semantic simpering cares to take her. The most remarkable thing is the intention that presides over her undertaking, and that is to make Ockham's philosophical theses into the *consequence* of his conception of God's action, by reducing his years of philosophical labour to the rank of a secondary excrescence of his theological thought. It is sidereal, as inebriating as bad wine and above all a perfect illustration of the way university works: if you want to make a career, take a marginal, exotic text (William of Ockham's *Sum of Logic*) that is relatively unexplored, abuse its literal meaning by ascribing to it an intention that the author himself had not been aware of (because, as we all know, the unknown in conceptual matters is far more powerful than any conscious design), distort that meaning to the point where it resembles an original thesis (it is the concept of the absolute power of God that is at the basis of a logical analysis, the philosophical implications of which are ignored), burn all your icons while you're at it (atheism, faith in Reason as opposed to the reason of faith, love of wisdom and other bagatelles dear to the hearts of socialists), devote a year of your life to this unworthy little game at the expense of a collectivity whom you drag from their beds at seven in the morning, and send a courier to your supervisor.

What is the purpose of intelligence if it is not to serve others? And I'm not referring to the false servitude that high-ranking state officials exhibit so proudly, as if it were a badge of virtue: the façade of humility they wear is nothing more than vanity and disdain. Cloaked every morning in the ostentatious modesty of the high-ranking civil servant, Étienne de Broglie convinced me long ago of the pride of his caste. Inversely, privilege brings with it *true* obligations. If you belong to the closed inner sanctum of the elite, you must serve in equal proportion to the glory and ease of material existence you derive from belonging to that inner sanctum. What would I do if I were Colombe Josse, a young student at the École Normale with all my future before me? I would dedicate myself to the progress of Humanity, to resolving issues that are crucial for the survival, well-being and elevation of mankind, to the fate of Beauty in the world, or to the just crusade for philosophical authenticity. It's not a calling, there are choices, the field is wide. You do not take up philosophy the way you enter the seminary, with a credo as your sword and a single path as your destiny. Should you study Plato, Epicurus, Descartes, Spinoza, Kant, Hegel or even Husserl? Aesthetics, politics, morality, epistemology, metaphysics? Should you devote your time to teaching, to producing a body of work, to research, to Culture? It makes no difference. The only thing that matters is your intention: are you elevating thought and contributing to the common good, or rather joining the ranks in a field of study whose only purpose is its own perpetuation, and only function the self-reproduction of a sterile elite – for this turns university into a sect.

Profound Thought No. 14

Go to Angelina's
To learn
Why cars are burning

Something really fascinating happened today! I went to see Madame Michel to ask her to bring some post for Colombe up to the apartment once the courier delivers it to her lodge. In fact it's Colombe's master's thesis on William of Ockham, it's a first draft that her supervisor was supposed to read and send back with comments. What's really funny is that Madame Michel told Colombe to get lost because she rang at the lodge at seven in the morning to ask her to bring up the package. Madame Michel must have told her off (the lodge opens at eight) because Colombe came back to the apartment like a fury, ranting that the concierge was an old bag and who did she think she was, anyway, and have you ever seen such a thing? Maman seemed to recall suddenly that yes, indeed, in an advanced, civilised country, you don't go disturbing concierges at any old hour of the day or night (and she would have done better to remember that before Colombe went down there), but that didn't calm my sister down, and she went on bleating that just because she'd messed up on the time didn't mean this non-entity had the right to slam the door in her face. Maman just let it go. If Colombe were my daughter – Darwin forbid – I would have slapped her on both cheeks.

Ten minutes later Colombe came into my room with a really gooey smile on her face. Now that is one thing I really cannot stand. I'd even rather she yelled at me. 'Paloma, sweetie, can you do me a really big favour?' she cooed. 'No,' I answered. She took a deep breath, ruing the fact that I am not her personal slave, why she could have had me horsewhipped, which would have made her feel a lot better – what an irritating snotty-nosed kid. 'Let's do a deal,' I added. 'You don't even know what I want,' she retorted with a scornful little smirk. 'You want me to go and see Madame Michel,' I said. She sat there with her mouth open. She's told herself for so long that I'm thick that she's finally ended up believing it. 'I'll do it if you don't play loud music in your room for a month.' 'A week,' said Colombe. 'Then I won't go,' I said. 'OK,' said Colombe, 'go and see that old bag and tell her to bring me Marian's package the minute it gets to her lodge.' And she went out, slamming the door behind her.

So I went to see Madame Michel and she invited me in for a cup of tea.

For the time being, I'm testing her. I didn't say much. She gave me a strange look, as if she were seeing me for the first time. She didn't say anything about Colombe. If she were a real concierge, she would have said something like, 'Yes, well, your sister there shouldn't go around thinking she can get away with whatever she likes.' Instead, she gave me a cup of tea and talked to me very politely, as if I were a real person.

The television was on in the lodge. She wasn't watching it. There was a programme about kids burning cars in the banlieues. When I saw the images I wondered what it is that makes a kid want to burn a car. What is going on in their heads? And then this thought came into my mind: what about me? Why do I want to set fire to the apartment? Journalists talk about unemployment and poverty; I talk about the selfishness and duplicity of my family. But these are all hollow phrases. There has always been unemployment and poverty and pathetic families. And yet, people don't go burning cars or apartments every day of the week. Honestly! I decided that, in the end, they were all false pretexts. Why do people burn cars? Why do I want to set fire to the apartment?

I didn't get an answer to my question until I went shopping

with my aunt Hélène, my mother's sister, and my cousin Sophie. In fact we had to go and buy a present for my mother's birthday, which is next Sunday. The pretext was a visit to the Musée Dapper, but we went straight to the interior design boutiques in the second and eighth arrondissements. The idea was to find an umbrella stand and buy my present for Maman as well.

As to the search for an umbrella stand, it was endless. It took three hours but, if you ask me, all the stands we saw were absolutely identical: either really basic cylinders, or things with ironwork like you'd find in an antique shop. And all of them ridiculously expensive. Don't you find it disturbing, on some level, to think that an umbrella stand can cost two hundred and eighty-nine euros? And yet that is what Hélène paid for a pretentious object in 'fatigued leather' (my foot: rubbed with an iron brush, maybe) with saddlemaker's stitching, as if we lived on a stud farm. And I bought Maman a little black lacquer box for her sleeping tablets, from an Asian boutique. Thirty euros. I already thought that was really expensive but Hélène asked me if I wanted to get something else to go with it, since it wasn't a lot. Hélène's husband is a gastroenterologist, and I can guarantee that, in the realm of medical doctors, gastroenterologists are not among the poorest . . . All the same, I like Hélène and Claude, because they are . . . well, I don't know quite how to put it . . . they have integrity. They are satisfied with their life, I think, at least they don't play at being something they're not. And they have Sophie. Sophie has Down's syndrome. I'm not the sort who gets all sentimental around people with Down's syndrome the way some people in my family do – they think it's good manners, even Colombe joins in. The consensual script reads: they are handicapped but they are so endearing, so affectionate, so touching! Personally, I find Sophie's presence somewhat hard to take: she dribbles, she cries out, gets moody, has her whims and doesn't understand anything. But that doesn't mean I don't admire Hélène and Claude. They themselves say that she is

251

difficult and that it is a real ordeal to have a daughter with Down's syndrome, but they love her and do a great job looking after her, I think. This, along with their integrity – well, the result is that I really like them a lot. When you see Maman playing at being the hip, well-adjusted modern woman, or Jacinthe Rosen playing at having been born with a silver spoon stuck in her mouth, it makes Hélène, who is playing at nobody at all, and who is content with what she has, seem really likeable.

Anyway, after the rigmarole with the umbrella stand, we went to eat some cakes and drink hot chocolate at Angelina's, a tea room on Rue de Rivoli. You'll tell me that nothing could be further removed from the topic of young people in the banlieues burning cars. Well, not at all! I saw something while we were at Angelina's that offered me a lot of insight into other things. At the table next to ours there was a couple with a baby. The couple were white and their baby was Asian, a little boy they called Théo. They struck up a conversation with Hélène and chatted for a while. Obviously they had in common the fact that their children were different, that is why they noticed each other and began to converse. We learned that Théo had been adopted, he was fifteen months old when they brought him home from Thailand – his parents had died in the tsunami, along with all his brothers and sisters. I was looking around and thinking, how will he manage? Here we were at Angelina's after all: all these well-dressed people, nibbling preciously at their exorbitantly priced patisserie, who were here only for . . . well, for the significance of the place itself – belonging to a certain world, with its beliefs, its codes, its projects, its history and so on. It's symbolic. When you go to have tea *chez Angelina*, you are in France, in a world that is wealthy, hierarchical, rational, Cartesian, policed. How will little Théo manage? He spent the first months of his life in a fishing village in Thailand, in an Eastern world dominated by its own values and emotions, where symbolic belonging might be played out at village feasts celebrating the rain god, where

252

children are brought up with magical beliefs, etc. And now here he is in France, at Angelina's, suddenly immersed in a different culture without any time to adjust, with a social position that has changed in every possible way: from Asia to Europe, from poverty to wealth.

Then suddenly I said to myself, Théo might want to burn cars some day. Because it's a gesture of frustration and anger, and maybe the greatest anger and frustration come not from unemployment or poverty or the lack of a future but from the feeling that you have no culture, because you've been torn between cultures, between incompatible symbols. How can you exist if you don't know where you are? What do you do if your culture will always be that of a Thai fishing village and of Parisian *grands bourgeois* at the same time? Or if you're the son of immigrants but also the citizen of an old, conservative nation? So you burn cars, because when you have no culture, you're no longer a civilised animal, you're a wild beast. And a wild beast burns and kills and pillages.

I know this is not a very profound thought but after that I did have a profound thought, all the same: I asked myself, what about me? What is my cultural problem? In what way am I torn between two incompatible beliefs? And in what way am I a wild beast?

And then I had an enlightened thought, thinking of Maman's incantatory care of her house plants and Colombe's phobic manias and Papa's stress over Mamie being in a retirement home, and a whole lot of other things like that. Maman thinks you can conjure your destiny just by going 'pschtt', and Colombe thinks you can push your cares to one side just by washing your hands, and Papa thinks he's a bad son who will be punished because he's abandoned his mother: in the end, they too have magical beliefs, the beliefs of primitive people, but unlike the Thai fishermen, they can't accept them, because they are rich-educated-Cartesian-French-people.

253

And I am probably the biggest victim of all of this contradiction because, for some unknown reason, I am hypersensitive to anything that is dissonant, as if I had some sort of absolute pitch for false notes or contradictions. This contradiction and all the others . . . As a result, I don't feel I belong to any belief system, to any of these incoherent family cultures.

Maybe I'm the symptom of the family contradiction, and so I'm the one who has to disappear, if the family is to prosper.

4. The First Principle

By the time Manuela comes down from the de Broglies' at two o'clock, I have put the thesis back into its envelope and dropped it off at the Josses'.

This gave me the opportunity for an interesting conversation with Solange Josse.

You will recall that as far as the residents are concerned I am a stubborn concierge who lurks somewhere at the blurry edges of their ethereal vision. Solange Josse is no exception to this rule, but because she is the wife of a socialist member of parliament she nevertheless makes an effort.

'Good morning,' she says as she opens the door and takes the envelope I hand to her.

An effort, as I said.

'You know,' she continues, 'Paloma is a very eccentric little girl.'

She observes me, checking to see if I am familiar with this word. I assume a neutral expression – one of my favourites, for its wide latitude of interpretation.

Solange Josse may be a socialist but she does not believe in mankind.

'What I mean is that she is a bit strange.' She articulates carefully, as if talking to someone who is hard of hearing.

'She is a very sweet child,' I say, taking it upon myself to inject a bit of philanthropy into the conversation.

'Yes, yes,' replies Solange Josse in the tone of someone who would like to get to the point but must first overcome a number of obstacles stemming from the other person's lack of culture. 'She's a sweet little girl but she often behaves rather strangely. She loves to hide, for example; she disappears for hours.'

'Yes, she told me.'

A slightly risky reply, compared with the strategy that advocates saying nothing, doing nothing, understanding nothing. But I think I can play the part without betraying my nature.

'Oh, she told you?'

Suddenly Solange Josse sounds rather vague. How can she find out what the concierge has inferred from what Paloma might have said? The question mobilises her cognitive resources, causing her to lose her concentration and making her look quite absent-minded.

'Yes, she told me,' I reply. You have to admit I have a certain gift for laconicism.

I catch a glimpse of Constitution behind Solange Josse, sneaking slowly up to the door with a blasé look on his face.

'Oh, watch out, the cat,' she says.

And she comes out onto the landing and closes the door behind her. Don't let the cat out or the concierge in: this is the first principle of socialist ladies.

'Anyway,' she continues, 'Paloma told me she would like to come to your lodge from time to time. She daydreams a lot and likes to settle somewhere and do nothing. To be honest, I really would prefer she did that at home.'

'Ah.'

'But from time to time, if it's not a bother . . . That way at least I'll know where she is. She drives us all mad, making us look all over for her. Colombe is up to here in work and she's not too keen on having to spend hours moving heaven and earth to find her sister.'

She opens the door a crack, ascertains that Constitution has moved on elsewhere.

'Are you sure you don't mind?' she asks, her mind already elsewhere.

'No,' I reply, 'she won't disturb me.'

'Oh, good, good,' says Solange Josse, whose attention is now most definitely being solicited by a far more urgent and interesting matter. 'Thank you *so* much, it's very kind of you.'

And she closes the door.

5. The Antipodes

After that, I get on with my duties as concierge and, for the first time all day, I have time to think. Yesterday evening comes back with a curious aftertaste. After a pleasant aroma of peanuts come the stirrings of a dull anxiety. I try to ignore it by concentrating on watering the house plants on every landing in the building: this is the very type of chore that I situate in the antipodes of human intelligence.

At one minute to two, Manuela arrives, looking as excited as Neptune when he espies some courgette peel in the distance.

'Well?' she says several times impatiently, handing me some madeleines in a little round wicker basket.

'I'm going to need your services again,' I say.

'Oh, really?' she says, insisting heavily, almost unintentionally, on the *real*.

I have never seen Manuela looking so excited.

'We're having tea together on Sunday, and I'm in charge of the pastries,' I explain.

'Ooooh,' she says, radiant, 'the pastries!'

And immediately pragmatic:

'I have to make you something that will keep.'

Manuela works Saturdays until lunchtime.

'On Friday night I'll make you a *gloutof*,' she declares, after a brief pause for reflection.

The gloutof is a rather voracious Alsatian cake.

But Manuela's gloutof is ambrosia as well. Everything that

258

is dry and heavy about Alsace is transformed by her hands into an aromatic masterpiece.

'Will you have time?' I ask.

'Of course,' she says, over the moon, 'I always have time for a gloutof for you!'

And so I tell her everything: how I arrived, the still life, the sake, Mozart, the gyozas, the zalu ramen, Kitty, *The Munekata Sisters* and everything else.

If you have but one friend, make sure you choose her well.

'You are amazing,' says Manuela, when I have finished my story. 'All the idiots in this building, and now you – for once there is a decent gentleman here – you are the one who is invited to his place.'

She gulps down a madeleine.

'Ha!' she exclaims suddenly, insisting heavily on the '*h*'. 'I'll make you a few whisky tarts!'

'No, please don't go to so much bother, Manuela, the . . . gloutof will be plenty.'

'So much bother? But Renée, you are the one who has been going to a lot of bother for my sake all these years!'

She pauses for a moment, as if trying to remember something.

'What was Paloma doing here?' she asks.

'Well, she was taking a rest from her family.'

'Oh, the poor kid! You must admit that with that sister of hers . . .'

Manuela's feelings about Colombe – she would gladly burn her bag-lady hand-me-downs and then send her out into the fields for a little cultural revolution – are unequivocal to say the least.

'The little Pallières boy stands there gaping whenever Colombe walks by,' she adds. 'But she doesn't even see him. He should put a bin bag on his head. Oh, if only all the young women in the building were like Olympe . . .'

'That's true, Olympe is a very sweet girl.'

'Yes, she's a good sort. Neptune had the *runs* on Tuesday, you know, and she really took care of him.'

One mere run on its own would have been far too stingy.

'I know, we need a new carpet in the hallway. They're delivering it tomorrow. No harm done there, the other one was dreadful.'

'You know,' says Manuela, 'you can keep the dress. The lady's daughter said to Maria, Keep everything, and Maria told me to tell you that she's giving you the dress.'

'Oh, that's very kind, but I can't accept.'

'Don't go on about that again,' says Manuela, annoyed. 'In any case, you'll have to pay for the dry cleaner's. Just look at that, it looks like an *orange.*'

The orange, it would seem, is a virtuous type of orgy.

'Well then, please thank Maria for me, I'm really very grateful.'

'It's better that way. Yes, yes, I'll thank her for you.'

Two sharp knocks at the door.

6. Baby Porpoise

It is Kakuro Ozu.

'Hello, hello,' he says, bursting into the lodge. 'Oh, hello, Madame Lopes,' he adds, upon seeing Manuela.

'Hello, Monsieur Ozu,' she replies, almost shouting.

Manuela is a very enthusiastic sort.

'We were having tea, will you join us?'

'Ah, with pleasure,' says Kakuro, grabbing a chair. And when he sees Leo: 'Oh, what a fine specimen! I didn't see him properly the other time. A regular sumo!'

'Have a madeleine, they're made with *orgy*,' says Manuela, who is getting everything mixed up, as she pushes the basket in Kakuro's direction.

The orgy, it would seem, is a vicious type of orange.

'Thank you,' says Kakuro, as he takes one.

'Marvellous!' he exclaims, the moment the madeleine has disappeared down his throat.

Manuela wriggles on her chair, blissfully happy.

'I have come to ask your opinion,' says Kakuro, after four madeleines. 'I am in the midst of an argument with a friend over the issue of European supremacy in matters of culture.' He sends a graceful wink in my direction.

Manuela ought to be more indulgent with the Pallières boy in future: she is sitting there gaping.

'He leans towards England, and obviously I am for France. So I told him I knew someone who could settle the matter between us. Would you mind being the referee?'

'But I'm a judge and being judged at the same time,' I say, sitting down, 'I can't vote.'

'No, no, no, you're not going to vote. Just answer my question: what are the two major inventions of French and British culture? Madame Lopes, I'm fortunate indeed this afternoon, you can give me your opinion too, if you would.'

'The English . . .' Manuela begins, in fine fettle; then she pauses. 'You go first, Renée,' she says, suddenly remembering, no doubt, that she is Portuguese, and that she ought to be more careful.

I reflect for a moment.

'Where France is concerned: the language of the eighteenth century, and soft cheese.'

'And England?' asks Kakuro.

'Oh, England will be easy,' I say.

'Pooding-ghe?' says Manuela, spicing the dessert with her accent.

Kakuro bursts out laughing.

'No, we need something more.'

'Then the roog-eby,' she says, savouring every syllable.

'Ha, ha,' laughs Kakuro, 'I totally agree with you! And you, Renée, what do you suggest?'

'Habeas corpus and lawns,' I laugh.

And this sends us off into another fit of giggles, including Manuela, who heard 'baby porpoise', which is strictly beside the point, but it makes her laugh all the same.

At that very moment, someone knocks at the lodge.

How extraordinary that this lodge which yesterday was of no interest to anyone seems today to be the focus of global attention.

'Come in,' I say without thinking, in the heat of the conversation.

Solange Josse looks in round the door.

All three of us look at her questioningly, as if we were guests at a banquet being disturbed by an ill-mannered servant.

She opens her mouth, then thinks better of it.

Paloma looks in round the door at the height of the lock.

I remember myself and get to my feet.

'May I leave Paloma with you for an hour or so?' asks Madame Josse, who has recovered her composure, albeit her curiosity needle has gone right off the gauge.

'Bonjour, Monsieur Ozu,' she says to Kakuro, who has risen to his feet and come to shake her hand.

'Bonjour, chère Madame,' he says kindly. 'Hello, Paloma, how nice to see you. Well, dear friend, she'll be in good hands, you can leave her here with us.'

How to send someone gracefully on their way, in one lesson.

'OK . . . well . . . yes . . . thank you,' says Solange Josse, stepping slowly back, still somewhat stunned.

I close the door behind her.

'Would you like a cup of tea?' I ask Paloma.

'I'd love one.'

A true little princess among high-ranking party members.

I pour her half a cup of jasmine tea while Manuela plies her with the few remaining madeleines.

'What did the English invent, do you think?' Kakuro asks her, still at it with his cultural contest.

Paloma sits lost in thought.

'The hat, as a symbol of stubborn resistance to change,' she says.

'Excellent,' says Kakuro.

I note that I have probably greatly underestimated Paloma, and that I will have to dig deeper but, since destiny always rings three times, and since all conspirators are doomed to be unmasked some day, there is once again a drumming at the window of the lodge, and I am distracted from my thoughts.

Paul Nguyen is the first person who does not seem to be surprised by anything.

'Good morning, Madame Michel,' he says, then, 'Hello, everybody.'

'Ah, Paul,' says Kakuro, 'we have definitively discredited England.'

Paul smiles gently.

'Very good,' he says. 'Your daughter just rang. She'll call again in five minutes.'

He hands him a mobile phone.

'I see,' says Kakuro. 'Well, ladies, I must take my leave.'

He bows.

'Goodbye,' we offer in unison, like a virginal choir.

'Well,' says Manuela, 'that's a job well done.'

'What job?' I ask.

'We've eaten all the madeleines.'

We laugh.

She looks at me thoughtfully and smiles.

'It's incredible, isn't it?'

Yes, it is incredible.

Renée, who now has two friends, is no longer so shy.

But Renée, with her two friends, feels a sudden undefined terror welling up inside.

When Manuela has gone, Paloma curls up in Leo's armchair in front of the television, quite at home, and looking at me with her big serious eyes she asks,

'Do you believe that life has meaning?'

7. Deep Blue

At the dry cleaner's, I had had to confront the wrath of the lady of the premises.

'Spots like this on such a quality item!' she had grumbled, handing me a sky-blue receipt.

This morning I hand my rectangle of paper to a different woman. Younger and dozier. She hunts endlessly through the serried rows of hangers, then brings me a lovely dress in plum linen wrapped tightly in transparent plastic.

'Thank you,' I say, picking up said item after an infinitesimal hesitation.

To the chapter of my turpitudes I must now add the abduction of a dress that does not belong to me, in place of one stolen from a dead woman, by me. The evil is rooted, moreover, in the infinitesimal nature of my hesitation. If my vacillation had been the fruit of a sense of compunction linked to the concept of ownership, I might yet be able to implore St Peter's forgiveness; but I fear it is due to nothing more than the time needed to ensure the feasibility of my misdeed.

At one o'clock Manuela stops by the lodge to drop off her gloutof.

'I wanted to come earlier, but Madame de Broglie was looking at me out of the corner.'

According to Manuela, the corner *of her eye* is a superfluous clarification.

As far as gloutofs are concerned: nestled amidst a profusion of rustling deep-blue tissue paper are a magnificent Alsatian cake, succulent with inspiration; some whisky tarts so delicate you dare not touch them for fear they will break; and some almond tuiles crisply caramelised on the edges. The sight of these treasures instantly causes me to drool.

'Thank you, Manuela,' I say, 'but there will only be the two of us, you know.'

'Well then, just get stuck in right away.'

'Thanks again, really, it must have taken you a lot of time.'

'Fiddle-dee-dee. I made two of everything and Fernando has you to thank.'

This broken stem that for you I loved

I wonder if I am not turning into a contemplative aesthete. With major Zen tendencies and, at the same time, a touch of Ronsard.

Let me explain. This is a somewhat special 'movement of the world', because it's not about a movement of the body. But this morning, while having breakfast, I saw a movement. *The* movement. Perfection of movement. Yesterday (it was Monday), Madame Grémont, the cleaning lady, brought Maman a bouquet of roses. Madame Grémont spent Sunday at her sister's, and her sister has a little allotment garden in Suresnes, one of the last ones, and she brought back a bouquet of the first roses of the season: yellow roses, a lovely pale yellow, like primroses. According to Madame Grémont, this particular rose bush is called 'The Pilgrim'. I already like that for a start. It's loftier, more poetic, less sappy, than calling a rose bush 'Madame Figaro' or 'Un amour de Proust' (I'm not making this up). OK, I won't go into the fact that Madame Grémont gives roses to Maman. They have the same relationship that all progressive middle-class women have with their cleaning ladies, although Maman really thinks she is the exception: a good old rose-coloured paternalistic relationship (we offer her coffee, pay her decently, never scold, pass on old clothes and broken furniture, and show an interest in her children, and in return she brings us roses and brown and beige crocheted bedspreads). But those roses . . . they were something else.

I was having breakfast and looking at the bouquet on the kitchen counter. I don't believe I was thinking about anything. And that could be why I noticed the movement; maybe if I'd been preoccupied with something else, if the kitchen hadn't been quiet, if I hadn't been alone in there, I wouldn't have been attentive enough. But I was alone, and calm, and empty. So I was able to take it in.

There was a little sound, a sort of quivering in the air that went 'shhhh' very very very quietly: a tiny rosebud on a little broken stem that dropped onto the counter. The moment it touched the surface it went 'puff', a 'puff' of the ultrasonic variety, for the ears of mice alone, or for human ears when everything is very very very silent. I stopped there with my spoon in the air, totally transfixed. It was magnificent. But what was it that was so magnificent? I couldn't get over it: it was just a little rosebud at the end of a broken stem, dropping onto the counter. And so?

I understood when I went over and looked at the motionless rosebud where it had fallen. It's something to do with time, not space. Sure, a rosebud that has just gracefully dropped from the flower is always lovely to look at. It's so artistic: you could paint them over and over again! But that doesn't explain *the* movement. The movement . . . and we think such things are spatial.

In that split second, while seeing the stem and the bud drop onto the counter, I intuited the essence of Beauty. Yes, here I am, a little twelve-and-a-half-year-old brat, and I have been incredibly lucky because this morning all the conditions were ripe: an empty mind, a calm house, lovely roses, a rosebud dropping. And that is why I thought of Ronsard's poem, though I didn't really understand it at first: because he talks about time, and roses. Because beauty consists of its own passing, just as we reach for it. It's the ephemeral configuration of things in the moment, when you can see both their beauty and their death.

Oh my gosh, I thought, does this mean that this is how we must live our lives? Constantly poised between beauty and death, between movement and its disappearance?

Maybe that's what being alive is all about: so we can track down those moments that are dying.

8. Contented Little Sips

And now it is Sunday.

At three in the afternoon I make my way to the fourth floor. The plum-coloured dress is slightly too big – a godsend on a gloutof day – and my heart feels as tight as a kitten rolled into a ball.

Between the third and fourth floor I find myself face to face with Sabine Pallières. Over the last few days whenever she has run into me she has openly and disapprovingly scrutinised my puffy hair. I might mention that I have abandoned the idea of hiding my new appearance from the world. But such determination puts me ill at ease, however liberated I might be. Our Sunday encounter is no exception to the rule.

'Good afternoon, Madame Pallières,' I say, carrying on up the steps.

She answers with a stern nod as she considers my sconce and then, noticing how I am dressed, she stops short on the step. A wave of panic assails me, deregulating my sudatory glands and threatening my stolen gown with the infamy of underarm rings.

'As you are heading that way, would you water the flowers on the landing?' she asks in an exasperated tone of voice.

Must I remind her? It is Sunday . . .

'Are those cakes?' she asks suddenly.

On a tray I am carrying Manuela's masterworks wrapped in navy-blue tissue paper, and I realise that in Madame Pallières's eyes this far surpasses my dress and that it is hardly my

270

pretension to elegance which is arousing Madame's condemnation, but the idea of some wastrel's greedy appetite.

'Yes, an unexpected delivery,' I say.

'Well then, make use of it to water the flowers at the same time,' she says and resumes her irritated descent.

I arrive at the fourth floor and find it somewhat awkward to ring the bell, as I am also carrying the video cassette, but Kakuro opens his door diligently for me and immediately relieves me of my cumbersome tray.

'Oh my goodness,' he says, 'you don't mess around, my mouth is watering already.'

'You'll have to thank Manuela,' I say, and follow him into the kitchen.

'Really?' He removes the gloutof from the mass of blue tissue paper. 'It's an absolute gem.'

I suddenly realise that there is music in the background.

It isn't very loud, and it is coming from some hidden speakers that diffuse the sound throughout the kitchen.

Thy hand, Belinda, darkness shades me,
On thy bosom let me rest,
More I would, but Death invades me;
Death is now a welcome guest.
When I am laid, am laid in earth,
May my wrongs create
No trouble, no trouble in thy breast;
Remember me, but ah! forget my fate,
Remember me, remember me, but ah! forget my fate.

This is the death of Dido, from Purcell's *Dido and Aeneas*. In my opinion, the most beautiful music for the human voice on earth. It is beyond beautiful, it is sublime, because of the incredibly dense succession of sounds, as if each were linked to the next by an invisible force and, while each one remains distinct, they all melt into one another, at the edge of the human voice, verging on an animal cry. But there is a beauty in these sounds that no animal cry can ever attain, a beauty born of the subversion of phonetic articulation and the transgression of the careful verbal language that ordinarily creates distinct sounds.

Broken steps, melting sounds.

Art is life, playing to other rhythms.

'Let's go,' says Kakuro, who has set cups, teapot, sugar and little paper napkins on a big black tray.

I precede him down the corridor and, following his instructions, open the third door on the left.

'Do you have a VCR?' Such had been my question for Kakuro Ozu.

And he had replied, 'Yes,' with a cryptic smile.

The third door on the left opens onto a miniature cinema. A large white screen, a host of mysterious shiny devices, three rows of real seats covered in deep-blue velvet, a long low table opposite the front row, and walls and ceiling covered in dark silk.

'Actually, it was my profession,' says Kakuro.

'Your profession?'

'For over thirty years, I imported high-end audio equipment to Europe, for luxury establishments. It was a very lucrative business, but above all marvellously entertaining for someone like me who is enchanted by the least little electronic gadget.'

I settle into a wonderfully plush seat and the show begins.

How to describe such moments of bliss? To be watching *The Munekata Sisters* on a giant screen, in gentle darkness, nestled against a soft backrest, nibbling gloutof, and drinking scalding tea in contented little sips. From time to time Kakuro pauses the film and we both begin to talk about this and that, camellias on the moss of the temple and how people cope when life becomes too hard. Twice I go off to greet my friend the *Confutatis* and return to the screening room as if to a warm cosy bed.

This pause in time, within time . . . When did I first experience the exquisite sense of surrender that is possible only with another person? The peace of mind one experiences on one's own, one's certainty of self in the serenity of solitude are nothing in comparison to the release and openness and fluency one shares with another, in close companionship . . . When did I first feel so blissfully relaxed in the presence of a man?

Today is the first time.

9. Sanae

At seven o'clock, after much conversation and drinking of tea, I am ready to take my leave, and as we are passing through the living room I notice, on a low table next to a sofa, the framed photograph of a very beautiful woman.

'She was my wife,' says Kakuro quietly, seeing that I am looking at the picture. 'She died ten years ago, from cancer. Her name was Sanae.'

'I am sorry. She was . . . a very beautiful woman.'

'Yes,' he replies, 'very beautiful.'

There is a brief silence.

'I have a daughter, who lives in Hong Kong,' he adds, 'and already two grandchildren.'

'You must miss them.'

'I go there fairly often. I love them very much. My grandson, who is called Jack – his father is English – and who's seven, told me on the phone this morning that yesterday he caught his first fish. It's the event of the week, you can be sure of that!'

Another silence.

'I believe you are a widow,' says Kakuro, escorting me to the front door.

'Yes, I've been a widow for over fifteen years.'

There is a catch in my throat.

'My husband was called Lucien. It was cancer, too . . .'

We stand by the door, and look at each other with sadness.

'Good night, Renée,' says Kakuro.
And with a trace of our earlier light-heartedness:
'This has been a fantastic day.'
Melancholy overwhelms me, at supersonic speed.

10. Dark Clouds

You are a sorry idiot, I say to myself as I remove my plum-coloured dress and discover some whisky icing on a buttonhole. What were you thinking? You're only a penniless concierge. Friendship across class lines is impossible. And anyway, what have you been thinking, you poor fool?

What have you been thinking, poor fool? I say it over and over as I proceed with my evening ablutions then slide between the sheets, after a short battle with Leo, who does not want to yield any terrain.

The lovely face of Sanae Ozu is dancing before my closed eyes, and I see myself as a sad old thing, abruptly reminded of a joyless reality.

My heart restless, I nod off.

The next morning, I feel something not unlike a hangover.

Nevertheless, the week goes by like a charm. Kakuro puts in a few spontaneous appearances to solicit my talents as an arbiter of taste (ice cream or sorbet? Atlantic or Mediterranean?) and I find the pleasure of his refreshing company unchanged, despite the dark clouds passing silently above my heart. Manuela has a good laugh when she sees the plum-coloured dress, and Paloma has taken over Leo's armchair.

'I'm going to be a concierge some day,' she informs her mother, and Madame Josse herself looks at me with a fresh gaze mingled with caution when she comes to drop off her progeny at the lodge.

'May God preserve you from such a fate,' I reply with an amiable smile in Madame's direction. 'You're going to be a princess.'

Paloma is displaying in equal measure: a candy-pink T-shirt that matches her new glasses; the pugnacious air of girl-who-will-be-a-concierge-some-day-in-the-face-of-everything-especially-my-mother.

'What's that smell?' she asks.

There's a problem with the sewage in my bathroom and it stinks like a barracks full of soldiers. I called the plumber six days ago, but he did not seem especially interested in coming.

'The drains,' I reply, not terribly inclined to pursue the matter.

'Failure of liberalism,' says Paloma, as if I had not said a thing.

'No, it's a blocked drain.'

'That's what I mean,' says Paloma. 'Why hasn't the plumber come yet?'

'Because he's busy with other clients?'

'Not at all,' she retorts. 'The correct answer is: because he doesn't have to. And why doesn't he have to?'

'Because he doesn't have enough competition.'

'Exactly,' says Paloma triumphantly, 'there is not enough regulation. Too many rail workers, not enough plumbers. Personally, I would prefer the kolkhoz.'

Woe is me, a knock on the windowpane interrupts this captivating discussion.

It is Kakuro, with an indescribably solemn air about him.

He comes in and sees Paloma.

'Good morning, young lady,' he says. 'Well, Renée, shall I come by later?'

'If you like. How are you?'

'Fine, fine,' he replies.

Then, suddenly resolved, he takes the plunge, 'Would you like to have dinner with me tomorrow evening?'

'Uh . . .' I feel panic sweeping over me. 'It's just that . . .'

It is as if my vague intuitions of the last few days are suddenly taking shape.

'I would like to take you to a restaurant that I'm particularly fond of,' he continues, with the air of a dog hoping for a bone.

'Restaurant?' I say, feeling the full force of panic.

On my left, Paloma makes a little squeaking sound.

'Look,' says Kakuro, who seems somewhat ill at ease, 'I really would like you to come. It's . . . it's my birthday tomorrow and I would be happy to have you as my dinner partner.'

'Oh,' I say, incapable of adding anything.

'I'm leaving to see my daughter on Monday, so I'll have a party with the family there, of course, but tomorrow evening . . . if you would . . .'

He pauses briefly, looks at me hopefully.

Is it just my impression or is Paloma experimenting with apnoea?

Silence settles briefly over the room.

'Look,' I say finally, 'really, I am sorry. I don't think it would be a good idea.'

'But why ever not?' asks Kakuro, visibly disconcerted.

'It's very kind of you,' I say, hardening my tone, for it has a tendency to go soft, 'I am very grateful, but I'd rather not, thanks all the same. I am sure you have friends with whom you can celebrate the occasion.'

Kakuro is looking at me, speechless.

'I . . .' he says eventually, 'I . . . yes of course but . . . well . . . really I would very much like . . . I don't understand.'

He frowns.

'Well, I just don't understand.'

'It's better this way,' I say, 'believe me.'

And, walking towards him to nudge him gently in the direction of the door, I add,

'We'll have other opportunities to chat, I'm sure.'

He retreats, looking like a pedestrian who has lost his pavement.

'Well, it's a great pity,' he says, 'I was so looking forward to it. All the same . . .'

'Goodbye,' I say, gently closing the door in his face.

11. Rain

The worst is over, I say to myself.

But I have not reckoned with a candy-pink destiny: I turn around and find myself face to face with Paloma. Who does not look the least bit pleased.

'May I ask what on earth you are playing at?' she asks, in a tone that reminds me of Madame Billot, my very last schoolteacher.

'I'm not playing at anything at all,' I say weakly, aware of how childishly I have behaved.

'Do you have anything special planned for tomorrow evening?'

'Well, no, but that's not why . . .'

'Then may I ask why, exactly?'

'I don't think it would be a good thing.'

'And why not?' asks my police commissioner.

Why not?

Do I really know, to be honest?

Just then, without warning, the rain starts to fall.

12. Sisters

All that rain . . .

Where I grew up, in winter, it used to rain. I have no memories of sunny days: only rain, a weight of mud and cold, dampness sticking to our clothes and hair; even when you sat by the fire it never really went away. How often since then have I thought back to that rainy evening, how many recollections, over more than forty years, of an event that re-emerges today, beneath that pouring rain?

All that rain . . .

My sister was named after an older child who'd been stillborn, who, in turn, had been named after a deceased aunt. Lisette was lovely, and even as a child I was aware of the fact, although my eyes had not yet learned to determine the shape of beauty, but only to divine its rough outline. As no one spoke in my home, nothing was ever even said; but in the neighbourhood people gossiped and when my sister went by they would comment upon her beauty. 'So pretty and so poor, fate is a brutish thing,' the seamstress would mumble as we passed on our way to school. As for me, ugly and ungainly in mind and body, I would hold my sister's hand and Lisette would walk, her head held high, and as she passed she let them voice all the dire destinies predicted for her, for each of them had their own version.

At the age of sixteen she left for the city to look after some rich people's children. For a whole year we did not see her. She came back to spend Christmas with us, bringing strange gifts (gingerbread, brightly coloured ribbons, little pouches of lavender); she had the bearing of a queen. Could a rosier, livelier, more perfect face than hers exist? For the first time, someone was telling us a story, and we hung on her every word: we were avid for the mysterious awakening, and were eager to hear more from the lips of this farm girl who had become the maid of powerful people. She would tell us about a strange and richly coloured and shining world, where women drove cars and went home at night to households filled with appliances that did the work of human beings, or gave them the news of the world, all you had to do was turn the knob . . .

When I think back on all that, I take the measure of how destitute we really were. We were only thirty-five miles or so from the city, and there was a market town scarcely ten miles away, but we lived as people did during feudal times, without amenities or hope, so entrenched was our belief that we would always be backward peasants. No doubt even today in some remote rural backwater there are still some old people who have been cut off and have no idea of modern life, but in our case we were all relatively young, and when Lisette began to describe the city streets all lit up for Christmas, we were discovering that there was a whole world out there whose existence we had never even imagined.

Lisette went off again. For a few days, as if through some sort of automatic inertia, we continued to talk a little bit. For a few evenings, at the dinner table, my father commented on his daughter's stories. 'Them's some hard, strange stories.' Then silence and shouts rained down on us again, like a plague upon the unfortunate.

When I think back . . . All that rain, all those deaths . . . Lisette bore the name of two women who had died; I had been given the name of only one, my maternal grandmother, who died shortly before my birth. My brothers all had first names of cousins who had been killed in the war and my mother too had inherited her name from a cousin who had died in childbirth and whom she had never known. This was the wordless existence we were living, in a world of the dead, when one November evening Lisette came back from the city.

I remember all that rain . . . The sound of it drumming on the roof, the paths running with water, the sea of mud at the gate to the farm, the black sky, the wind, the horrible feeling of endless damp weighing upon us as our life weighed upon us: neither consciousness nor revolt. We were sitting huddled together by the fire when suddenly my mother got to her feet, throwing the rest of us off balance; we watched in surprise as, driven by some obscure impulse, she headed to the door and flung it open.

All that rain, oh, all that rain . . . Framed in the door, motionless, her hair clinging to her face, her dress soaked through, her shoes caked with mud, staring lifelessly, stood Lisette. How did my mother know? How did this woman who, while never mistreating us, never showed us that she loved us, either by deed or word – how did this coarse woman who brought her children into the world in the same way she turned over the soil or fed the hens, this illiterate woman, so exhausted by life that she never even called us by the names she had given us – to the point where I at times wondered if she even remembered them – how did she know that her daughter, half-dead, neither moving nor speaking but merely staring at the door without even thinking of knocking, was just waiting in a relentless downpour for someone to open it and bring her into the warm room?

Is this a mother's love, this intuition of disaster in one's heart, this spark of empathy that resists even when human beings have been reduced to living like animals? That is what Lucien said: a mother who loves her children always knows when they are in trouble. Personally, I do not much care for this interpretation. Nor do I feel any resentment towards that mother who was not a mother. Poverty is a reaper: it harvests everything inside us that might have made us capable of social intercourse with others, and leaves us empty, purged of feeling, so that we may endure all the darkness of the present day. Nor do I nurture any sturdy illusions: there was nothing of a mother's love in my mother's intuition, merely the translation into gesture of her certainty of misfortune. A sort of native consciousness, rooted deep in the heart, which serves to remind poor wretches like us that, on a rainy night, there will always be a daughter who has lost her honour and who will come home to die.

Lisette lived just long enough to give birth to her child. The infant did what was expected of it: it died within three hours. From this tragedy, which to my parents seemed to be part of the natural order of things, so that they were no more – and no less – moved by it than if they had lost a goat, I derived two certainties: the strong live and the weak die, and their pleasure and suffering are proportionate to their position in the hierarchy. Lisette had been beautiful and poor, I was intelligent and indigent, but like her I was doomed to a similar punishment if I ever sought to make good use of my mind in defiance of my class. Finally, as I could not cease to be who I was, either, it became clear to me that my path would be one of secrecy: I had to keep silent about who I was, and never mix with that other world.

From being silent, I then became clandestine.

Quite abruptly I realise I am sitting in my kitchen, in Paris, in this other world where I have made my invisible little niche, a world with which I have been careful never to mix, and I am weeping great warm tears while a little girl with an incredibly warm gaze is holding my hand, gently caressing my knuckles.

And I also realise that I have said it all, told her everything: Lisette, my mother, the rain, beauty profaned and, at the end of it all, the iron hand of destiny giving stillborn infants to mothers who die from wanting to be reborn. I am weeping plump, hot, long, good tears, sobbing tears, and while I am troubled, I am also incomprehensibly happy to see the transfiguration of Paloma's sad, severe gaze into a well of warmth where I can soften my sobs.

'My God,' I say, regaining my composure somewhat, 'my God, Paloma, how silly I am!'

'Madame Michel,' she replies, 'you know, you are giving me hope again.'

'Hope?' I say, snuffling pathetically.

'Yes,' she says, 'it seems it might be possible to change one's fate after all.'

We sit there for countless minutes holding hands, not speaking. I have become friends with a lovely twelve-year-old soul to whom I feel very grateful, and however incongruous this connection may be – asymmetrical in age, condition and circumstances – nothing can taint my emotion. When Solange Josse comes to the lodge to fetch her daughter, Paloma and I look at each other with the complicity of indestructible friendship, and say goodbye with the certainty we shall meet again soon. I close the door behind them, and sit down in the armchair by the television, with my hand on my chest. And I find myself speaking out loud: maybe this, then, is what life is all about.

Profound Thought No. 15

If you want to heal
Heal others
And smile or weep
At this happy reversal of fate

You know what? I wonder if I haven't missed something. A bit like someone who's been hanging out with a bad crowd and then discovers another path through meeting a good person. My own personal bad crowd: Maman, Colombe, Papa and their entire clique. But today I was with a really good person. Madame Michel told me about this traumatic event in her life: she has been avoiding Kakuro because she was traumatised by the death of her sister Lisette, who was seduced and abandoned by some rich man's son. Don't fraternise with rich people if you don't want to die: since then this has become her survival technique.

Listening to Madame Michel, I asked myself something: Which is more traumatic: a sister who dies because she's been abandoned, or the lasting effects of the event – the fear that you will die if you don't stay where you belong? Madame Michel could have got over her sister's death; but can you get over the staging of your own punishment?

Above all, there was something else I felt, something new, and as I write it I am very moved – proof is I had to put my pen down for two minutes, so I could cry. This is what I felt: listening to Madame Michel and seeing her cry, but above all seeing how it made her feel better to be able to tell her story to me, I understood something. I understood that I was suffering because I couldn't make anyone else around me feel better. I understood that I have a grudge against Papa, Maman and above all Colombe because I'm incapable of being useful to them, because there's nothing I can do for them. They are already too far gone in their sickness, and I am too weak. I can see their symptoms clearly but I don't have the skills to treat them and so as a result that makes me as sick as they are, only I don't see it. Whereas when I was holding Madame Michel's hand I could feel how I was sick, too. And one thing is sure, no matter what: I won't get any better by punishing the people I can't heal. I might have to rethink this business about fire and suicide. Besides, I may as well admit it: I don't really feel like dying, I want to be able to see Madame Michel and Kakuro again, and his unpredictable little great-niece Yoko, and ask them for help. Of course I'm not going to show up saying, please, help me, I'm a little girl who is suicidal. But I feel like letting other people be good for me – after all, I'm just an unhappy little girl and even if I'm extremely intelligent, that doesn't change anything, does it? An unhappy little girl who, just when things are at their worst, has been lucky enough to meet some good people. Morally, do I have the right to let this chance go by?

Sigh. I don't know. This story is a tragedy, after all. 'There are some worthy people out there, be glad!' is what I felt like telling myself, but in the end, so much sadness! They end up in the rain. I really don't know what to think. Briefly, I thought I had found my calling, I thought I'd understood that in order to heal, I could heal others, or at least the other 'healable' people, the ones who can be saved – instead of moping because I can't save other people. So what does this mean – I'm supposed to become a doctor? Or a writer? It's sort of the same thing, isn't it?

And for every Madame Michel, how many Colombes are out there, how many dreary Tibères?

13. In the Pathways of Hell

After Paloma left I didn't know which way to turn, and sat in my armchair for a long time.

Then, taking my courage in both hands, I dialled Kakuro Ozu's telephone number.

Paul Nguyen picked up on the second ring.

'Yes, hello, Madame Michel. What can I do for you?'

'Well, I would like to speak with Kakuro.'

'He's not in, would you like him to call you when he gets back?'

'No, no,' I said, relieved to be able to go through an intermediary. 'Could you tell him that, if he hasn't changed his mind, I would be happy to have dinner with him tomorrow evening?'

'With pleasure,' said Paul Nguyen.

I put the phone down and flopped back into the armchair, and for the past hour have let myself be carried away by confused but pleasant thoughts.

'It doesn't smell too good in your place, now does it?' says a soft male voice at my back. 'Isn't there anyone who can come and fix it?'

He opened the door so quietly that I didn't hear him. A nice-looking young man with rather dishevelled brown hair and a brand-new denim jacket and the large eyes of an amiable cocker spaniel.

'Jean? Jean Arthens?' I ask, scarcely believing my eyes.

'Yep,' he replies, leaning his head to one side, the way he used to.

But that is all that lingers of the human wreck, that ravaged young soul in the emaciated body he used to be: Jean Arthens, once so very close to the abyss, has visibly opted for rebirth.

'You look great!' I say, with my broadest smile.

Which he returns in kind.

'Well, good morning, Madame Michel, it is a pleasure to see you. It suits you,' he adds, pointing to my hairstyle.

'Thank you. What brings you here? Would you like a cup of tea?'

'Ah . . .' he begins, with a hint of his old hesitancy, 'yep, I'd love one.'

I prepare the tea and he sits down on a chair and looks at Leo, eyes wide with astonishment.

'Was this cat of yours always so fat?' he enquires, not meaning it in a nasty way.

'Yes. He's not terribly athletic.'

'It's not him that smells so bad, is it?' With an apologetic expression, he sniffs the cat.

'No, no, there's something wrong with the plumbing.'

'You must find it strange that I've just shown up here like this, especially as we never really talked much, uh, I wasn't very talkative in those days . . . well, in my father's days.'

'I'm happy to see you and above all to see that you seem to be doing well,' I say with sincerity.

'Yep . . . I had a close shave.'

We take little sips of scorching tea, simultaneously.

'I'm cured now – well, I'd like to think I'm cured, if you ever can be cured. But I'm keeping off drugs, I've met a nice girl – well, a fantastic girl, rather, I must say' – his eyes open wide and he sniffles slightly as he looks at me – 'and I've found a little job I like.'

'What are you doing?'

'I'm working at a ship's chandler's.'

'Parts for boats?'

'Yep, and it's a fun job. It's kind of like being on holiday, there. People come in and tell me about their boat, the seas they're about to sail, the seas where they've been, I like that, and then I'm happy to have a job, you know.'

'What do you actually do in your job?'

'I'm sort of the factotum, stock man and messenger boy, but I'm learning as I go along, so now from time to time they give me more interesting things to do like repair sails or shrouds, or put together the inventory of provisions.'

Just listen to the poetry of the language: *provisioning a sailing boat . . .* providing what is needed, with a vision to the future. To those who have not understood that the enchantment of language comes from such nuances, I shall address the following prayer: beware of commas.

'And you too look like you're doing well,' he says, with a kindly gaze.

'Really? Well, there have been a few changes that have been good for me.'

'You know, I didn't come back here to see the apartment or the people, here. I'm not even sure they'd recognise me; I even brought my ID card, just in case you yourself didn't recognise me. No, I came because there's something I can't remember, something that helped me a lot, already when I was sick and then afterwards, when I was getting better.'

'And you think I can help?'

'Yes, because you were the one who told me the name of those flowers one day. In the flowerbed, over there' – he points towards the far side of the courtyard – 'there are some pretty little red and white flowers, you planted them there, didn't you? And one day I asked you what they were but I wasn't able to remember the name. And yet I used to think about those flowers all the time, I don't know why. They're nice to look at, and when I was in a really bad way I would think about those flowers, and it did me good. So I was in the neighbourhood just now and I thought, I am going to ask Madame Michel, maybe she can tell me.'

Slightly embarrassed, he waits for my reaction.

'It must seem weird, eh? I hope I'm not scaring you, with this flower business.'

'No, not at all. If only I'd known the good they were doing you . . . I'd have planted them all over the place!'

He laughs, like a delighted child.

'Ah, Madame Michel, you know, it practically saved my life. That in itself is a miracle! So, can you tell me what they're called?'

Yes, my angel, I can. Along the pathways of hell, breathless, one's heart in one's mouth, a faint glow: they are camellias.

'Yes,' I say. 'They are camellias.'

He stares at me, wide-eyed. A tear slips across his waiflike cheek.

'Camellias . . .' he says, lost in a memory that is his alone. 'Camellias, yes.' He repeats the word, looking at me again. 'That's it. Camellias.'

I feel a tear on my own cheek.

I take his hand.

'Jean, you cannot imagine how happy I am that you came by here today.'

'Really?' He looks astonished. 'But why?'

Why?

Because a camellia can change fate.

14. From Passageway to Pathway

What is this war we are waging, when defeat is so certain? Day after day, already wearied by the constant onslaught, we face our terror of the everyday, the endless passageway that, in the end – because we have spent so much time walking to and fro between its walls – will become a destiny. Yes, my angel, that is our everyday existence: dreary, empty, and mired deep in troubles. The pathways of hell are hardly foreign; we shall end up there one day if we tarry too long. From a passageway to a pathway: it is an easy fall, without shock or surprises. Every day we are reacquainted with the sadness of the passageway and step by step we clear the path towards our mournful doom.

Did he see the pathways? How is one reborn after a fall? What new pupils restore sight to scorched eyes? Where does war begin, where does combat end?

Thus, a camellia.

15. His Shoulders Soaked with Sweat

At eight o'clock, Paul Nguyen comes to my lodge, his arms loaded with packages.

'Monsieur Ozu has not come back yet – there's a problem at the embassy regarding his visa – so he asked me to bring all of this to you,' he says, with a lovely smile.

He places the packages on the table and hands me a little card.

'Thank you,' I say. 'Would you like something to drink?'

'Thank you, but I still have a great deal to do. I'll take you up on your invitation another time.'

He smiles again, and there is something warm and happy about his expression: this does me untold good.

Alone in the kitchen I sit by the packages and open the envelope.

'Suddenly on his shoulders soaked with sweat he felt a pleasant and airy sensation that he could not initially explain; but during the pause, he noticed that a huge black cloud drifting low in the sky had just fallen to earth.'

Please accept these few gifts with simplicity.

Kakuro

The summer rain on Levin's shoulders as he is scything . . . I raise my hand to my chest, touched in a way I have never been. One by one, I open the packages.

A wraparound dress in a pearly grey silk, with a high round neck and a black satin martingale belt to fasten it.

A purple silk scarf, light and bracing like the wind.

Low-heeled court shoes, in leather of so fine and soft a grain that I lift one to my cheek.

I look at the dress, the scarf, the shoes.

Outside, Leo is scratching at the door, meowing to come in.

I begin to cry, quietly, slowly, a trembling camellia in my breast.

16. Something Must Come to an End

The next morning at ten there is a knock on the glass.

A sort of immense beanpole, dressed all in black with a navy-blue woolly hat on his head and military boots that must have seen duty in Vietnam. It happens to be Colombe's boyfriend, a world specialist in the use of the ellipsis in stock polite formulas.

'I'm looking for Colombe,' says Tibère.

Appreciate, if you will, how ridiculous this sentence is. I am looking for Juliet, said Romeo, is nevertheless more ceremonious.

'I'm looking for Colombe,' thus spake Tibère, who fears nothing, save shampoo; this becomes apparent when he removes his head covering, which he does, not because he is courteous but because it is very warm.

It is May, by Jove!

'Paloma said she was here,' he adds.

And concludes, 'Shit, what the fuck.'

Paloma, you are enjoying yourself.

I send him promptly on his way and become immersed in strange thoughts.

Tibère . . . such an illustrious name for such a pathetic demeanour . . . I think of Colombe Josse's prose, the silent corridors of the Saulchoir . . . and my mind finds itself in Rome . . . Tiberius . . . The memory of Jean Arthens's face suddenly takes me unawares, then I see his father, and that outdated lavaliere of his, so ridiculous . . . So many quests, all these different worlds . . . Can we all be so similar yet live in such disparate worlds? Is it possible that we are all sharing the same frenetic agitation, even though we have not sprung from the same earth or the same blood and do not share the same ambition? Tiberius . . . I feel weary, to be honest, weary of all these rich people, all these poor people, weary of the whole farce . . . Leo jumps from his armchair and comes to rub up against my leg. This cat, made obese only by virtue of charity, is also a generous soul who can feel the irresolution of my own. Weary, yes, I am weary.

Something must come to end; something must begin.

17. The Travails of Dressing Up

At eight o'clock I am ready.

The dress and the shoes fit perfectly (14 and 4).

The shawl is Roman (60 cm wide and 2 m long).

I dried my hair, which I had washed 3 times, with the BaByliss 1600-watt hairdryer, and combed it 2 times in all directions. The results are astonishing.

I sat down 4 times and got up again 4 times which explains why at present I am standing up and do not know what to do.

Sit down, perhaps.

From their box hidden behind the sheets at the back of the wardrobe I have brought out 2 earrings inherited from my mother-in-law, the monstrous Yvette – antique silver, dangling, with 2 pear-shaped garnets. I made 6 attempts before I managed to clip them properly to my earlobes and now must live with the sensation of having 2 potbellied cats hanging from my distended lobes. 54 years without jewellery do not prepare one for the travails of dressing up. I smeared my lips with 1 layer of 'Deep Carmine' lipstick that I bought 20 years ago for a cousin's wedding. The longevity of such a useless item, when valiant lives are lost every day, will never cease to confound me. I belong to the 8% of the world population who calm their apprehension by drowning it in numbers.

Kakuro Ozu knocks 2 times at my door.

I open.

He is very handsome. He is wearing a charcoal-grey suit consisting of straight-legged trousers and a jacket with a mandarin collar and ornamental frog fastenings in matching tones; on his feet are soft leather loafers that look like luxurious slippers. The effect is very . . . Eurasian.

'Oh, you look magnificent!' he says.

'Oh, thank you,' I say, touched, 'and you look very handsome yourself. Happy birthday!'

He smiles, and after I have carefully closed the door behind me, before Leo can manage to slip past, Kakuro extends an arm for me to place my slightly trembling hand on his elbow. Let us hope no one will see us, begs a voice inside, still resisting, the voice of Renée the clandestine. No matter that I have tossed a goodly number of my fears onto the bonfire, I am not yet ready to serve as copy for the Grenelle gossip columns.

Someone's in for quite a surprise.

The front door, where we are heading, opens before we have even reached it.

It is Jacinthe Rosen and Anne-Hélène Meurisse.

A pox upon it! What am I to do?

We are already upon them.

'Good evening, good evening, dear ladies,' twitters Kakuro, pulling me firmly over to his left, passing them quickly, 'good evening, dear friends, we are late, lovely to see you, we are in a terrible rush!'

'Oh, good evening, Monsieur Ozu,' they simper, enthralled, turning in unison to follow us with their gaze.

'Good evening, Madame,' they say to me (to me), smiling with all their teeth.

I have never seen so many teeth all at once.

'Until we next have the pleasure,' whispers Anne-Hélène Meurisse, staring intently as we make our way through the door.

'To be sure! To be sure,' chirps Kakuro, pushing the door with his heel.

'Heavens,' he says, 'if we had stopped, we would have been there for an hour.'

'They didn't recognise me,' I say.

I come to a halt in the middle of the pavement, completely flabbergasted.

'They didn't recognise me,' I repeat.

He stops in turn, my hand still on his arm.

'It is because they have never seen you,' he says. 'I would recognise you anywhere.'

18. Flowing Water

All it takes is one experience of being blind in broad daylight and able to see in pitch dark to wonder what sight is all about. Why do we see? While climbing into the taxi that Kakuro had ordered, I think about Jacinthe Rosen and Anne-Hélène Meurisse, who noticed nothing of me beyond what they could see (on Monsieur Ozu's arm, in a world of hierarchy), and I am struck with incredible force by this proof that sight is like a hand that tries to seize flowing water. Yes, our eyes may perceive, yet they do not observe; they may believe, yet they do not question; they may receive yet they do not search: they are emptied of desire, with neither hunger nor passion.

And as the taxi glides through the early twilight, I become thoughtful.

I think of Jean Arthens, his scorched pupils illuminated with camellias.

I think of Pierre Arthens, his sharp eye, with the blindness of a beggar.

I think of these avid ladies, their greedy gaze unseeing, futile.

I think of Gégène, his sunken eyes with neither life nor force, seeing nothing beyond his own fall.

I think of Lucien, ill-suited to vision, because obscurity often, in the end, proves too strong.

I think even of Neptune, whose eyes are a dog's nose that does not lie.

And I wonder how well I myself can see.

19. They Shimmer

Have you seen *Black Rain*?

Because if you have not seen *Black Rain* – or, at a pinch, *Blade Runner* – it will surely be difficult for you to understand why, when we go into the restaurant, I have the sensation that I am on the set of a Ridley Scott film. There is that scene in *Blade Runner*, in the snake woman's bar, where Deckard calls Rachel from a videophone. There is also the call girls' bar in *Black Rain*, with Kate Capshaw's blonde hair and naked back. And those shots lit as if through a stained-glass window, with a brilliance of cathedrals, surrounded by all the penumbra of hell.

'I like the light in here,' I say to Kakuro as we sit down.

They have led us to a quiet little booth, filled with a solar light circled with shimmering shadows. How can shadows shimmer? They shimmer, that's all there is to it.

'Have you seen *Black Rain*?' asks Kakuro.

I should scarcely have believed that between two people there could exist such a congruity of tastes and thought patterns.

'Yes,' I say, 'at least a dozen times.'

The atmosphere is brilliant, bubbly, racy, plush, crystalline. Magnificent.

'We are going to have an orgy of sushi,' says Kakuro, unfolding his napkin with panache. 'I hope you don't mind, I've already ordered; I want you to discover what I consider to be the very best Paris has to offer in the way of Japanese cuisine.'

'I don't mind at all,' I say, my eyes open wide, because the waiters have placed before us several bottles of sake and myriad little bowls filled with clusters of tiny vegetables that have clearly been marinated in something bound to be very tasty.

And we begin. I fish for a piece of marinated cucumber, only nominally either marinated or cucumber, as it has been transformed into something that is delicious beyond description. With his auburn wooden chopsticks Kakuro delicately lifts a fragment of . . . mandarin orange? tomato? mango? and skilfully causes it to vanish. I immediately dip into the same bowl.

It is a sweet carrot for a gourmet god.

'Happy birthday, then!' I raise my cup of sake.

'Thank you, thank you very much!' We touch our cups together.

'Is this octopus?' I ask, for I have just found a crinkly little tentacle in a bowl of saffron-yellow sauce.

The waiter brings two thick little wooden trays, without edges, covered with pieces of raw fish.

'Sashimi,' says Kakuro. 'There is some octopus here, too.'

I am lost in contemplation of the masterpiece. The visual beauty of it is enough to take your breath away. I squeeze a little chunk of white and grey flesh between my clumsy chopsticks (that's plaice, elucidates Kakuro obligingly) and, determined to find ecstasy, raise it to my mouth.

Why do we go in search of eternity in the ether of invisible essences? This little whiteish chunk is a far more tangible morsel thereof.

'Renée,' says Kakuro, 'I am very happy to be celebrating my birthday in your company, but I also have a more pressing reason to have dinner with you.'

Although we have only known each other for three weeks or so, I am becoming familiar with Kakuro's reasons. France or

England? Vermeer or Caravaggio? *War and Peace* or our beloved Anna?

I wolf down another feather-light sashimi – tuna? – of a respectable dimension which might, I concede, have preferred to be divided in two.

'I did invite you to celebrate my birthday with me, but in the meantime, someone has given me some very important information. So I have something crucial to tell you.'

The piece of tuna has been absorbing all my attention, and does not leave me prepared for what is about to follow.

'You are not your sister,' says Kakuro, looking me straight in the eyes.

20. Gagauz Tribes

L adies.

Ladies, if of an evening you are invited by a rich and agreeable gentleman to dinner at a luxurious restaurant, be sure you behave at all moments with equal elegance. If you happen to be surprised, or annoyed, or disconcerted in any way, you must preserve the same refinement in your impassivity, and, should a turn of phrase astonish you, you must react with the distinction appropriate to such vexations. Instead, because I am a country bumpkin who gulps down sashimi as if it were spuds, I begin to hiccup spasmodically and, aghast at the prospect that the fragment of eternity might well have become lodged in my throat, I endeavour with all the distinction of a gorilla to spit it out forthwith. All around us, silence has fallen. After many eructations and a last and very melodramatic spasm, I finally succeed in dislodging the guilty morsel and, grabbing hold of my napkin, I lodge it there *in extremis*.

'Should I say it again?' asks Kakuro who – dash it! – seems to be enjoying himself.

'I . . . kof . . . kof . . .'

Kof kof is a traditional response in the fraternal prayer ritual of the Gagauz tribes.

'I . . . that is . . . kof . . . kof . . .' My conversation is evolving brilliantly.

Then, with a show of class that clearly seeks to best all my efforts thus far:

'Whaa??'

'I'll say it again to make myself perfectly clear,' says Kakuro, with the sort of infinite patience one exercises with children or, rather, the simple-minded. 'Renée, you are not your sister.'

And as I go on sitting there like a moron, staring at him:

'I'll repeat it one last time, in the hope that this time you won't choke on sushi that – I might mention – costs thirty euros a piece and normally requires a bit more care in its consumption: you are not your sister, we can be friends. We can be anything we want to be.'

21. All Those Cups of Tea

Toom toom toom toom toom toom toom
Look, if you had one shot, one opportunity,
To seize everything you ever wanted
One moment
Would you capture it or just let it slip?

That's Eminem. I confess that, in my capacity as prophet of the contemporary elite, I do on occasion listen to him when I can no longer ignore the fact that Dido has perished.

But, above all, I am greatly confused.

The proof of it?

Here:

Remember me, remember me
But ah forget my fate
Thirty euros a piece
Would you capture it
Or just let it slip?

That is what is going around inside my head, and it needs no commentary. The strange way that a tune can get stuck in one's mind will always amaze me (not to mention a certain *Confutatis*, patron saint of small-bladdered concierges), and it is merely with passing, though sincere, interest that I notice that this time it is the medley that has prevailed.

And then I burst into tears.

At the Brasserie des Amis in a dreary suburb like Puteaux, a patron who almost chokes, barely comes out of it alive and then bursts into tears, with her face in her napkin, would be priceless entertainment. But here, in this solar temple where sashimi is sold by the piece, my excesses have the opposite effect. A wave of silent reproach has enclosed me, and here am I, sobbing, my nose running, obliged to find refuge in an already seriously encumbered napkin in order to wipe away the marks of my emotion and attempt to hide behaviour that public opinion reproves.

Which only causes me to sob all the harder.

Paloma has betrayed me.

So, impelled by my sobs, it unravels in my bosom, this life spent in the clandestinity of a solitary mind, all these reclusive readings, all these winters of illness, all that November rain on Lisette's lovely face, all the camellias restored from hell and come to the rest on the moss of the temple, all these cups of tea in the warmth of friendship, all these words spelling wonder from the lips of my schoolteacher, these so *wabi* still lifes, these everlasting essences luminous with their own singular light, and these summer rains bursting in the delight of pleasure, snowflakes dancing the melopoeia of the heart, and then, in the jewel case of old Japan, the pure face of Paloma. I am weeping, weeping uncontrollably – thick round lustrous tears of happiness, while all around us the world is fading, leaving nothing to the senses beyond the gaze of this man in whose company I feel like somebody, and who has taken me gently by the hand and is smiling at me with all the warmth in the world.

'Thank you,' I manage to whisper.

'We can be friends,' he says. 'We can be anything we want to be.'

Remember me, remember me,
And ah! envy my fate.

22. Meadow Grass

I know now what you have to experience before you die: let me tell you. What you have to experience before you die is a driving rain transformed into light.

I did not sleep all night. After – and in spite of – my infinitely gracious outpourings, dinner was marvellous: smooth, full of complicity, with long, sweet silences. When Kakuro walked me back to my door, he kissed my hand for a long time, and that is how we said goodbye, without a word, with a simple, electric smile.

I did not sleep all night.

And do you know why?

Of course you do.

Of course everyone must know that along with everything else – that is, a seismic tremor suddenly turning a thawed-out life upside down – something more must be jogging through my little fifty-something schoolgirl's head. And what if I say it out loud: 'We can be anything we want to be.'

At seven o'clock I get up, as if propelled by a spring, catapulting my indignant cat to the other end of the bed. I am hungry. I am literally hungry (a colossal slice of bread staggering under the weight of butter and cherry plum jam only serves to sharpen my gargantuan appetite) and I am figuratively hungry: I am in a state of frenzied impatience to find out what will happen. I roam through my kitchen like a wild animal in a cage, I scold my cat who pays not the slightest attention, I indulge in a second round of bread-butter-jam, pace up and down putting things away that do not need putting away, and prepare myself for a third round of bakery consumption.

And then, all of a sudden, at eight o'clock, I calm down.

For no particular reason, and in the most surprising way, a great feeling of serenity trickles over me. What is happening? A mutation. I can see no other possible explanation; some people find themselves growing gills; in my case, it is wisdom.

I flop into a chair and life goes on its way.

A way which, incidentally, is hardly cause for exaltation: it occurs to me that I am still a concierge, and that at nine o'clock I have to go to Rue du Bac to buy some brass cleaner. 'At nine o'clock' is a whimsical addition: let's just say 'at some point during the morning'. But yesterday, as I was planning today's chores, I thought to myself, 'I'll go at around nine.' So I take my shopping bag and handbag and head out into the wide world in quest of a substance that will cause the ornaments in rich people's houses to shine. It is a marvellous spring day outside. From a distance I can see Gégène extricating himself from his cardboard; for his sake I am pleased there is fine weather ahead. I think briefly of how fond the old tramp was of that arrogant grand master of gastronomy, and it brings a smile to my lips: for those who are content, class struggle suddenly seems less important, I muse, surprised that my rebellious consciousness has yielded in this way.

And then it happens: Gégène staggers. I'm only a dozen steps away from him: I frown, concerned. He is staggering uncontrollably, as if he were on the slippery deck of a pitching ship, and I can see his face, his lost look. What is going on? I wonder, out loud, and hurry towards the pauper. Ordinarily Gégène would not be drunk at this time of day and besides, he holds his drink the way a cow does its meadow grass. Woe of woes, the street is almost deserted; I am the only person who has noticed the poor man teetering on his feet. He takes a few wobbly steps towards the kerb, stops, and then, when I am no more than six feet away, suddenly breaks into a run as if he were being pursued by a million demons.

And this is what happens next.

What happens next – like everyone, I wish it would never happen.

23. My Camellias

I die.

I know with a certainty that is close to divination that I am dying, that I am about to expire on Rue du Bac, on a fine spring morning, because a tramp named Gégène, suddenly overcome with St Vitus's dance, wandered onto the deserted street without a care for either man or God.

But that street was not so deserted after all.

I ran after Gégène, leaving my shopping bag and handbag behind me.

And then I was struck.

It was only as I was falling, after a stunned moment of utter incomprehension, before the pain crushed me, that I saw what had struck me. And now I am lying on my back, with an unrestricted view onto the side of a dry-cleaner's van. It had tried to avoid me and skidded off to the left, but too late: I bore the full brunt of its left front bumper. The blue logo on the side of the little white vehicle says 'Malavoin Cleaners'. If I could, I would laugh. The paths of God are all too explicit for those who pride themselves on their ability to decipher them . . . I think of Manuela, who will feel remorse until the end of her days over this death by dry cleaning – can it be anything other than a punishment for the double theft of which, through her great fault, I was guilty? Now the pain is overwhelming me; the pain in my body, radiating, sweeping through me, succeeding brilliantly in being nowhere in particular and everywhere at once, wherever my body has a nerve to feel; but also the pain in my soul, because I have thought of Manuela, whom I will leave behind, alone, and never see again, and this sends a stabbing pain straight to my heart.

They say that in the moment of your death, you see your entire life. But passing before my wide-open eyes – they can no longer make out either the van or its driver, the young woman who had handed me the plum-coloured linen dress and who is now crying and wailing without a care for propriety, nor do they see the passers-by who ran over after the accident and who are all talking to me non-stop with none of it making any sense – passing before my wide-open eyes that can no longer see the outside world is a procession of beloved faces, and as each one goes by, my thoughts are wrenching.

With respect to faces, the first one is a little muzzle. Yes, my first thoughts go to my cat, not that he is the most important one of all but, before the real torment and the real farewells begin, I need to be reassured regarding the fate of my four-legged companion. I smile to myself, thinking about the big fat windbag who has been my partner through these years of widowhood and solitude, and I smile sadly, tenderly, because, seen from death, our close relations with our domestic animals no longer seem to be something minor to be taken for granted, given their everyday nature; ten years of a lifetime have crystallised in Leo, and I take the measure of how the ridiculous, superfluous cats who wander through our lives with all the placidity and indifference of an imbecile are in fact the guardians of life's good and joyful moments, and of its happy web, even beneath the canopy of misfortune. Farewell, Leo, I say to myself, saying farewell to a life I did not think I would be so reluctant to lose.

I entrust the fate of my cat to Olympe Saint-Nice, with the

deep relief of knowing with the utmost certainty that she will take good care of him.

Now I can confront the others.

Manuela.
　　Manuela my friend.
　　Now that I am about to die I shall call you *tu* at last.
　　Do you recall all our cups of tea in the silk of friendship? Ten years of tea and saying *vous* to each other and, at the end of it, a warmth in my breast and a hopeless gratitude towards someone or something, life perhaps, for having graced me with your friendship. Do you know that it is in your company that I have had my finest thoughts? Must I die to realise this at last . . . All those hours drinking tea in the refined company of a great lady who has neither wealth nor palaces, only the bare skin in which she was born – without those hours I would have remained a mere concierge, but instead it was contagious, because the aristocracy of the heart is a contagious emotion, so you made of me a woman who could be a friend . . . How easy would it have been to transform the thirst of a poor woman like me into the pleasure of Art, to conceive a passion for blue china, for rustling foliage, for languid camellias and all the century's eternal jewels, all these precious pearls in the endless movement of the river, if you had not, week after week, offered your heart, and made with me the sacrifice to the sacred ritual of tea?
　　How I miss you, already . . . This morning I understand what it means to die: when we disappear, it is the others who die for us, for here I am, lying on the cold cobbles and it's not the dying I care about; it has no more meaning this morning than it did yesterday. But never again will I see those I love, and if that is what dying is about, then it really is the tragedy they say it is.

Manuela, my sister, may fate keep me from being for you what you were for me: a safeguard against unhappiness, a rampart against banality. Carry on with your life, and think of me with joy.

But in my heart the idea that I shall never see you again is infinite torture.

There you are, Lucien, on a yellowed photograph, as if on a medallion, the way I see you in my memory. You are smiling, whistling. Was it like this for you too, the feeling that it was my death and not your own, the end of our gazes long before the terror of going into the darkness? What remains of a life, exactly, when those who spent it together will now have both been dead for so long? Today a strange feeling has taken hold, that I am betraying you: by dying, I am truly causing you to die. Is it not enough in this ordeal to feel that others are becoming distant – must we also put to death those who were still alive only through us? And yet you are smiling, and whistling, and I too am smiling. Lucien . . . I did love you well, after all, and for that reason, perhaps, I deserve to rest. We'll sleep in peace in the little cemetery, in our village. You can hear the river in the distance. They fish for shad and gudgeon there. Children come to play, shrieking their heads off. In the evening, at sunset, you can hear the angelus.

And you, Kakuro, dear Kakuro, who made me believe in the possibility of a camellia . . . Only fleetingly do I think of you today; a few weeks do not provide the key. I hardly know you beyond the person you were for me: a heavenly benefactor, a miraculous balm against all the certainties of fate. How could it be otherwise? Who knows . . . I can't help but feel my heart ache over that uncertainty. And what if? And what if you had made me laugh again and talk and cry, washing away all those years of feeling tainted by sin, restoring to Lisette her lost honour through the complicity of an improbable love? What a shame . . . You are fading into the night, and at this moment, when I know I shall never see you again, I must give up all hope of ever knowing what fate's answer might have been . . .

Is this what dying is about? Is it so pitiful? And how much time is left?

An eternity, if I still do not know.

Paloma, my child.

Now it is your turn. You are last.

Paloma, my child.

I did not have any children, because it did not happen that way. Did I suffer because of it? No. But if I had had a daughter, she would have been you. And with all my strength I implore that your life be worthy of all that you promise.

And then, an illumination.

A true illumination: I see your lovely face, grave and pure, the pink frames of your glasses and the way you have of fiddling with the hem of your sweater, of looking me straight in the eye and stroking the cat as if he could speak. And I start to cry. To cry from the joy inside. What do these onlookers see as they bend over my broken body? I do not know.

But inside me, the sun.

How to measure a life's worth? The important thing, said Paloma one day, is not the fact of dying, it's what you are doing at the moment of your death. What was I doing at the moment of my death, I wonder, with an answer ready in the warmth of my heart.

What was I doing?

I had met another, and was prepared to love.

After fifty-four years of emotional and psychological wilderness, hardly touched by the tenderness of someone like

315

Lucien, who was little more than a resigned shadow of myself, after fifty-four years of clandestinity and silent victories inside the padded walls of a lonely mind, after fifty-four years of venting my futile frustrations upon a world and a caste I despised, after these fifty-four years of nothingness, where I met no one and was never with another:

Manuela, always.

But also Kakuro.

And Paloma, my kindred soul.

My camellias.

I would gladly share a last cup of tea with you.

And then a jolly cocker spaniel, his ears and tongue dangling, runs across my line of vision. How ridiculous . . . but I would still like to laugh. Farewell, Neptune. You are a ninny of a dog, but I suppose death makes us run off the rails somewhat; perhaps it's you I shall think of last. And if there is any meaning behind it, it is beyond my grasp.

Ah, no. Wait.

One last image.

How odd . . . I can't see any more faces . . .

It will be summer soon. It's seven o'clock. At the village church, the bells are ringing. I see my father, his back bent, his arms straining, he's turning the June earth. The sun is setting. My father straightens up, wipes his brow with the back of his sleeve, comes away home.

End of the day's toil.

It will soon be nine o'clock.

Peacefully, I die.

One Last Profound Thought

What to do
Faced with never
But look
For always
In a few stolen strains?

This morning, Madame Michel died. She was knocked over by a dry-cleaner's van, near Rue du Bac. I cannot believe I am writing these words.

It was Kakuro who brought me the news. Apparently Paul, his secretary, was walking up the street at the time. He saw the accident from a distance but when he got there it was too late. She wanted to help Gégène, the tramp on the corner of Rue du Bac and who was drunk as a lord. She ran after him but she didn't see the van. Apparently they had to take the driver to hospital, she was a nervous wreck.

Kakuro came and rang our bell at around eleven. He asked to see me and he took my hand and said, 'There's no way I can spare you this pain, Paloma, so I'll just tell it to you the way it happened: Renée had an accident, at about nine o'clock. A very serious accident. She's dead.' He was crying. He squeezed my hand very hard. 'Dear God, who is Renée?' asked my mother, alarmed. 'Madame Michel,' answered Kakuro. 'Oh!' she went, relieved. He turned away from her, disgusted. 'Paloma, I have to take care of a lot of not very cheerful things, but we'll see each other later on, OK?' he said. I nodded, and squeezed his hand very hard, too. We acknowledged each other in the Japanese manner, a quick little bow. We understand each other. We both feel so bad.

When he had gone, the only thing I wanted was to avoid Maman. She opened her mouth but I made a gesture with my hand, my palm raised towards her as if to say, 'Don't even try.'

She gulped but didn't come near, she let me go off to my room. When I got there I rolled myself into a ball on my bed. After half an hour Maman knocked gently on the door. 'No,' I said. She didn't insist.

Ten hours have gone by since then. A lot of things have happened in the building, too. I'll summarise: Olympe Saint-Nice rushed to the lodge when she heard the news (a locksmith came to open the door), so she could take Leo to her place. I think that Madame Michel, that Renée . . . I think that's what she would have wanted. I was relieved. Madame de Broglie took charge of the operations, under Kakuro's supreme command. It's odd how that old bag seemed almost nice. She said to Maman, her new friend, 'She was here for twenty-seven years. We're going to miss her.' Right away she organised a collection for the flowers, and said she would contact Renée's family members. Are there any? I don't know but Madame de Broglie will find out.

The hardest was Madame Lopes. Once again, it was Madame de Broglie who told her, when she came at ten to do the cleaning. Apparently she stood there for a few seconds, not understanding, her hand on her mouth. And then she collapsed. When she revived, a quarter of an hour later, she just murmured, 'Forgive me, oh, forgive me,' and then she put on her scarf and went home.

It's heartbreaking.

What about me? What do I feel? I may be chattering away about the little events at 7, Rue de Grenelle, but I'm not very brave. I'm afraid to go into myself and see what's going on in there. And I'm ashamed. I think I wanted to die and make Colombe and Maman and Papa suffer because I hadn't ever really suffered. Or rather, I was suffering but it didn't hurt and, as a result, all my little plans were just the luxury of some problem-free teenager. Poor little rich girl rationalising things, wanting to draw attention to herself.

But this time, for the very first time, it hurt, it really hurt. Like a fist in my stomach: I couldn't breathe, my heart aching fit to burst, my tummy crushed. An unbearable physical pain. I wondered if I'd ever get over the pain of it. It hurt so much I wanted to scream. But I didn't scream. What I feel now is that the pain is still there but it isn't keeping me from walking or talking, it's a feeling of complete helplessness and absurdity. So that's what it's like? All of a sudden all possibility just vanishes? A life full of plans, discussions just started, desires not even fulfilled – it all vanishes in a second and there's nothing left, nothing left to do, and there's no going back?

For the first time in my life I understood the meaning of the word 'never'. And it's really awful. You say the word a hundred times a day but you don't really know what you're saying until you're faced with a real 'never again'. Ultimately you always have the illusion that you're in control of what's happening; nothing seems definitive. I may have been telling myself all these weeks that I was going to commit suicide, but did I really believe it? Did my decision really make me understand the meaning of the word 'never'? Not at all. It made me understand that it's in my power to decide. And I think that even a few seconds before dying, 'never again' would still just be empty words. But when someone that you love dies . . . well, I can tell you that you really feel what it means and it really really hurts. It's like fireworks suddenly burning out in the sky and everything going black. I feel alone, and sick, my heart aches and every movement seems to require a colossal effort.

And then something happened. It's hard to believe, it's such a sad day. At around five I went down to Madame Michel's lodge (I mean Renée's lodge) with Kakuro because he wanted to get some of her clothes to take them to the hospital morgue. He rang at our door and asked Maman if he could speak to me. But I had guessed it would be him, I was already there. Of course I wanted to go with him. We took the lift down, not speaking. He looked very tired, more tired than sad, and I thought, That is what suffering looks like on a wise face. It's not apparent; it just leaves traces that make you look very very tired. Do I look tired, too?

In any event, Kakuro and I went down to the lodge. But while we were crossing the courtyard we stopped short, both of us at the same time: someone had begun to play the piano and we could hear very clearly what they were playing. It was Satie, I think, well, I'm not sure (but anyway it was classical).

I don't really have any profound thoughts on the matter. Besides, how can you have a profound thought when your kindred soul is lying in a hospital refrigerator? But I know we stopped short, both of us, and took a deep breath and let the sun warm our faces while we listened to the music drifting down from above. 'I think Renée would have liked this moment,' said Kakuro. And we stayed there a few more minutes, listening to the music. I agreed with him. But why?

Thinking back on it, this evening, with my heart and my stomach all like jelly, I have finally concluded, maybe that's what life is about: there's a lot of despair, but also the odd moment of beauty, where time is no longer the same. It's as if those strains of music created a sort of interlude in time, something suspended, an elsewhere that had come to us, an always within never.

Yes, that's it, an *always* within *never*.

Don't worry, Renée, I won't commit suicide and I won't burn a thing.

Because from now on, for you, I'll be searching for those moments of always within never.

Beauty, in this world.